A Wa

“Can you get some heavy-duty backup? Not muscle. But somebody you can trust to watch your back?”

“If this is about drug smuggling, count me out.”

“Drugs? No. You just need a good person for backup. Okay. There’s one more wiggle here. Keep watching CNN.”

“I’ve seen that desert thing ten times.”

“You tape it?”

“I did.”

“There’s going to be another videotape some time today.”

“I don’t understand.”

“Me neither. But my sources tell me there’ll be a second videotape. That’s all I know, but the client wants to make sure you watch it.”

“Bobby. Tell me if you know the answer to this one.”

“What’s the question?”

“Another batch of dead immigrants in the middle of somewhere. A videotape of nothing, in the middle of somewhere else. How are they connected?”

“The client says you’ll know why once you see the tape. Gotta go.”

And just like that, he hung up.

Other Books by
David Cole

THE KILLING MAZE
BUTTERFLY LOST

Stalking Moon

David Cole

AVON BOOKS
An Imprint of Harper Collins*Publishers*

This is a work of fiction. Names, characters, places, and incidents are products of the author's imagination or are used fictitiously and are not to be construed as real. Any resemblance to actual events, locales, organizations, or persons, living or dead, is entirely coincidental.

AVON BOOKS
An Imprint of HarperCollins*Publishers*
10 East 53rd Street
New York, New York 10022-5299

ISBN: 0-380-81970-8
www.avonbooks.com

First Avon Books paperback printing: January 2002

Printed in the U.S.A.

10 9 8 7 6 5 4 3 2 1

for Deborah

Many thanks to Marco Lopez, Jr., Mayor of Nogales, Arizona, and his office staff, especially Press Secretary Juan Pablo Guzman. In Tucson, thanks to Dr. Katrina Mangin; Dr. Vanessa Olsen; Cynthia Dagnal-Myron, teacher and writer; students at Pueblo High School; Sinclair Browning; and Heather Irbinskas. Dr. Marc Becker, one of my colleagues at www.nativeweb.org gave continual advice on Mexico, maquiladoras, and the Zapatista political movement. In Syracuse, Nancy Priest is my ever-reliable consultant, Rosemary Pooler a true supporting angel; this book wouldn't exist without Drs. Dennis Brown and James Blanchefield. Thanks also to the continual support of my agent, Jessica Lichtenstein, of Joelle Delbourgo Associates. Jennifer Fisher (Avon Books) and Clarissa Hutton (HarperCollins) are every writer's dream editors.

All the errors are mine alone.

Adventure most unto itself
The Soul condemned to be;
Attended by a Single Hound—
Its own Identity.

—EMILY DICKINSON, *The Single Hound*

chat room

ROZAFA4bluedog: > in new york, how i find the money sender?

LUNA13: > take train a to meet Liliana

ROZAFA4bluedog: > please, what is train a?

LUNA13: > subway to washington heights

ROZAFA4bluedog: > is it safe?

LUNA13: > the water man can NOT find you

ROZAFA4bluedog: > please, is it safe?

LUNA13: > safe, my sister

ROZAFA4bluedog: > how much to send dollars? how much?

LUNA13: > trust the money sender, he will help you

ROZAFA4bluedog: > after the water man, who can I trust?

LUNA13: > my sister, if you do not trust me, then who?

ROZAFA4bluedog: > is it safe?

LUNA13: > sister, from this day, you are free

1

One of my cell phones rang at 4:15 in the morning.

Scrubbing sleepiness from my eyes, I sat up from the leather couch where I'd fallen asleep. My ears crackled as I yawned. The phone rang and rang, tones from a three-note chord rippling down and up. I had six cell phones scattered around the penthouse suite, each with a different call pattern, but by the time I found the right one on the bathroom sink, it had stopped ringing.

I carried the cell past my unused master bedroom. Still too sleepy to bother with putting in my contact lenses, I found my work glasses with the fake abalone-patterned frames and put them on.

My suite was on the top floor of the Las Vegas Hilton. I pulled back the drapes from the living room window wall, squinting through the work glasses at blurred streaks of dawn light shooting in from the east. Below me, Desert Inn Road was half in neon, half in darkness. I took a fresh water bottle from the minibar and waited for the cell to ring again. When I got back to the couch, the sunlight and neon glow outside backlit the window wall. Twenty feet long, ten feet high, the plated glass window shimmered from the vibrations of my footsteps on the oak parquet floor, the glass itself a half-inch thick and slightly tinted, so that while it admitted lights from outside, it also reflected the bluish screens of my twelve computer monitors. Since without my glasses I could only focus up to three feet, all the lights blurred together.

Neat. Out of focus means not having to absorb details. The combination of colored lights reminded me of an LSD trip at the Grand Canyon during my crazy teenager rebel years. But that was so long ago that the memories of hallucination were themselves fuzzy and uncertain.

I cracked open the water bottle just as the cell rang again.

"Check CNN," Bobby Guinness said abruptly. "They arrested him in Madrid."

"Hello to you too," I said, coughing as the water went down the wrong way.

Bobby didn't bother with pleasantries. Not that he was unpleasant. Just too busy to bother. I liked that in him, since I didn't have many social skills either.

"Turn on CNN."

Fumbling for my TV remote and wincing at the amazing streaks of pain through my arthritic right shoulder, I grabbed my vial of Vicodin pills, but realized it was too early in the day to go down that route. The station I found was running a dog food commercial. A puppy skidded on kitchen tiles and hit some stacks of toilet paper, bounced off, changed direction to his food bowl.

I hit the Mute button.

"Am I going to see his face?"

"I checked with Interpol. He was arrested. Your end of the payment will be at the usual place. Look, forget him. You got CNN yet?"

Without my contacts in, I couldn't focus on the TV remote dial pad and kept hitting the wrong input numbers and getting a home shopping channel.

"What *is* my end?"

I sat on the floor and scrunched toward the TV until things came into focus.

"Fifty, fifty-five. Come on, I've got something hot. You awake yet?"

"I'd've liked to have seen his face," I said. "After six weeks, I was getting ditzy just looking at a digitized photo."

"Keep checking, if you want to see him. Maybe they'll run a spot. I've leaked info about his arrest, all the media knows where to get a live shot."

CNN showed a videotape of some backcountry desert road, stretching toward a midafternoon horizon. Low desert with little water. Even the creosote bushes were barely two feet high.

"This is what you woke me up for?"

"You watching?"

"I'm looking at a desert. Why?"

"Got another job. Depending."

"Depending on what?"

Bobby rarely wasted words, never stayed on the phone longer than he had to. I never knew where he was calling from, didn't even know where he lived.

"You ever track somebody through chat rooms? Message boards? AOL Instant Messenger? Peer-to-peer stuff, like Napster?"

"Very difficult to do," I said. "Who's the contractor? What's the fee?"

"Gotta get back to you on that. There's a wiggle I haven't figured yet."

"But you're not going to tell me about it? Or who's wiggling?"

"Can't say. Listen, um, you awake yet? You dressed?"

"Yup. Nope."

"Get dressed quick. Your plane leaves in fifty minutes."

Now *that's* the kind of comment that wakes you up real quick.

"What plane?"

"Back to Tucson."

"I can't dump this job yet," I protested.

"Somebody else will be there about now to shut things down."

"Bobby, whoa. I thought that finding these online gambling hackers was a major contract."

"You close to them yet?"

I looked at several of the computer screens, reading search results.

"Canada. Maybe Manitoba. That's all I've got so far."

"Okay. Just pack up and get to McCarran airport."

The doorbell chimed.

"He's here," I said. "You sure about this? Why are you pulling me out?"

"Can't say yet. But it's major. I'll call you in a day. Maybe two. Plus I'm dumping this cell number. You dump yours. Will call you back on seven minus four, two plus three."

"Bobby, why am I watching this CNN thing about the desert?"

"Um. I have to be honest. Don't know yet. Client just said to watch the videotape, wait for details about the women."

"What women?"

The CNN newsreader came back on the screen. I hit the Mute button, turned up the volume to hear what she was saying.

"Four bodies have been discovered in what Border Patrol officials describe as particularly brutal conditions southeast of Yuma in the Cabeza Prieta National Wildlife Refuge. Yesterday's temperature ran as high as 115 degrees. In this part of the Sonoran Desert, there is virtually no shade, no water, no safety."

"You get that?" Bobby said.

I muted the TV.

"Didn't say anything about women."

"Keep watching when you get home."

"Tell me why this is important. Is it the Cabeza part?" "

I was using an ID kit with the name Laura Cabeza and wondered if I was blown.

"Nope. Just get back to Tucson, and I'll get back to you. What do you think of this CNN announcer, the woman with the crooked smile?"

"Brown hair, bangs, brown sweater set?"

"She's really sexy, but not so smart. Give me that call-in

talk show blonde with the wandering eye. Now she's what I call intelligent."

He hung up.

Before I could get to the door, I heard the bolt slide back and the door opened. A teenage girl stood there with a hotel room lock booster. Head shaven, golden rings of all thicknesses and diameters sprouting from both ears, she wore a Running Rebels tee-shirt, khaki shorts, and a pair of battered Doc Marten Classic 1490 Series 10-eyehole boots. She pulled the electronic card out of the door, wrapped the cable strap around the booster keypad, and shoved it into a purple backpack. Techno music buzzed from her headset as she tugged a six-pack of Mountain Dew from the backpack. She twisted one can free from the plastic and handed the rest to me.

"Put these in the refrigerator," she shouted, head bobbing to the beat.

Walking past me into the living room, she immediately sat down at one of the computers and ignored me completely as she scanned several monitors.

"Hey!" I lifted off her headset. "Who are you?"

"Kimberley."

Her head moved from side to side, her face always level as it slid first over her right shoulder and than the left one. She clamped her headset back on, fumbled at the volume control on her belt pack. As the music blasted, she extended both arms straight out to her sides and began undulating like a Cambodian dancer.

"You can leave any time," she shouted. "I've got it now."

I *hate* leaving a contract unfinished.

2

I lived in a small *casita* on the back acres of Heather Aguilar's ranch. Two large rooms connected by French doors, a bathroom hooked off the bedroom, a kitchen tacked onto the back of the living room, mesquite ramadas sheltering windows on all four sides against the fierce southern Arizona summer sun, with a swamp cooler on the roof instead of air conditioners.

Casitas are small, contained, controllable homes.

Just big enough for one person, small enough for *only* one person.

My plane from Vegas was on time, the flight was short, and I was home before nine o'clock that morning. I brought back two weeks of dirty laundry and my six cell phones and the still-present dissatisfaction of not finishing the job, coupled with uneasiness about a new contract that was somehow connected to dead immigrant women.

After brushing my teeth, I moved into the living room and pulled out my Pilates track. Three mourning doves fluttered onto the mesquite thatching and began cooing. I started a CD of Tohono O'odham *waila* chicken scratch music, cranked up the sound, and settled onto the Pilates bed, arranging my body carefully to start my series of postures and poses.

I've never bought into the New Agers' stuff about chanting, prayer, candles, or incense stalks. *Waila* songs are like polkas. The beat is steady, the button-key accordions playing simple tunes against a background of fiddles, guitars, and drums. Instead of jazzing me up, the steady rhythms helped focus my breathing. All I wanted was focus, deep relaxation, body awareness, strength, and flexibility.

By the fifth CD track, "Lemonades Verde Cumbia," I slid effortlessly and mindlessly on the Pilates. Stress-busting without pharmaceutical enhancement.

I *am* happy.

I often focused my daily energy entirely on watching birds. A curve-billed thrasher *whit-wheeting* his way between mesquite and cholla, chunking into the topsoil for bugs. Red-tailed hawks and kestrels in a grove of ancient saguaro cactus within binocular range. A string of Gambel's quail babies toddling after mom, *chi-ca-go-go, chi-ca-go-go,* their head plumes bobbing asymmetrically while they scooped up water.

That kind of thing.

Sheer delight in the details of the bird's wing. The sky, the heat, the day itself.

I never knew, you see, that life *could* be simple.

What an odd discovery at the age of forty-three.

I'd always sought, at times I'd *relished,* a complicated, wrapped-tight lifestyle. Pushing right to the physical and psychological edges of a thing. Pushing beyond and over the edges, when I had to. Absolutely ignoring awareness that complications might work against me. That was, once, my lifestyle.

Now my biggest complications are only small details, small decisions.

Like working on how to get air out of my Appaloosa's gut so I can cinch the saddle tight. Don't knee Palo like some macho cowboy, Heather Aguilar insisted. Just walk him a bit. Gently. Let him get used to breathing, then pull up the cinch strap another notch or two.

Some afternoons my sense input cranked *way* down beyond having to think. I delighted in small sensations. Deciding *which* tea to brew. Deciding whether to drink that tea in the upland meadow, under scrub oaks, or in one of my many gardens.

Life in the slow lane. Instead of hurdling anxieties to meet deadlines and shortcutting my paranoia of not being private enough, my heart was light, the personal orbit of my daily lifestyle reduced to the languid, hot delights of the Sonoran Desert.

Am I loopy or what? I thought. It's an incredibly giddy feeling, to be happy after so many years, so many decades of anxiety, depression, whatever. Being happy is cool, being simple is the key.

As simple as a lazy teenager's diary. Life condensed to primal activities, each a single sentence, phrase, or word. Clean the stable. Currycomb Palo. Pilates. Cooking.

Find the person.

Fill the contract.

Take down the score.

Bobby Guinness helped simplify my work as an information midwife.

One job a month, no more. Nonnegotiable fees in the mid-five-figures. Half in advance, half when I found the person or the hidden bank accounts or whatever digital information I needed to find. I never advertised. Clients came to me by reference through Bobby. Before him, I'd rejected nineteen of twenty skip tracing jobs, waiting for whatever seemed right.

No, not quite that. Whatever seemed *safe.*

Find the person. Fill the contract. Take down the score.

Just like the movie *Heat*. Bobby Guinness was my Jon Voight.

Bobby knew what I could do, knew what digital scores he could line up for me, each score drawing on what I already knew how to do with some new digital challenge. I'd always been able to find *anybody*. Now I had better techniques, a better playing field on the Internet, more dollars to purchase more information.

Bobby Guinness wasn't even his real name. When he first contacted me nine months before, he was Bobbie McCue. We successively went through Jack Armstrong, Eddie Fast, Bruce Springsteen, and Marlon Coppola.

I'd never met him personally. We'd arranged a coded system for changing cloned cell phone numbers, and he dumped his active number at random intervals.

CNN played without sound while I concentrated on Pilates technique. Grace. Control. Precision. Breathing. Exercise without exhaustion. Honestly, I could sell the stuff. My friends Meg and Heather had long since given up listening to me talk about it.

I was looking for a face. In handcuffs, in a police car, in a perp walk, a face I knew only from digital information and several blurred and altered photographs.

My biggest job ever. Low six-figure payoff. Took me five weeks to track him across three continents, and I found him in Madrid because he couldn't live without some Swedish woman in his bed. I got his cell phone records, I got her name, I found her, and by tracking her air travel, I found him. Let the government find the money he'd stolen with his phony pump and dump stock scheme. I didn't care about that, but it was so much money that his arrest would make CNN for sure.

But that wasn't the main story today.

Every half-hour CNN played the desert videotape. A typical consumer video camera, no particularly high resolution, no real concern for image quality. No titles or credits. The picture had been shot from the vehicle's front seat. From the shape of the hood, I guessed it was a large SUV, probably a Chevy Suburban. The time-date stamp in the lower right corner read:

July 24 2002
4:44:17 pm

It still wasn't the image I wanted, not the man in handcuffs, so I didn't bother to turn the sound on until later. The Border Patrol had covered fifty square miles of Sonoran Desert with trackers, helicopters, spotter planes, even satellite images. They couldn't find the dead women, they didn't even know if the videotape was shot in the US or Mexico.

But seven more bodies had been found in the Cabeza desert. All men and boys, dead of exposure to the sun. Two others had been medivacked to the Yuma hospital, barely alive, seriously dehydrated.

A media chopper followed the tracks southward, the cameras zooming in on empty water jugs, abandoned pieces of clothing, and an endless stream of lightweight plastic supermarket bags that marked the highway to nowhere.

3

Seven minus four. Two plus three.

Next morning after breakfast I unstuck Bobby's magnet from my refrigerator door, where I stored it with some other pretty innocuous stuff. Recipes for never-made chile burritos, a two-armed saguaro cactus like the one Snoopy stands next to in the *Peanuts* comic strip, plus some business calling cards I picked up once on a trip to Atlanta and Houston. Bobby had created a magnetic advertising placard for Altamont Construction. No address, just a phone number without an area code and a message in the standard quotation marks, as though this punctuation enhanced the quality of the business.

"No job too small"

I unboxed a brand new Kyotera digital cellular phone and carefully cloned in a new number based on the phone number of the refrigerator magnet card and Bobby's code phrase.

Cloning is much harder than it used to be. When you make a call on your cell phone, it sends out three discrete chunks of digital information—the serial number of the actual phone, your account number, and a randomly generated identifier code, something so encrypted that it was almost impossible to duplicate because it changed at random intervals. Of course, nothing about Internet or wireless security is absolute.

Some hacker, somewhere, crunches decoding possibilities until security is breached. In my case, Bobby Guinness had purchased some cloning software from a contact in Kazakhstan. It currently worked with Pacific Bell cellular accounts. When PacBell got hit with too much illegal cell activity, it would switch its encryption scheme, and then Bobby would obtain another block of telephone company cellular frequencies.

Seven minus four. Two plus three.

Seventh number minus four, second number plus three.

Bobby took care of the legitimacy of the phone numbers. I never used my phone to make calls, only to hear from him. Five minutes after I finished snapping the plastic case back together, it rang.

"You think about what I asked?" he said abruptly, as though we were continuing the conversation from earlier, even though a whole day had passed.

"I'm thinking . . . who was that girl in Vegas?"

"Smart kid. She found them, by the way."

"Found who?"

"The gambling hackers. You were right about Manitoba. These guys worked for a computer repair company. Not too smart covering their tracks."

"How did she find them? I sure couldn't."

"Does it really matter? Listen. This new contract's shaping up really quick."

"So?"

"Chat rooms and message boards? You think about getting into them?"

"Yeah. Well, it's really difficult."

"Isn't it like hacking into email servers?"

"Not really. Two reasons. First, it's this peer-to-peer stuff. Doesn't use the standard Internet protocols, where everything has a designated location number. AOL Instant Messenger and Napster. Whole new world. People connect to each other in real time, but not through fixed computer locations. The only real way to track this stuff is to be online at the same exact time, plus know *where* the people are. Difficult."

"What else?" he asked.

"There are just too many of these connections. Too many people. The AOL Instant Messenger system alone has thousands of users, hundreds of thousands of messages a day. Later today I'll see what more I can find out. But I've never used this stuff, so I can't say what the learning curve will be, how long it will take."

"What will you need?"

Each of our scores had different technical problems, sometimes with hardware and software, sometimes with setting up illegal shell accounts on computers around the world so I could hack without leaving a substantial chase.

"Minimum, half a dozen more computers. I'd have to hack into AOL computers to look at their log files, and AOL is really snooty about that. First I'll have to get the logfiles for a fixed period of time, then write a computer program to search them for whatever name you want. But I'll need to build a massive computer network handling all that data."

"How long to build it?"

"Depends what the client wants and how soon it's wanted."

"Here's the wiggle. Funky. I've got two people wanting to pay for the same job."

"Bobby, I don't understand."

"Two different clients. Each approached me separately. I know they've got no idea somebody else is asking for the same information."

"That *is* funky. So?"

"The first client, a package is coming your way."

"At my mail drop?"

"The second client," he continued, ignoring my question, "you're going to have to meet her."

"No. I don't personally meet clients."

"Not even for two hundred thousand?" He sucked in his breath, the sound rasping in my earpiece. "That's a minimum."

Well. Incredible. My biggest score ever. I could take months off work, I could retire for a year, I could bliss out in northern Thailand with that kind of money. The phone connection buzzed the way it does when somebody on a portable or wireless phone shifts body position and the uplink can't quite maintain the connection.

"Okay. I'll meet. Where do I go? What state?"

"No airplanes necessary. Your own neighborhood. Client's nearby. Meet her tomorrow night 4:22. She prefers Nogales. I told her you'd pick Tucson."

"Yes. Arizona Desert Museum."

He hesitated so long I thought there was a problem.

"Just checking her cell phone, had to leave a message on her voice mail about the meet. Okay. Gotta go."

"Wait! What's the job?"

"Something connected to that videotape on CNN. Today, when you get the package, you'll understand a lot more. Um, I've *got* to go."

"Um," I said. "There you go again."

"Don't have time to talk."

"Whoa, Bobby. Whoa. What's the hurry here? I know you by now. I know when you've got something unpleasant to tell me about a score."

"What's the tell?" he asked after a while.

"I'm not telling you anything. I'm *ask*ing."

"No. You know, um, like gamblers. Poker players. Get a good card, they lick their lips, sniff, hunch their shoulders, whatever. It gives away information to the other players so they can fold."

"That's called a tell?"

"Yes. Look, I'm really curious. I need to know if I've got a tell, a giveaway on the phone. Nobody's ever said that to me before."

"When you're holding back something, you say 'um.' "

"Um," Bobby Guinness said faintly.

"See?"

A long, long silence. But I waited, knowing he was trying to figure out just how much more data to give me.

"Okay," he said finally. "Things here are getting complicated."

"*Bad* complicated? Or just . . . more difficult?"

"Both. First off. There's a Mexican factor."

"Is there data about that in the package I'm getting?"

"Second off. The package is being hand-delivered."

I was stunned.

"How do you know where I live?"

"That's my business. To know all about people. But . . . um . . ."

Uncharacteristically, he was at a loss for words. I heard a swoosh of static as he shifted his head, a momentary buzzing, like a large moth at the screen door.

"I'm going to freak you out here, I think. Tell you the truth, *I'm* freaked."

"What?"

"You're going to find out anyway," he said, "once the package arrives."

"Find out what?"

"I'm not Bobby Guinness."

Where is this going? I thought, unable to think clearly at all.

"Well. I am Bobby to you. But I'm just a voice, just a person who calls himself Bobby Guinness. Actually, I'm a cutout. I work for . . . for the real Bobby. Who's coming to see you in the next day or so. Bringing the package."

"A cutout? I don't think I like this contract at all."

"You will, once you hear the money that's involved. It's going to be a percentage, not a straight fee. Twenty percent of at least thirty million dollars."

"Jesus!"

"So. You cool? You freaked? What?"

"How will I recognize the real Bobby, or whatever his name is."

"You'll know. Listen, there's one more thing. Two more. One of the keys here is a person who uses chat rooms and AOL Instant Messenger. User name is LUNA13."

"Wait." I grabbed a red Magic Marker pen. "Spell that out."

I wrote it on my palm.

"The score depends on you tracking down the actual person."

He waited, silent. I heard the buzzing again and realized he was nervous, probably pacing back and forth, uncertain how I was taking all this. I turned my palm this way and that, as if by changing the angle of my hand I could somehow find meaning in the user name.

"Nearly impossible," I said finally, thinking of the permutations. "LUNA13. That could be anybody. Anywhere. It could even be a group of people."

"Yes. Well. You said *nearly* impossible. Second thing. Can you get some heavy-duty backup? Not muscle. But somebody you can trust to watch your back?"

"If this is about drug smuggling, count me out."

"Drugs? No. You just need a good person for backup. Okay. There's one more wiggle here. Keep watching CNN."

"I've seen that desert thing ten times."

"You tape it?"

"I did."

"There's going to be another videotape some time today."

"I don't understand."

"Me neither. But my sources tell me there'll be a second videotape. That's all I know, but the client wants to make sure you watch it."

"Bobby. Tell me if you know the answer to this one."

"What's the question?"

"Another batch of dead immigrants in the middle of

somewhere. A videotape of nothing, in the middle of somewhere else. How are they connected?"

"The client says you'll know why once you see the tape. Gotta go."

And just like that, he hung up.

4

The Internet is a chaotic, anarchic mess.

Your identity is supposed to be protected.

It's not.

In the past few years, hundreds of public and private agencies have published intense amounts of personal information. $59.95 to check out the hot date you just met in a singles bar. $79.95 to run a credit check on that new plumber you were thinking of hiring. $35.00 for software to install on your kid's computer to see if they visit porn websites. Or install it on your wife's computer to privately capture her email, find out if she's got a boyfriend.

If you use cash for everything, you're partially safe. Unless you've got a driver's license and a registered vehicle, a social security number, or even just an account at your supermarket where you can save on in-house items by swiping your store card. If you visit a doctor, dentist, even a veterinarian, they've got records that they may share—deliberately or innocently—with similar offices.

But all of this information is based on the Internet as its method of exchanging digital information that has been codified. AOL and Napster changed all that.

Instead of sending a message to a specific email address, which can be tracked, people use AOL Instant Messenger to "chat" with friends. Unlike your email connections, these chats have no specific digital identifier that leaves traces.

Your friend pages you, you open a chat window, you can even move into a private chat room. Once you stop chatting, the connection is broken. Even if you start chatting again in ten seconds, the connection may be entirely different.

Most websites have fixed addresses. Napster could have set up thousands of music files on a monster computer bank, but instead, Napster software circumvented the law requiring royalty payments by having people literally connect to somebody else's computer for however long it took to swap music files.

Peer-to-peer connections. That's the term.

God, I hated them. Anybody could be talking to anybody anywhere on the Internet, but the fixed digital locators no longer existed.

So far, I'd avoided anything involving peer-to-peer connections. So far, I thought as I carefully set up AOL Instant Messenger software on one of my secret computer accounts on a Japanese corporate network in Osaka.

I could have picked a hundred other chat room possibilities, but I figured the odds were enormous that LUNA13 used AOL. Instant Messenger was incredibly simple to use. You create your own "buddy" name, you set up chat possibilities with other buddies. All I needed to do was to add LUNA13 to my Buddy List.

An hour later, having done many searches for that user name, I found nothing.

I switched plans and launched a variety of probes at the AOL computers in Vienna, Virginia. AOL didn't like that.

At least I found out the Internet Protocol addresses of some of the AOL computers. I emailed one of my hacker contacts to see if she had any information on installing a Trojan Horse program on AOL computers, so I could capture user login identities and passwords. I'd never had an Internet challenge I couldn't solve. But this was a whole new, surprising world for me. I wasn't sure I could do the job.

Most surprising, to me, was the total lack of anxiety about my not knowing what to do. A new feeling for me. No anxiety. No panic attack because I thought I'd fail.

Cool.

I turned on CNN again. The desert videotape story now ended with two pictures. The women looked vaguely European, perhaps from Eastern Europe. Names appeared underneath the pictures, and in a flash my entire simple life vanished. I stared at one of the women's pictures and her dyed reddish hair, and memories I had worked so *hard* to suppress came flooding back as bright as sunlight off a mirror, blindingly straight into your eyes.

It was another videotape of the same desert. The quality was better, the camera angles different, and it wasn't shot through a windshield. More like the person was out on the hood of the vehicle, or actually standing on the desert floor. But I was transfixed and horrified by one of the photographs.

Fumbling for the TV remote so I could turn it *off* fast enough, I couldn't get that red hair out of my sight. My mind went through one of those memory sequences where one thing triggers another and another and another.

Dyed raspberry hair.

Meg Arizana.

Meg with the shotgun.

The rattlesnake in Tuba City.

Kimo Biakeddy. Me with the shotgun, walking to meet Kimo. Remembering *exactly* what I was thinking that late, terrifying night.

I shut off the TV and unplugged the set. Totally irrational, I thought, can't unplug reality, so unplug the device. Totally stupid, but I knew myself so well, knew I'd *have* to turn on the TV to watch the pictures over and over. Somehow it was connected with my new contracts, and I'd already decided to turn them down.

When the package arrived, I'd tell the delivery agent No Go!

I'd cancel the meeting with the other client.

Nobody was going to die again from something I set in motion.

God*damn*it! Nobody!

5

And there she was, riding toward me.

Meg Arizana.

Eating a late breakfast, I saw three riders crest a rise and move through the line of oaks behind my stable. I recognized Meg's uneasy riding style and fought a wave of nausea, remembering her agony at killing Audrey Maxwell, who burst into my Tucson home only because I'd stripped away all her power and money.

Never give voice to your demons, I tell you. They may come true.

The other two riders also looked uncomfortable, bobbling around like beginners with the jerky uncertainty of trusting their bodies atop large animals. A woman and a young girl. Threading between three huge saguaros, they rode directly to where I sat under the ramada.

The woman struggled with a boot caught in a stirrup, clasped the saddle horn, and vaulted off the horse. She wore a flowered scarf tied tightly around her head and knotted at the back, but as she landed and stumbled for a moment, the scarf flew off. Her head was totally bald. A portable radio flew out of her front shirt pocket, but she made no attempt to grab it. She grasped the scarf in her hand while running to the house.

"Where's your TV set?"

"Power's off," I said with some irritation.

"Turn it on."

"Why?"

"Do it!" she demanded. "I'll explain. Just turn on the power. Now!"

When I didn't move, she came outside and circled the house until she found the circuit breaker box. I heard her slam the main switch on. She was already in the living room before the screen door banged shut. Using the remote, she turned on the TV, but I'd run the volume control all the way down and she burst outside, slamming the screen door with such force that one hinge cracked, the spring broke with a sharp twang, and the door fell halfway to the ground.

"The sound," she barked at me. "How do I turn up the fucking sound?"

Not even waiting for an answer, she ran back inside and knelt inches from the TV screen and aimed the remote at the TV just as the raspberry hair jumped onto the screen. Flinging away the remote, she knelt in front of the TV and pressed a button until the anchorwoman's voice thundered out of the tinny speakers and set a small vase rattling somewhere in the kitchen. Immune to the volume, she sat with her face only inches from the TV and nodded with the story as she absentmindedly adjusted the scarf on her head.

Meg couldn't settle the three horses, but I quickly realized they were skittish because *she* was skittish and translated the nervous energy to them.

"How you doing?" I said.

"Off my meds," she answered in a high-pitched voice.

"Why?"

Meg was bipolar, although far more manic than depressive. The last time I'd stayed with her at one of her Tucson safe houses for abused women, I'd watched her swallow a ten-pill cocktail in the morning, another at supper.

"Drinking, smoking weed. Peyote. Like that."

Her horse pawed the dirt, tugging the reins. She jerked in response and the horse wheeled around, wild-eyed. I saw a shotgun sheathed in a leather case.

"Meg! What the hell is that?"

"Part of my new look. Check this out."

She turned around, lifted her fluffy white blouse to show a holstered Glock at the small of her back, tucked underneath her skirt.

"Why?" I asked again. "I never thought I'd see you with a gun. Ever."

"Part of the package. Since Columbine, I've been trying to understand these young kids."

"By going off your meds?"

"Sure. Teenage girls are always depressed. I'm getting more of them in my safe houses, but it's a witch's brew. Teenage depression amped up by crossing the border illegally and then being robbed and raped by the *coyotes*. There's a lucky one."

She nodded her head at the teenage girl who sat cross-legged in the dirt with a video camera.

"But *why*, Meg? Why?"

"I have to experience why they're depressed so I can help them. I have to remember depression, remember the inertia, remember . . . anyway, that's the reason."

"That's not a reason, that's just an excuse."

"Don't push on me, Laura!"

"So you're off your meds. You're drinking, you're getting high. Are you eating? Sleeping? I remember you once telling me that when you get manic, you don't do either."

"I sleep an hour or two at a time. Today, I've been up all night. So far, I've had five double espressos, a six-pack of Coronas, some Cuervo Gold tequila shots, a flour tortilla, no, a *corn* tortilla, at least a dozen ibuprofens, five lines of coke, and three orgasms with some cowboy I met in a Catalina bar. My gut is roiling, I've got so much pure adrenaline pumping that I could damn near carry this horse instead of riding him."

"So you're still in the manic phase. What's going to happen when it rolls downhill so fast you can't get away from the depression?"

"Look," she pleaded, "don't ask, okay?"

"Meg. Just tell me why you're doing this?"

"Please, Laura. I can see you're concerned and probably worried. I don't watch myself in the mirror any more, so I'm probably a lot wilder-looking than I realize. I appreciate that you care, that you love me, that you want to help me. But I have to go through this. Even if I really don't understand why, I have to do it. Okay?"

"And why the guns?"

She pirouetted, flouncing up her blouse to show off the handgun in back.

"I killed somebody," she said with a grin that stretched too wide. "Changed my life when I blew away Audrey Maxwell. Even got the same kind of shotgun. The Mossberg. I go places, Laura, I've just got to be packing."

"Packing," I said quietly.

"It means—"

"I know what it means. You used to hate guns. Hate what they did."

"So now it's a love-hate thing. Give me some space with this, Laura. Okay?"

"Okay," I said finally. I tried to hug her, but she squirmed out of my embrace.

As the girl panned her camera around my yard, I caught her face in profile. It was the teenager who'd come to the Vegas hotel.

"Who are they?" I said quietly to Meg.

"Emerine. Mother and daughter. The kid's name is Alex."

She must have seen the strange look on my face.

"You recognize her?"

"And the mother?" I said, avoiding her question.

"Mari. She shoots video documentaries. Said she wanted to do something about illegal immigration, how it's affecting the ranchers down near the border. You know, those people that are getting overrun with immigrants stealing water and food. We've been riding near Sonoita and Patagonia, but she wants to go further south. I told her, no way we're going near the border. But she just started writing me another check, and every time I said no, she wrote a bigger check."

"What kind of cancer?" I asked.

"Left breast. She's still got two more chemo treatments. When her hair fell out, the daughter shaved her own head. For support, she told me. To be with my mom. I think it's silly, but hey . . . what do I know? Never had a kid. Did you?"

"I thought you had a daughter. Loiza?"

"Oh. Yeah, well, she says she's really not my daughter. That's a whole other story, and I'm *so* not going to talk about it. That kid and her mother, they've paid me a ton of money for a ride tomorrow. She thought maybe you'd like to come along. That's why we're here today."

"Come watch," the woman inside shouted at us.

"Well, kid," Meg said anxiously to me. "How's your day so far?"

The anchorwoman wasn't smiling, but you could tell she was excited by the story, that she was smiling inside at her chance to be at the center of the network action.

"This new videotape contains violent images," she said. "You may not want to watch, especially if you have children watching with you."

"No kids here," the teenager said.

"Shut up, Alex. It's starting again."

"I'll shut up, Mom, if you don't crank up the fucking volume again."

"Mari," Meg said to the woman. "You need to chill out here just a little bit."

Mari shook her head so abruptly that her bandanna flew off her head again. She was totally cancer-patient bald but not in any way concerned about her appearance. The daughter knelt beside her and lovingly adjusted the scarf, then nestled into her mother's lap. Alex had a New York Mets baseball cap turned backward on what was obviously a shaved head. Both wore identical Orvis khaki shorts, pale green tank tops, Nike sports bras, off-white calf-high socks and L.L. Bean hiking boots.

"They've got another tape," Alex said excitedly. "Cool!"

A white placard with hand-lettered words appeared on the screen.

"This is Albanian," the anchorwoman said in a voiceover. "Translated, it reads 'You want freedom?' "

The four of us watched, silent, on edge.

Two naked bodies lay twisted on the desert floor. CNN's editors had created digital blurs over the women's faces, breasts, and genitals. Not entirely naked, I realized. Shreds of clothing clung to parts of the bodies. Bits of green, red, blue, yellow, perhaps part of a blouse, a skirt, jeans, a bra, but hard to identify as actual clothing. More like confetti pasted onto the bodies.

Not all confetti.

Both bodies had multiple scratches, bruises, wide patches of skin rasped totally off, bloody bits of confusion that CNN had *not* bothered to cover with their flickering digital blurs. Both women lay haphazard, arms and legs out at odd angles, one woman's head bent sideways at an impossible angle. Both had a rope tied around their ankles, the rope extending a few feet.

The camera panned one hundred and eighty degrees. Nothing but desert. The lens zoomed into a patch of jumping cholla cactus, and I realized that the women had been repeatedly dragged through the cactus patch.

I couldn't watch any more, but just at that moment the videotape ended abruptly. The two women's pictures again appeared.

Veraslava Divodic.

My eyes flicked quickly to the other photo.

Ileanna Fortescu, with raspberry hair.

"Please," I said. "I don't want to watch this. I'm turning off the TV."

"Not yet," Mari said. "I'll explain."

I cut my eyes to Meg. She stared down at her folded

hands, her mouth pressed so tight her lips flattened out to a thin line.

Another lettered sign appeared.

" 'Death,' " the anchorwoman said. " 'Death. That is your freedom!' "

Without warning, the anchorwoman's face went into a fade, and an instant later we were watching a Toyota four-wheel-drive SUV roaring up a mountain road. Alex reached slowly toward the TV set and hit the Power button.

We sat in silence, all of us staring unfocused at the darkened screen.

I have crossed some strange, emotional border, I thought. I'm lost in a completely different country. Facts are so elusive that "truth" and "myth" crisscross from one moment to the next. I felt a touch on my shoulder.

"I'm sorry," Mari said quietly. "I'm really sorry for bursting into your house and hijacking your television. Hijacking your quiet day."

"It's okay."

"No, it's not. But I get crazy from the chemo treatments . . . and I just kinda lose it if I'm excited. I heard the story on my transistor radio while we were horseback riding. I saw on my wireless PDA that a second videotape had been released. I asked Meg where we could find a television, and she said you lived close by."

She shrugged in apology.

"Hey," she said. "Whadya say, early tomorrow morning you come for a horse ride with us?"

"I've got another question," I said.

"Okay."

"A private question."

"Honey," Mari said to her daughter, "why don't you and Meg go outside?"

When they'd left, Mari started to say something, but Alex burst back through the screen door.

"You cool, Mom?"

"Yes. I'm fine, now that I'm out of the sun."

"No. I mean, are you cool, are you feeling okay? Do you need me for anything?"

She sat at her mom's feet and they locked eyes, entered a private universe.

"I'm fine, Alex."

"Okay. Then Meg is going to take me riding for a bit. Wants to teach me how to steer the horse. Or guide him. Whatever. Be gone for an hour. That okay?"

"Yes."

Alex left. Mari studied me again, pulling off the scarf to scratch her head. She blinked as a wave of pain shuddered through her body. She held her eyes shut tight and began breathing deeply, rhythmically, until the pain subsided.

"Who is she?"

"My daughter."

"Alex."

"Alexandra. When she was born, I was in Egypt and was actually reading Durrell's *Alexandria Quartet.*"

"She told me her name was Kimberley."

"One of her user names. She's Kimberly, Ashley, Amber, Lucianna, and a lot of other names I don't even remember. When I ask why she switches her name so much, she says 'Like, *Mom*, it's chat room stuff, LIKE, you *never* use your real name in there.' "

"She's right," I agreed. "Listen. You'd better tell me why you're here. Okay?"

"I'm going to freak you out," she said, smiling weakly.

"Doesn't bother me," I said. "The cancer, I mean."

"Not that."

I waited.

"What?" I finally said.

"Well. Okay, then. Here goes. I'm the package you've been waiting for."

"The package," I said, not understanding what she meant, and she saw it.

"Bobby Guinness. Said you'd get a package today."

"So?"

"Well. I'm the package."

"This is totally fucked," I said. "I can't deal with all of this."

"There's more."

Oh, Jesus Christ, I thought. God*damn*it, just go away, woman, just leave me alone.

"I'm also Bobby Guinness."

6

"That's kinda weird, no?"

She got up and went into the kitchen. I heard her clinking through bottles in my refrigerator, and she returned with a Diet Coke. Zipping her fanny pack open, she took out a baggie and carefully selected five pills.

"Some days, I think I need the sugar more than the pills."

I could see several Zuni fetishes in the baggie.

"What are those?"

She lined them up between us.

"Bear. Healing, curative powers. Owl. Carries prayers to the clouds, prayers for clouds, for rain, for blessings. This guy here, he's my favorite. Mountain lion, carved from amber. Safe journey. Successful journey. Here. Take him."

"I can't do that," I protested.

She pressed the small figure into my hands. Scarcely an inch and a half long, with carefully delineated paws, his tail looped over his back and down the left side. Small, pale blue turquoise eyes, and a turquoise heartline running across his left side.

"I've got three more like him. Take it. For your journey."

"Okay. But . . . what journey?"

"Don't think real trips. More cosmic. Life's a journey. Enjoy the ride."

"Life's a beach, and then you die."

"Please," she said. "I *am* dying."

"I don't like talk like that."

"It is what it is."

"Why are you here?"

An upturned palm, eyes sideways, a slow smile. Lost in her world for a moment, but the smile faded as she locked eyes with mine.

"I don't understand all this," I said.

"Simple. My cancer has metastasized."

"How bad is it?"

"You don't want to know. And it doesn't matter."

"Of course it matters."

"Well, sure, but I don't want to talk about it. Alex thinks I'm okay, because I told her that the mastectomy was successful. No cancer cells at the margins. There were cells everywhere. But she thinks I'm in remission, thinks I'm going to recover, and for now I want her to keep believing that. I'll tell her the truth, when I figure it's the right time. But forget that for a while, okay?"

"I just met you," I said. "I'm hardly going to tell any of this to your daughter."

"More important, you need to know, you need to *trust* that I'm really the person behind Bobby Guinness, behind all the scores we've pulled down this past year."

She rubbed her right shoulder and grimaced.

"You got any pain pills?"

I jumped up like a marionette and she smiled.

"Not the cancer. I jammed my shoulder, getting off that damn beast out there."

"Vicodin," I said. "Percocet. OxyContin. Codeine number three."

"Heavy duty," she said.

"I fell off my horse a few months ago. Had some serious sprains, aggravated my arthritis. When I need it, I take a Vicodin."

"Just some ibuprofen," she said. "I can't take anything stronger. The chemotherapy treatments fuck me up so bad, if I take anything else I'm flat out of the world for a day or two."

I brought her a bottle of generic ibuprofen and she swallowed four tablets.

"So? Do you trust me? Want to ask a few trick questions?"

"I believe you. Trust—that's another thing. I mean, what are you doing here? And who's that man I always talk with?"

"Donald Ralph," she said with a smile. "That's a whole other story, how I hooked up with him. What you need to know is that this is my last score."

"Jesus Christ, Mari. You're hitting me with *waaaaaay* too much stuff here."

"I know. I *know*. But we've got to move quickly. Can you—can you just put aside questions about me, about the cancer? Just talk business? Like you were talking to Bobby instead of me?"

"Is Mari your real name?"

"Yes. I am really Mari Emerine. My husband, Dennis, was a helicopter pilot, killed in Desert Storm. I was in Desert Storm. An army captain. Intelligence. Electronic surveillance, digital recognition software, all that stuff."

"Surveillance."

"Actually, intelligence. Intel, for short. You've seen the live video. Satellite recon, laser-guided missiles and bombs. Totally useless in the real world. But the concept of intelligence, that's discipline. Alex can do anything with a computer. Better than you, maybe. But she has no discipline, no real skills, no real experience. I hear she found those hackers who were manipulating some of the Caribbean online gambling sites."

"So I hear," I said. "But I still don't understand much of this."

"Almost done with my life story, all right?"

"Sure. But I've got to tell you, Mari. I don't think I want in on this contract."

"Somehow," she said, avoiding my comment, "somehow I picked up whatever weird cancerous stuff the US government sprayed during Desert Storm. Two years ago, when it was obvious the government wasn't going to acknowledge that it caused my cancer, I had to look for a way to make a lot of money. I set up my network, recruited people like you."

"How did you find me?"

I had to know, you see, had to know how she found me.

"Anybody who does what you do leaves tracks."

"Not me."

"I'm here. Isn't that proof enough?"

Actually, it was devastating. If she could track me, anybody could. Against my will I started running through all the different identity kits I'd created, thinking it was time to move on and be somebody else.

"But I phased out everybody else. Now, they're all out of the loop. You're the best, and you're all I've got left."

"Why me?"

"Why not? Wait. I've got something for you."

We went out to the horses. She pulled a envelope from a saddlebag and looked around my garden area.

"Can we sit in the sun?"

"It's ninety degrees. Can you tolerate the sun?"

"I need heat. Warms my bones, warms my blood."

We sat in ancient lawn chairs next to an old wooden cable spool that Heather Aguilar had made into a table. She bent her head toward a creosote bush, got down on her hands and knees.

"What's this?" she asked, pointing at a round hole about an inch in diameter. "You got big ants around here?"

"Some kind of mouse."

She poked a finger into the hole.

"Hey! It's closed up about two inches down."

"They seal in humidity."

"Cool!" she said with real excitement and curiosity. "What kind of mice?"

"Cactus mouse. Pocket mouse. Plain old house mouse."

She sat at the table again, ripped open the envelope, took

out four sheets of paper, and handed them to me, watching as I leafed quickly through them. They were financial records of what looked like the transfer of money from Mexican banks to places in the Cayman Islands and Switzerland.

"You want me to track this money?"

"For starters, yes. Here's some background. What do you know about the Zedillo government that got voted out in Mexico?"

"Nothing except who lost and who won."

"Vicente Fox. He's trying to clean up a lot of corruption. Some of it related to government and military officials who embezzled money from their agency funds. Some of it related to police corruption, payoffs from smuggling drugs and people. My client is a private citizen. He just wants to get the money back."

"He?"

"Why did you ask that?"

What's in a name? I thought. Anybody can be anybody.

"You're right," she said. "A man contacted me originally, but the client could be anybody. Forget gender. Just look at the money trail."

I ran my fingers down the pages.

"This in pesos? Dollars?"

"Dollars, pesos, francs, marks, Dutch guilders, some Asian currencies I can't even pronounce. I figure, rounded to top dollar, hundreds of millions. My client isn't asking to get it all back. Just what I can find. My fee is twenty percent of what they recover. No questions asked by the Mexican government. Can you trace these things?"

"Difficult."

"But not impossible. I know what you did with that medical insurance scam last year in Tucson. I know how much you got back, so I know you can dance your way through any bank account in the world."

"Who's your client?" I asked.

"I don't even know. He's got or *she's* got cutouts, just like me and Bobby."

"Who is this guy, this Donald Ralph?"

"Don, actually. He's also a Vietnam vet, plus he's a paraplegic. Kinda like one of those guys you see in computer geek movies, the guy who runs his wheelchair within a circle of computers and telephones and all other kinds of gadgets."

"Like the guy in *The Matrix*."

"Yeah. But that's a kid movie. Why did you watch it?"

"For the technology. About your client—"

"The client's not important. But the urgency comes from the fact that President Fox is reported to be closing in on indictments of some of the embezzlers. My client thinks this will make them transfer the money again, maybe several times. We need to monitor offshore banks, look for the cash, then grab it. Can you get there first, Laura?"

It was the first time she'd used my name.

"Maybe," I said. "It's just not that easy. I'm used to finding cash, but there are a ton of island countries that have banks. Some of them are really *small* islands."

"Yeah. But you find people by first finding how they spend money."

"You said there were two clients. This is the first. Who's the person you wanted me to meet?"

"First I should explain a little more about who I am. Why I do what I do. You probably thought that I—no, that Bobby Guinness—had a very big operation going. But the truth is that I've focused almost entirely on very carefully selected scores. Maybe three a month. I've closed all the rest of them out. You're the only person left, as I told you. So when this second score was pitched to me, I was all ready to say no when the client told me it was connected to smuggling, probably headquartered in Nogales."

"Drugs?"

"People. Women. I wanted to say no to the score, but . . . I've discovered that money isn't the prime motivator any more."

"I'm in this just for the money," I said. "I know *my* motives. What are yours?"

"Changing."

"From what?"

"When my own army, my own government denied that they've killed me, I thought what the hell, if their morality is fucked, so is mine. That's how I got into the gray areas between what's digitally legal and what's not."

"Like me."

"I don't know if I'm like you," she said. "I really don't know you at all. But with the cancer, I seem to have gotten back my ethics. My morality. My sense of being a mother, responsible for a teenage daughter's future. Plus, I've got no health insurance. Since the US government denies that I got this cancer from Desert Storm, they won't pay for my treatments, which cost a hell of a lot of money when you're uninsured."

"You haven't sold me yet."

"On the contract?"

I nodded.

She upended the envelope, squeezed the sides, and shook it. A small scrap of paper fell out and floated to the ground. I reached down to get it.

LUNA13.

"That's the user name Bobby gave me," I said. "Sorry. Donald."

"Yeah," she said, draining the Diet Coke can and getting up for another. "That's where you come in. I can tell you in excruciating detail anything you want to know about cancer. But computers? The Internet? Hacking into bank accounts? That's you, baby. Listen. I've got to move around, catch my breath."

I followed her into the kitchen.

"Can I ask you another question?" I said.

"Sure."

"I just wondered . . . does the chemo affect your judgment?"

"You want to know if I'm wacky about these two scores?"

"Wouldn't you ask the same question of me?"

"The chemo seriously fucks up my head. Almost every

day. But listen, if you take all those drugs you told me about, then your body, or maybe just your head, is screwed up in some way that you just push underneath your mind and don't think about. I'm no different."

"Fair enough," I said after a while. "Fair enough."

"So. LUNA13. There must be millions of user names on the Internet. How do you go about finding the one name you want?"

"Not easy at all. You got specific email addresses, right?"

"Sure."

"A user name . . . it's not as specific as an email address. Or a website URL."

"Why not?"

"Have you ever been in a chat room?"

"Alex has. I think her current user name is boogie4ever."

"Exactly. People make up these user names, but you can't tell the players by their fantasies. Luna. Could be anything. Anybody."

"It's Spanish for moon," she said after a while.

"It's also a moth. Listen, Mari. It could take me weeks to find who the person is. Months. Maybe never."

"I understand that. If you want up-front money, let me know. One last thing. Remember Don asking if you knew somebody who could watch your back? Not just muscle, but street smarts? Probably knows Mexico? Speaks Spanish?"

I immediately thought of Rey Villaneuva, and as I did so, she smiled.

"I know who you're thinking about."

"Not a chance."

"I *know* you, Laura. I know a lot about you. I know about that nasty business in Tucson last year. I know about Mr. Villaneuva. Can you get him?"

"Maybe."

She drained the second Diet Coke, glanced around the kitchen looking for my trash bucket, lined herself up, and tossed a jumpshot. The can clinked on the bucket's rim and clattered around on my tile floor.

"Losing more muscles," she said with a grimace. "A month ago, I'd've made that shot. So. There's one more thing. This little ride Heather has arranged for me. I've got a tip-off that I have to check out. I want you to come along. But first, can you find Villaneuva today? See if he'll help us?"

"Maybe," I said, my eyes down and to the right, realizing I knew where he was.

"Out*stand*ing!" she said.

"How much does Alex know?" I said. "About what you do."

"Not much. But then she's a teenager. She picks up things from anywhere, so she might realize that I have a whole other life. In time, she'll learn. I've made my peace with the cancer, so I forget the impact it has on other people. Let's be up front. You want to know how bad my cancer is. You want to know how fast you've got to find this money, and you're about to tell me that it could take weeks or months."

I *did* want to know, but how could I ask such direct questions?

"Well. Truth or dare. I've got six weeks at the outside. But even if I die, you'll be able to get the money for Alex. That's all that's important."

"That's all?" I said weakly.

"Of course not," she snapped.

A series of muffled explosions echoed back and forth among the hills.

"What the hell is that?" I said.

"Shotgun. Do people hunt on this property?"

Meg, I thought.

"It's my friend. Sorry."

"My daughter is qualified in all kinds of weapons, but she wouldn't shoot anything without checking with me first."

"Your daughter shoots? Guns?"

"After Columbine, I vowed my daughter would know everything I knew. Come on. Let's go see what they're shooting at."

Meg and Alex strolled toward us, the sun bright behind them, darkening their bodies into shadow puppets. But I could see Alex was cradling the shotgun as Meg gestured wildly with both hands.

"Your friend's got a drug problem," Mari said.

"More than you know," I answered. "She's out of control."

"Oh, I don't think so." Mari narrowed her eyes against the sun, raised her right hand like the brim of a cap over her eyes. "She *wants* you to think that, but I've seen a lot of people about to slide over the edge. They get a wild look, their eyes don't focus on things very well, they don't smile a lot. Your friend? Nope. She's playing some game I don't yet understand, but she's perfect for what I want to do."

"And that's what?" I asked.

"You'll see. Better that I don't try to explain it. Just wait."

7

"That kid really knows how to shoot."

"Jesus, Meg. How could you let her near your guns?"

"Said no. Three times. The kid's a natural. Reminds me of you."

"I don't even own a gun."

"Didn't mean that. She's great with guns. From listening to her talk nonstop, I guess she's great at computers."

"So?"

"You're both outsiders, Laura."

"What does that mean?"

"Look at you. Living out in the middle of nowhere. Traveling off to jobs where you bunker up in some hotel, staring at computer screens."

"I'm happy with that."

"Laura, you've got a serious lack of social skills."

"Yeah," I grinned. "But I'm getting better at it."

"Are you?" she said, with a long stare ending in a sudden quiver of her cheek muscles. "Whoa. Time for downers."

She uncapped a vial, dropped three small yellow pills into her right hand, and flung them into the back of her mouth. She swallowed with a shudder.

"Valium. Takes the edge off."

We watched Mari and Alex ride over a hill and disappear, leading Meg's horse. Meg begged off riding back to Heather's stables after I promised to drive her there. I thought she was just weary of riding, but she had something else in mind.

"You going down to see Rey?"

"No," I lied.

"He's got this thing for you, Laura."

"Come on."

"He talks to me about it."

"Whatever."

"He's changed, Laura. You should give him a chance."

"No thanks."

"Hey. When was the last time you had sex?"

I blushed and she grinned.

"No big deal," she said. "I'm screwing two guys right now. I want it. I need it."

"Not me."

"Not yet, you mean. So. You going to see him?"

On my way to Nogales to see Rey about backup for the client meet later in the afternoon, I thought about everything Mari had told me. I'd decided to at least meet the client, and then I'd decide whether to take the contracts.

Or not.

Meg was right about one thing. It wasn't so much a matter of lacking social skills as it was the need to acquire them. Meet people. Make a few friends. Move out of my *casita*, move into a neighborhood. Totally new thoughts for me.

I blanked them out.

Mari had two clients, two possible contracts, two different kinds of work.

Embezzlement and smuggling.

The first thing was easy. I'd tracked so much money as it fluttered around the world that I knew just about every kind of Internet possibility for transferring funds.

But smuggling.

Living near the Mexican border, smuggling was a subject never more than day's news away from reality. Drugs were a major problem. But many smugglers were turning to people instead of drugs. This summer, even though it was only July, more immigrants had died in the Arizona deserts than any previous year. And for the first time national media regularly featured stories about immigrants being smuggled from other continents into Mexico, across the US border, and to states in the northeast, the south, and even to isolated states like North Dakota.

I couldn't figure Mari's interest in smuggling people. She'd told me a lot, but in some ways, she'd told me very little.

Pulling into Nogales, driving mostly on autopilot, I almost blundered into the one-way street that funneled traffic into the border crossing point. I swerved abruptly into a no-parking zone, narrowly missing a Ford pickup loaded with laborers. They laughed at my driving, swearing good-naturedly after me and raising beer cans in salute.

Ahead of me, past the US and Mexican customs plazas, the roadway into the Mexican city of Nogales slanted up through the notch between two hillside *colonia* neighborhoods. Groups of shacks and huts intermingled with sturdier houses, unpaved streets, power lines and sewers weaving randomly through the rough neighborhoods. Buenos Aires, one of the tougher *colonias*, lay directly in front of me. I'd heard that many smugglers operated out of the houses.

It was the border that so threatened me. Once beyond it, my entire existence depended on totally different circumstances, and I wasn't sure I wanted to risk being involved, particularly if it meant I had to deal with the drug and smuggling cartels. Many Mexicans accepted their rough existence with a shrug. *Fatalismo*, they'd say. Life down here, it is what it is.

Seeing a break in traffic, I pulled away from the curb and went looking for Rey.

8

"Drop your gun!" the man screamed, squeezing his left forearm around the neck of the young woman in front of him. Both of them wore cammie jumpsuits and hockey helmets with clear plastic visors.

"Fucking *drop your gun* or I'll fucking blow her fucking head off."

Gunshots echoed loudly throughout the old factory building. A uniformed policeman crouched in the Weaver stance, his body turned sideways at a thirty-degree angle, left hand underneath and supporting the grips of his paint gun. Hesitating, he bobbed and weaved as he tried to get a line of sight. The visor of his hockey helmet was misting up from sweat.

"Oh, for Christ's sake," Rey said with disgust. "Shoot the son of a bitch."

"I might hit her."

"He's going to kill her anyway. Shoot him before he shoots you."

The policeman still hesitated. Rey quickly drew his own paint gun and aimed it at the gunman, who immediately swung his own paint gun around the woman's right arm and fired. A large blob of red paint splattered onto the policeman's visor, knocking his head back. He staggered in obvious pain and dropped to his knees. Rey backed off ten feet and fired his paint gun at the policeman's left thigh. Blue paint splashed all over the leg and crotch of his cammies and he shouted in pain.

"Ice it down," Rey said.

"Are you crazy?" the policeman shouted. "What did you do that for?"

"Next time there's a hostage situation, you'll remember. The hostage is dead anyway. Forget about lawsuits, forget about looking for your best shot, just unload. What's your standard weapon?"

The policeman ripped off his helmet and flung it across the room. He tried to stand up, but his leg gave out, and he slumped to the concrete floor. Rey knelt beside him and put a hand on his shoulder.

"I know you don't like me much, right now. I know you're hurting. Just focus on this thought. You're alive."

"Ah, fuck you."

"And you're angry as hell. That's okay with me. Now come on, stand up."

He offered an arm, but the policeman refused assistance and tottered to his feet.

"Enough of this shit," he said.

"Not a chance. We're running this again, from the top."

The gunman in cammies took off his helmet and began wiping the visor clean.

"Captain," the policeman said, "I can hardly stand up. Forget this shit."

"You can forget it, Officer. And you can forget working for the Pasadena Police Department. Make your choice, right now. Continue training and you continue your job."

The policeman's shoulders sagged, but he slowly nodded.

"What's your standard issue sidearm?" Rey asked again.

"Glock 17."

"God help you if you ever get in a real situation like this. In a high school, or an office building, whatever. But all the instincts ground into you from police academy, you've got to rebuild those instincts right here. You can't hesitate, you can't think, you don't even squeeze off a double tap and then wait to fire again. Confronted with the assassin, you empty your magazine as fast as you can squeeze them off. I don't care if you're using the Glock or an assault rifle, you empty the magazine and reload. Did you ever see that movie *Heat?*"

"What is this shit. You want me to watch a movie?"

"Los Angeles movie," Rey said patiently, ignoring the policeman's obvious anger. "Big bank robbery scene. Robert DeNiro, Val Kilmer, they don't hesitate firing their M-16s at policemen. Full automatic. New clip. Full automatic. Kill the son of a bitches, before they kill you. Got that? Watch the movie."

"Yeah, whatever."

"Watch it tonight," the captain said. "Go to a video store, rent the movie."

"There's no VCR in my hotel room."

"I've got the movie on DVD," Rey said. "Tonight, we can have a few beers, watch the movie. Okay?"

"Whatever."

"All right," Rey said. "I'll give you all fifteen minutes to reset, then we're running the whole scenario again."

As the three of them left the warehouse space, Rey carefully set his paint gun on the floor, avoiding me for a minute. He took a deep breath and faced me. A sudden spasm of gunfire echoed through the building and he held up a hand, palm toward me, and went to an electronic console to flick a switch. The gunfire stopped abruptly.

"Sorry. Part of the training atmosphere. It's a tape loop. I forgot it was on."

"Hey," I said.

"Hey."

"Been a while."

"Eleven months."

"How you been?"

"Ah, shit," he said. "I've been dreaming about this day

forever, and here you are, and all of a sudden I'm the same hopeless, nervous, useless son of a bitch I was at Miguel's funeral. Come on. Let's get out of here."

We ate burritos and chile rellenos at a rusted metal table outside Pico's Taco Delight on the Northside of Nogales. The restaurant was built into an old Texaco station, its ancient paved driveway cracked and spotted with patches of grass and weeds. Bougainvillea vines grew from a jury-rigged PICO'S sign built over the forty-year-old rooftop. The red bougainvillea flowers spilled down onto the gas pumps.

Rey avoided talking, ordering another burrito supreme, then a third Negra Modelo. I couldn't stand the silence any longer.

"What?" I said. "What's the problem?"

"You show up like this. No calls for months, I don't even know where you live, and boom, you just show up. I don't do well with surprises like that."

"Would it be different if I was a client?"

"Client? For my SWAT training?"

"Not for that. For, say, protection."

"Hey! Are you in trouble?"

"No. I need somebody to watch my back. Ever since Tigger died, I've never used anybody else. I get all my work through my computers, cell phones, mail drops. I don't meet clients any more. But tonight, I *have* to meet a client. I need somebody watching my back, doing surveillance, following the client when he leaves me."

"That's why you came to see me?"

"You sound disappointed."

He drained the beer bottle, seemed ready to order another, but checked himself.

"It's . . . it's hard for me, seeing you all of a sudden. I get all these weird feelings, I'm not sure what to think about you."

"Hey," I said lightly, "just because I'm here doesn't mean we're engaged."

I thought he'd laugh, but his face screwed up even tighter

for an instant and then shifted to a neutral expression, as though he'd decided to distance himself from me.

"Backup. Surveillance. I don't know, Laura. Hell, I don't even know if your name is still Laura."

"Yes."

"You've changed."

"How?" I was surprised.

"You're so . . . confident. In charge. I remember you as a neurotic mess."

"Thanks a lot."

"I remember you as not being much happy about your life."

"Do I seem happy now?"

"Funny thing is, you do."

"Look, Rey. I'm glad to see you." I reached across the table and grabbed both his hands. "I knew where you were all these months. I knew you took your part of the money and bought that warehouse, started the SWAT school. I knew all of that. But when it came to letting you know where I was living, I couldn't allow that."

"So where are you living?"

"Up near Sonoita. But I don't have time to talk about it. It's almost one o'clock. By three I've got to be set up in Tucson for the client meeting with a backup person in place. I've got my routines and I need to follow them, but I'm rusty."

"Yeah. Well. I remember what happened to your last backup person."

"That's a low shot."

"I didn't mean it that way. About Tigger. I just . . . I don't know what you need me to do, that's all. But if you're asking for backup, that means it could be trouble."

"Unlikely." I thought about Tigger and sighed. "Possible. But unlikely."

He lined up the three beer bottles side by side. Picking up one bottle, he slid another sideways, and shuffled their order like a three-card monte dealer. He rearranged them again, tops together at the center, bottles radiating out sixty degrees apart.

"I'm not being honest here. I'm not telling you what I'm feeling."

"Jesus Christ, Rey. You *never* told me what you were feeling!"

"Well, things change. I've changed. You've changed. Here's the thing. You showing up here, you've jumpstarted all my memories about you. I don't know if I want that. I don't know if I want you in my life."

"That's honest. Why?"

He shrugged and tried to balance one bottle on top of another.

"You see how many beers I've had in just twenty minutes? Three. I've been dealing with alcoholism for the past six months. I've been managing. Surviving."

"You belong to AA?"

"That's a bunch of crap. Twelve steps, higher power, my ass. *I'm* the power over my own life. I manage. A beer a day, that's my survival rate. And look at me. I see you and I'm already three beers down."

"Are you telling me you don't want to be there today?"

"Forget I brought it up. I'll be sober. Just tell me, what time's the meet."

"Four-twenty."

"Where?"

"The Desert Museum."

He lined up his three beer bottles, chinking them with his spoon, nodding his head in time to the rhythm.

"Okay. I'll meet you in the parking lot at three. I've got a dark blue Jeep Wrangler, ragtop and roll bars."

"What's your fee?"

"Jesus Christ, Laura. You think I'd do this for money?"

"It's strictly business," I said with my best Al Pacino godfather imitation, and he finally smiled.

"Nothing personal?"

"Of course it's personal. I don't trust anybody else. I don't even *know* anybody else I'd trust as a backup, not since Tigger."

"Okay. Tonight we'll handle the business end. I'll follow the client, give you the rundown on whatever I find out. You got particulars?"

"No idea who it is. Thanks, Rey."

"One other thing. Nobody knows me by that name. I am Ramón Vargas."

"Are you serious?"

"You taught me a lot, Laura. Maybe when we can work out how to talk about things, I'll tell you what's happened to me since I last saw you. But remember. To anybody, to *every*body. You don't know where to find Rey Villaneuva."

"Ramón Vargas. That's the Charlton Heston character."

"*Touch of Evil*. You see the director's cut?"

"Rey. This is unreal."

"Ramón."

"Whatever."

"No," he insisted, almost tapping me on the chest he was so serious. "I've got my own devils about being somebody else. For a while. Okay?"

"Has this got anything to do with Meg?"

"How do you know that?"

"I guessed."

"You're spooky, Laura. Yeah. It's kind of about Meg. And Amada."

"Why did she change it from Loiza?"

"When Meg got—crazy—last month, when she got on this Columbine kick about depressed teenagers and went off her meds, Amada couldn't stand it any more and came to live with me."

"Amada."

"Loved one. That's what it means in Spanish."

"I know. It's just a little strange. Changing her name and all."

"That's *her* business," Rey snapped. "We've both learned from you, Laura. Keep our lives private. Change our names. Just like you."

Okay. My legacy. Convincing my friends to have secret identities.

"Four o'clock," he said, standing up so quickly he jiggled the table and the beer bottles fell over and rolled off onto the dirt. "Let me get you back to your car, and I'll run those Pasadena cops extra ragged and tell 'em it was your idea."

"Why Ramón Vargas?" I asked.

"I wanted to see what it was like," he finally said.

"To be anonymous," I said, knowing this was what he meant.

"Yeah. To be somebody you're not. I spent five months at my father's place drinking and shooting apart that screening on his porch. You remember that day we visited and he paid me no mind, just kept shooting holes in that screen? After I buried him, I must have worked through fifty boxes of cartridges, blasting that screen while I blasted my head with tequila. One day I shot clean through one of the main roof supports and the porch collapsed on my head. So I got sober, bought a new identity, and opened my business in Nogales. True story. Nobody knows who I am."

"I do," I said. "Except you've changed. You don't avoid talking about things. You don't throw me lines from some movie and leave me to figure out what you mean."

He avoided my question, watching an old woman push a fruit and vegetable cart down the dusty street. The cart was almost empty except for a few limes and several dozen bruised plantains. The woman hesitated in front of us, her head tilting sideways at me. I caught her eyes and quickly looked away, but not quickly enough. She silently held five plantains in the palms of her gnarled, brown hands. Rey gave her several pesos and she started to push the cart away as she furtively glanced up and down the street.

"*Cocaína*?" she whispered. "*Heroína?*"

"Are you selling drugs?" I said, incredulous.

"Nieve? Chiva?"

Thinking we were buyers, she unfastened the straps of her skirt to display several cloth bags hanging underneath. Rey flicked a hand, urging her away.

"Arrestado," he threatened.

"Carajo!"

With her curse, the woman spit at his feet and pushed her cart rapidly down the street. He laid the plantains on the cigarette-scarred tabletop, dusting his hands together, winding his fingers into knots.

"Yeah. Well. It is what it is. DeNiro says that to Pacino. In *Heat*."

"So you haven't totally changed."

"Except now I realize what I'm doing. It's like acting, this thing of mine. By being Ramón Vargas, instead of being myself, I get this weird freedom to say things I wouldn't. Is that how you feel when you use another name?"

"This whole conversation is weird," I said. "What I really want to know is if Meg is going over the edge."

"No. She's not. I had my really bad times, I got out of it okay. Now it's her turn. But she's going to be okay. Just give her some time."

"You've both changed. How did that happen?"

He rubbed his temples, hard, first with his fingers and then actually pressing his knuckles so tight against his skin that when he took his hands away he left whitened dimples on his darkened skin.

"The simple answer is Columbine High School. But, really, Meg's been sheltering abused women for almost ten years. She now has safe houses all over Arizona, and more and more of the women showing up there are illegals. Undocumented workers, that's the politically correct new term. And most of these women are incredibly depressed, even though they've just been offered freedom from abuse. I guess Meg felt she could help them even more if she just understood why they were so depressed."

"And the guns?" I asked. "A year ago she had such a horror of gun violence."

"She killed a woman, Laura. The killings at Columbine just set off an explosion in her head. *She* had killed, *she* was alive, and she felt enormously guilty. It's ironic, no? I stopped using guns, she started."

"Except you teach people to kill."

"Only because it saves lives," he insisted.

Kill to save lives.

A paradox of our times, I thought. Life is short enough, but if you kill somebody quickly, you grant longer lives to others.

9

Rey leaned against the left side of his Wrangler, put his hands straight out onto the hood, and started what looked like bench presses in reverse. His body rigidly straight, he lowered himself slowly to within an inch of the hood and held himself there for thirty seconds, pushed himself vertical, and repeated the whole routine.

I watched him for ten minutes and couldn't stand it any more. Parked three rows away, I slammed my pickup door hard, the sound like a pistol shot. A family of five, getting out of a van thirty feet away, looked abruptly around the parking lot, the woman with a hand to her mouth, looking anxious. Rey finished his last pushoff and waited for me to join him.

Diamond-lensed sunglasses covered his eyes. The sunglass temples didn't go above his ears but were positioned higher on his head, on either side of an Arizona Cardinals gimme cap. He wore a light blue tank top tucked neatly into unpressed khaki Docker slacks. The tank tops straps were extra wide, about two inches, and I wondered if he'd had it specially made. Everything fit tight against his body.

His hair had just been restyled in a fade cut. Razored almost to the skin, from neck to an inch or so above his ears, then cut progressively longer until the inch-and-a-half top hairs. I couldn't remember his hair being totally black and wondered if he dyed it. He extended his arms out from his sides and turned completely around.

"I hope you didn't want firepower," he said.

"No. Not really."

"Good. I don't shoot guns any more. What's the drill?"

I wanted to ask why a paint gun was different than a Glock, but I thought I'd better let that one slide, not knowing what he'd been through in the past eleven months to deal with his explosive tendency to solve problems with violence. His voice was pitched lower, his tones more neutral than when we'd spoken a few hours earlier.

"What's the drill?" he repeated.

Okay, I thought, for now we'll play it just like a business agreement. I took out my equipment toolboxes from the back of the crewcab. I gave him a cell phone, a belt holster, and a plug-in wire for microphone and earpiece.

"Do you have a shirt? A jacket?"

"Why?"

"I don't want people to notice how wired up you are."

He took a canvas jacket from the Wrangler backseat and shrugged it on. Once he'd rigged the holster on his belt, I helped him adjust the wire, but he immediately took the whole thing off.

"Too hot, too unnatural, wearing this jacket. Besides, if this place is anything like the world, half the people in there will be talking on cell phones."

I spread a map of the Desert Museum on top of the Wrangler's hood and pointed to the Desert Walk in the far eastern section of the property.

"It's getting near closing time. Not too many people will be out this way, but there'll still be a lot of visitors, so you can mingle in anywhere."

I unslung my Nikon camera bag.

"You know how to use this?"

"Nikon F5. Autofocus, rapid shutter. Long lens. You got plenty of film?"

"Four rolls of thirty-six exposures. Should be enough. And here, take this."

I unslung the binocular case from my other shoulder. He nodded in admiration.

"Ten by forty-two. Birding glass. I'll just be another *turista, qué no*."

"Exactly."

"So what does this client look like?"

"No idea. So you'll have to pick him up when I start the meet. When it gets near the meet time, I'll call your cell phone from mine. When the meet's over, you follow him out to the parking lot, get pictures of the vehicle, then follow him."

Following the Desert Museum map, I wandered to the far end of the highlands trail and sat on a rustic oak bench across from the bear enclosure. With the waterfall adding background noise, I figured it was the easiest spot to avoid anybody listening without getting so close I'd notice them. Fastening my cell phone microphone cord, I couldn't help looking about to see where Rey was located.

I punched in the numbers of his phone and hit TALK.

"Yes," he said immediately.

"You've got me?"

"Yes."

"Camera ready? You've glassed me with the binoculars?"

"Just get it on," he said shortly. "I'm going to start talking to my girlfriend."

"Don't make another call, Rey. Stay with me."

"Jesus, Laura. There's no girlfriend. But I'm standing here with this phone to my ear. I've got to make up some kind of conversation. Just don't pay attention."

"Where are you?"

"Twenty away. Around the curve, in front of the Mexican gray wolves."

"Stay out of sight."

"So are they."

"Say what?"

"The wolves. A dozen people standing here to see those wolves, but they're holed up in back. Probably sleeping. Fine thing. Here I've lived in Mexico half my life, spent months in the desert, never seen a wolf."

I took out my earpiece, spread the Desert Museum map on my knees, and looked at my watch. 4:19.

A young couple strolled by the bear enclosure. They walked slowly, hand in hand, toward me. I jammed the earpiece into my left ear.

"Rey. Heads up."

"I see them."

They were young, maybe mid- to late-twenties, both wearing faded denim jeans and tee-shirts. The front of his tee had a graphic of a two-door lowrider coupe painted a vivid cranberry with lots of yellow pinstriped patterns. When he turned for a moment, I read the back of the shirt, which said 82 OLDS CUTLASS. Her yellow tee had nothing on it. She wore it over her jeans with a Navajo silver concho belt tied loosely around her waist. A soft leather purse hung from a strap over her left shoulder

She was extraordinarily beautiful.

They ambled along the path, looking around. She was cool and ignored me. He couldn't. Standing finally at the edge of the bench, she swiveled slowly in a complete circle, looking to see who else was around. Since it was only a half-hour before closing, visitors were walking away from us to the exits.

"Who are you?" she said without looking at me.

"Call me whatever you want. It really doesn't matter."

"I shall call you . . . Ishmael."

She spoke with an obvious European accent, but she looked Hispanic.

"Ishmaela," she said with a smile. "You've read *Moby Dick?*"

"I saw the movie," I said. "And who are you?"

"Another Ishmaela," she said wistfully as she sat next to me. "Luis. Can you go back over to find the wolf?"

"You'll be all right?"

"Luis, it's only thirty feet away. Yes. I'll be all right."

He left us alone. She avoided looking at me, and a line of sweat came down just outside her left eye. She wiped it away with a quick, nervous gesture. Looking me in the face, she frowned at the wire that ran from my earpiece.

"Oh, Mary and Joseph," she said. "Please, *please* tell me that you're not a cop."

"Just a cell phone."

"Cops use cell phones. I'm leaving."

"No, no. It's connected to my backup man, okay?"

"I don't trust you."

"I don't trust you either. But here we are."

She looked down and to the left. Her lips moved slightly as she thought things through for herself, then she looked up.

"Okay," she said.

"This is a weird moment for both of us. So take a few breaths, look me over all you want for a minute or two, then tell me what you want from me. You're a potential client. That's all I care about."

"You saw the videotape, on the news?" she blurted.

"Yes. Did you know them?"

"No. Yes. No."

She began to cry. I let her sob for a moment. She opened her purse and took out some tissues and blew her nose.

"I didn't know them by name. I'm not even sure I met them. But there are hundreds of us from Albania."

After a few moments, she reached into her purse again and took out several sheets of paper listing names, addresses, and phone numbers. I glanced at them quickly.

"Which one is you?"

She pointed. I put that sheet on top.

"Xochitl Gálvez?" I stumbled over the words. "That's your name? How do you pronounce that?"

"Zo-*shee*-til *Gal*-vez."

"That doesn't sound Albanian," I said.

"It's not. My real name isn't important."

Pulling a cell phone from her purse, she displayed it in the palm of her hand. "This phone number is where I work. A restaurant called Nonie, the Creole restaurant in Tucson. On Grant near Campbell. You can find me there from Tuesday through Saturday nights. You know the place?"

"No."

Loudspeakers crackled.

"The Desert Museum will be closing in fifteen minutes. Please make your way to the exits, and thanks for spending your day with us."

The announcement echoed across the grounds from several loudspeakers. A gentle woman's voice, not insistent, just informational.

"I don't understand what you want of me," I said.

"You know about the *coyotes* and you know about the people who cross the border illegally."

"Yes."

"There are many ways to come across. Me, I came through the water tunnels. Hundreds of people every day gamble on those tunnels. They pay lots of money, they hope they've found an honest *coyote*. Most of us have crossed several times, but La Migra caught us and sent us back. The Albanian women discovered a special connection, and once we believed we were safe in this country, we began to organize."

"Is there a group in Mexico?" I asked. "Somebody who helps?"

"It's called *Basta Yo*. They get us across, they get us new papers, and then we all help each other."

"My Spanish isn't very good. *Basta*, I know what that means. 'Enough.' "

"*Basta Yo* is a workers' organization. Like the Zapatistas in Chiapas. *Basta Yo* is organized in Sonora, first for Indian women and mestizos. They are involved with foreign women, they help us get out of Mexico illegally. A special *coyote* arranges these things. He takes only special clients. Women only, like me. My Mexican identity papers were fake. But very good fakes. This *coyote* from *Basta Yo*, he worked only with Albanian women. But things have changed."

"How?" I asked.

"Somebody called the water man."

"What does that mean?"

"I don't know. Probably somebody connected with those tunnels."

"Wait," I protested. "I'm really confused. There are two competing groups that smuggle women across the border?"

"Yes."

"And this new connection, this 'water man' or whatever, he takes money but doesn't really do what he's paid for?"

"No, no, no. He brings in women from Albania, Russia, Rumania, from all over Eastern Europe. They paid enormous amounts of money to get as far as Mexico. Thirty thousand dollars. Fifty thousand. But once they got to Mexico, they found out they owed the water man so much money that he demanded immediate payment. If they didn't pay, they could go to the US and work as strippers. As whores. Sex slaves."

"Wait a minute," I said. "I'm not a detective, like, a private investigator who goes out looking for real people. Everything I do is on computers. I find out where people live, but I never see them personally, and I *really* don't want to get involved in something so dangerous as messing with the Mexican drug cartels. You need to hire somebody else."

"But it does involve computers."

"Xochitl!" I complained, "you're really not making much sense."

"Okay, okay," she said excitedly, holding my arm when I started to stand up. "Listen to my story, to the story of my sisters, my friends. Then decide if you want to help me or not. Okay?"

"Make it a short story."

"In Albania, there are organized criminal gangs which control illegal trafficking in women and children. Albanians are desperately poor. Mothers and fathers sometimes cannot feed their young daughters. Teenage daughters. Maybe as old as eighteen, but maybe as young as twelve or thirteen. So men offer to marry these girls, take them to the big cities, give them a stable life with good food, clothing, a nice apartment. Except there really is no marriage. In the earlier years, the girls were smuggled by boat from Albania to Italy, where they were sold to other men as prostitutes."

"You were sold this way?" I asked.

"Three times. From one man to another. By auctions. All girls would be stripped down to their underwear, sometimes, even not underwear. Just naked. The men would feel our bodies, make bids, pay in cash. Some men demanded sex before they would bid."

"Jesus Christ, Xochitl. That's slavery. You became a slave?"

"Yes. But please, my story is not *the* story. Hundreds of girls are kidnapped like this every month. Many thousands a year, not just from Albania, but all over eastern Europe and Asia."

"If you were smuggled into Italy, how did you come to Mexico?"

"Many of the smuggler's boats were seized, so the trafficking cartel started to use, um, what do you call them, ship containers?"

"Inside the containers?" I gasped. "You came to Mexico by ship, living inside a metal container? How long were you trapped inside?"

"Two, three weeks, I'm not sure. Thirty of us in one container. Very little food and water. Buckets for toilets. We landed at Vera Cruz, where there was another auction, and groups of girls were sent to different places in Mexico. With fifty other girls, I was bought by the water man. He took us to Nogales."

"And you want me to find this water man?"

"Yes."

"No way," I protested.

"His money. You find his money. Others will take care of the man."

"Do you know his name?"

"No. But we just learned there is a money trail. Isn't that what you do? Find money in secret bank accounts?"

"Yes. But usually I also know the name of the person who has the money."

She took one last scrap of paper from her purse and handed it to me.

LUNA13.

"This is how we talk among ourselves."

I fingered the scrap of paper.

"LUNA13? What does that mean?"

She hesitated for a very long time before taking a Palm Pilot V from her bag.

"Chat rooms. Message boards. Things like that."

Extending the thin antenna, she began working the keypad, keeping it out of my line of vision. A series of message exchanges took place quickly. She handed me the Palm Pilot. Although the screen was tiny, barely an inch and a half square, I could clearly see the user name and message.

LUNA13: > give this to her
RoadSkyRunner: >

"That's you?" I said, watching the tiny blinking cursor. "That's your user name?" She nodded. "What does he want from me, this LUNA13, whoever she is."

"Just answer anything. You will get a message."

RoadSkyRunner: > hey
LUNA13: > can you help us?
RoadSkyRunner: > how?
LUNA13: > Xochitl told you about the murdered women?
RoadSkyRunner: > yes
LUNA13: > You can track down people who have disappeared, that's what you do?
RoadSkyRunner: > what people?

"The Desert Museum is closing in five minutes."

This message was crisper, more businesslike than the earlier one. Get out now, they were saying. Sorry about that, but get out.

RoadSkyRunner: > we can't stay here much longer—what people?
LUNA13: > do you see policia?
RoadSkyRunner: > no, no—the museum is closing, we have to leave.
LUNA13: > Ok. Here's what you do. Write down this email address. RoadSkyRunner@aol.com
RoadSkyRunner: > you're going to send me email?
LUNA13: > Remember how they caught that man Kopp? Who killed the abortion doctor and ran to Europe?
RoadSkyRunner: > yes, i remember how they found him
LUNA13: > Do that tonight. The list of names will be there.

She logged off. Xochitl held out her hand for the Palm Pilot.

"I don't understand," she said, "about the email messages."

"James Kopp. He murdered an abortion doctor and fled to Europe. He and his supporters used AOL in a very original way. Instead of emailing each other to set up his escape route, they just put messages in the Draft folder. Everybody read the messages, but nobody sent emails."

"Aha!"

She stashed the Palm Pilot in her bag and stood up.

"Whoa!" I protested. "Whoever that was talking to me, she said nothing about a money trail. She sounded like I'm expected to find who murdered those women."

"I apologize," Xochitl said. "There wasn't enough time to discuss things. You follow the money trail back to the water man. He's the one who ordered the murder of those two women as a warning. He knows we are close to him, sniffing at his money, trying to take him down and stop his smuggling cartel."

"And what do you expect me to do?" I asked.

"You saw the messages on the videotape? In Albanian?"

"Yes."

"That's a warning to all the other women still in Mexico and the ones in the US. You *can't* escape from us, you *can't* get away. If you try, you will die. Like Ileana. Like Veraslava. Whatever name they want to use, it doesn't matter. It's a warning."

"Sounds more like a death threat."

"Exactly."

"I'm not sure what I can do," I said. "I'm not sure that I trust you."

"Do whatever you can." She spoke softly, without insistence, sadness, or even anger. "I paid a fee just to meet you. If you can do more work, I will pay more money to your boss. Mr. Bobby McCue. He's who I dealt with for the business end."

"How did you find him?"

"Money. I paid somebody who paid somebody else. It goes down a chain until the answer comes back."

"Who gave you Bobby's name?"

"That doesn't matter. My friend from the chat room, she also has connections to people like you. She got names of people who may be involved with the slavery ring. *Policía* in Sonora, politicians from the old Zedillo government. I was hoping . . . we thought, maybe you could secretly read their email, you could find out who controls the smuggling. Then we can learn how they bring the women into Mexico, and how they get them across the border."

"The Desert Museum is closed."

I saw a museum guard coming purposefully toward us. We stood up.

"If I find the people who run the smuggling ring, what will you do?"

"Kill them," she said quietly. "Free the women."

"I want no part of that."

She took my hand, and I dreaded the contact for a moment, thinking I was going to get a tearful plea for help. But she just shook my hand, pumping it twice, and then let go. She walked to Luis, and they both hurried away. As the museum guard approached me, I waved at him and started toward the exit.

"I'm on them," Rey said. "Already got two rolls of film, and I'll get their car and license plate. Call you late tonight when I find out where they live."

"Don't bother with the car. We've got to talk."

The parking lot emptied fast, and we waited until no cars were left nearby.

"How well do you know Nogales?" I asked.

"Arizona or Mexico?"

"What's the difference?"

"The Arizona city is only twenty-two thousand people. Across the line, three hundred thousand, double what it was just five years ago. With any one hundred thousand of them changing every month."

"What are these water tunnels that the smugglers use?"

"They're huge," he said. "Big enough to drive a tractor through. They start about a mile inside Mexico and come up all over on the Arizona side."

"Have you ever heard of a smuggler called the water man?"

"Nope."

"Maybe it's not a man but a group."

"Could be one of the tunnel gangs," he said.

"The drug tunnels, the ones that go right into people's homes?"

"No. The water tunnels. Lots of kids hang out in the tunnels. *Vatos, cholos*, some really bad kids. But kids are more into petty crimes, not smuggling."

"Is there water in these tunnels?"

"Really *bad* water," he said with disgust. "And it runs north. The whole aquifer flows north into the US, just like the Santa Cruz river. During the monsoon season, rainwater floods the tunnels, brings all kinds of contaminated water across the border."

"Rey. Do illegals come through these tunnels?"

"All the time. A few hundred a day."

"Do the *coyotes* smuggle people through the tunnels?"

"No need. Everybody knows they can walk through, squeeze through a curbside drainage gate and be in Arizona. One fat guy, he got stuck. The fire department had to pry open the drain and let him out."

"So you don't think the tunnels have anything to do with a smuggler called the water man?"

"I'll ask around. Laura, can you tell me what this is all about?"

"Somebody is trafficking in women as sex slaves. Not just smuggling them across the border. But owning the women. Selling them."

"Your client, the woman you just met. Was she one of them?"

"Yes. I'm not sure I trust her or trust her information. She *says* she belongs to a group that helps women escape from the sex trade. She *says* that the smuggling organization is responsible for the murdered women shown on TV."

"Luca Brazi," he said.

"What?"

"Luca Brazi sleeps with the fishes. A warning."

I touched his nose, pulled my hand back quickly.

"Sorry," I said sheepishly.

"You'd be surprised," he said, reaching for my hands, "at how I've changed. Let's go get some dinner."

"No. I've got work to do."

"Then let me follow you home. I'll cook a meal while you work."

But I was nowhere near ready for that.

10

A hacker contact told me about the AOL chat room server.

WOODCHIP5: > aol may be possible cuz their world is not enuff against my power
GIRLZ2HACK: > bux? 4 the programming code?
WOODCHIP5: > one time offer, twenty large, usual bank drop . . . can *probably* say again *maybe* guarantee access to their server farm for a twentyfour hour period, no more.
GIRLZ2HACK: > surprised you can get into aol at all
WOODCHIP5: > theyre paranoid about hackers. what you want, girl? cuz i can't get sysadmin level access, but from your msg i figure you want logfiles of user names?
GIRLZ2HACK: > yup yup, never done this b4
WOODCHIP5: > ive got access to program scripts u can launch from shell account and do realtime download, just remember, twentyfour hour period only then they close the gates that's all she wrote, sol

I called Bobby Guinness and left a voice mail message to set up the money transfer. I almost called him Don, but I figured that Mari might not have told him I knew his identity. My hacker friend replied in twenty minutes.

WOODCHIP5: > havent got money transfer but i know youre cool for it so im setting up the hack now . . . with minimum six-ten million chat sessions this is gunna be monster file transfers so im dumping it by realtime mode into web DIR, usual FTP & pwd protect, user mello69fello & pwd *34$&22@HZ* so check for it 1300zulu tomorrow & i will keep it there 24 only . . . girl, hope you got plenty of multi cpu boxes cuz itll take a lot of ton of em to crunch all this data

GIRLZ2HACK: > if its not aol, will the same hack work for msn, yahoo, whatever? i'm guessing no way

WOODCHIP5: > jose

GIRLZ2HACK: > you got hacks for those portals?

WOODCHIP5: > no got, can get, dont know how much bux you got for this stuff???

GIRLZ2HACK: > major bux if needed

WOODCHIP5: > tnx girl, wuz wonderin how i wuz gonna afford my new harley ;-)))

I figured I'd buy ten more computers, each with at least two Pentium V chips and tons of RAM. Knowing how to hack into Internet satellites, I knew I could easily get a complete download of the user logfiles.

This was tricky. AOL chat room people had their user names stored in a central AOL database. These people had chosen their user names, but in the process had also provided AOL with a chunk of personal information.

Supposedly *true* information, that is. But anybody who knew their way around chat room registration could create an AOL account with false data. So I wasn't counting on getting address or phone number information I could rely on. But AOL chats weren't as anonymous as users might think. All chats were recorded on backup computers in daily log files. Since the files were so huge, they were deleted on a regular basis to make room for newer data. But before they were deleted, AOL swept the messages for specific contexts, mostly related to Internet porn.

Before a day's log files were deleted, I'd download a copy. Once I'd broken them down into manageable chunks, the search task was easy.

Run the search program for one thing only.

LUNA13.

If I was lucky enough to get a hit, the hard work would start. There was nothing I could do for twenty-four hours. I was really fatigued, and my shoulder throbbed with pain. I took two Vicodin ES tablets. One wasn't enough any more. I soaked in my spa as the analgesic kicked in, the combination of hot water and mild narcotic relief making me so sleepy I started to doze. My head slipped on the plastic cushion and I woke up snorting water and thinking *Stupid, stupid, stupid.*

Rey called an hour later.

"She does work at Nonie," he said. "Man, do they have this fantastic gumbo! Guy's name is Luis Cabrera. I got shots of both of them, of his beat-up old pickup, and the license plate, which I'm having a friend run down now."

"Do they live together?"

Loud gunfire erupted on the phone, drowning out his answer.

"Rey, turn off that tape. I can't hear you."

"Running a training session. Here, I'll go into the next room."

The gunfire sounds faded and I heard a door shut.

"That better?"

"I was asking, do they live together?"

"Can't say, but I don't think he's a player. He dropped her off, went to a house in south Tucson. I followed him, but didn't go back to Nonie. I wanted to get the film processed. Tell me where you are, I'll come drop off the pictures."

No, I thought, I'm not really up to Rey knowing where I live.

"I'll come to Nogales tomorrow."

"Whatever. Bring five hundred."

"That's your fee?"

"You want to pay me more, please, be my guest. If you were a police department, I'd charge you three hundred an hour."

"Thanks, Rey. Did you find out anything about the water man?"

"Nobody on this side of the border ever heard that term. My contacts are asking around in Mexico. Don't count on it, though. Too many people down there will tell you anything, as long as money's involved. Listen . . . can we get together again?"

"For what?"

"Dinner? Whatever, I don't know. I just want to see you."

"Please, Rey. Don't complicate my life right now."

"Why not?"

The question so confused me that I hung up on him. The phone rang almost immediately, but I turned it off. Nice thing about cell phones, you don't have to unplug wires or leave receivers off the hook. Just turn them off.

Would be nice to do that with your memories.

11

Some time after four, the faint beginnings of sunrise backlit the cloud cover over the Patagonia Mountains. Thousands of feet overhead, three vapor trails stretched horizontally eastward. From Montham Air Force Base, the F-5 fighters soared straight up until they were so high that sunlight flickered on their wings. Lower, just above the Coronado National Forest, I saw small planes weaving in and out of the tree line, working a search grid controlled by a BlackHawk Border Patrol helicopter.

"Busy day," Meg said, punching in numbers on her dashboard scanner. "Let's see what's happening."

"I got it, Mom," Alex said, leaning out the backseat window and tracking the helicopter with a digital video camera. "What are those dinky little planes?"

"Remote controlled drones," Meg said, fiddling with her scanner. "They've got video cameras, just like you. But all the radio chatter is encrypted. I don't know if it's routine or something major."

"That's enough, Alex. Save the battery."

"Aren't we kinda far south?" I asked Meg. "I thought we were going to ride up Adobe Canyon. Or Alamo."

"Yesterday, you said you were bored."

"You *said*, 'Let's go for a long *horse* ride in the morning.' Not a long drive."

"Yeah." Meg frowned at a road marker and began slowing

down. "But when I asked if you had anyplace in mind, you said 'Surprise me.' Whoa! What's this?"

A white Ford Expedition with Border Patrol markings sat at the edge of the frontage road turnoff. The tinted passenger-side window wound down, a face leaned out of the window as the patrolman talked into a hand-held radio.

"Jesus," Meg said quickly. "Put that camera back in the bag."

The scanner crackled and Meg turned up the volume.

"Cherry-red GMC 3500, four-door crew cab," the radio voice said. "Pulling a fifth-wheel horse trailer, headed south on 82. Just passed Gunner Road."

We rounded a curve. Meg checked her left-side mirror as we hit a straight patch of the road and continued south.

"Not following us," she said.

"That was Three R Canyon," Mari said from the backseat, a topo map spread across her thighs. "Isn't that where you wanted to take the horses?"

"Not when La Migra's around. I don't understand all this activity. It's the Fourth of July. It's supposed to be a holiday."

We passed more frontage roads, more white Ford Expeditions straddling the entrances and blocking all traffic. Meg continued south, and we passed the Nogales International airport and eventually turned east, driving in silence until we reached Kino Springs. The crew cab windows were all closed, the aircon fan buzzed at high speed, but once Meg turned off the engine, we heard a solid *chump-chump-chump* somewhere outside. I looked all around, saw nothing but the four-horse trailer swaying solidly behind us, its front end anchored firmly on the pickup bed.

"Upstairs," Meg said, sliding back the moon roof cover.

Alex started to unzip the camera bag, but Meg quickly stuck her right arm between the front bucket seats, pressing Alex's hands down hard.

"Company's coming," she said. "Smile, everybody."

A black helicopter hovered fifty feet above us. Meg stuck her right arm out the moon roof and waved.

"Who the hell is that?" I said.

"More Border Patrol. One of their unmarked Black-Hawks. They're making sure it's really me. I don't usually come this far south."

"Meg *Hon*ey!"

A voice on her scanner. She adjusted the squelch, gave a thumbs-down signal, and zipped her fingers across her mouth, warning us not to talk. She tilted her face slightly to the microphone clipped on her sweatshirt.

"Who's that?"

"Jake Nasso. Long way from home, Meg Honey."

"Not my fault, Jake. How come you guys blocked off FR 812 and 215?"

"Ahhhh, it's another busy day."

"Who's busy on a holiday?"

"Tucson Sector set a record for detentions. As of mid-night, three five oh niner apprehended. Douglas Sector, an-other record. One seven niner deuce. Half of Sonora seems to be coming across today. So. Where you headed, honey? And why?"

"Right here. Kino Springs. I've got paying customers from Missouri, they want to ride up into the Patagonias."

"You're right on the border, baby. You know we don't much like that. What kind of paying customers we talking about?"

"Documentary film crew. A TV special about the National Park System."

"Why don't you take them up north? Lots of parks in Utah."

"Jake, c'mon. They've *been* to Utah. I'm just trying to earn a living here. It's a holiday, for Christ's sakes. There's a nice trail at Kino, we'll just ride a few miles up Providencia Canyon, eat a late breakfast, be gone by noon."

"Okay, Meg. I don't like it, but just 'cause it's you, no harm, no foul. But we want you to turn on your GPS beacon."

She stabbed a green button on the dashboard.

"Gotcha. Listen. Be warned. Three times last night ranchers traded gunfire with *coyotes.* Shotguns, AK-47s, lots of attitude out there. We've intercepted five groups in the past hour, but a lot of illegals got away, and who knows where they are. Once you guys get on horseback, don't forget to squawk us and carry the portable beacon. We'll keep our eyes on ya, honey. You packing?"

"Say again?"

"I said, are you packing?"

"Mossberg 590."

"Outstanding weapon," he said. "But if you think you need to use it, you just squawk us the location and then ride like hell the other way. *Comprende?*"

"Roger that."

The chopper wobbled left and right, then spun sideways off toward the sunrise. I swiveled in my seat, staring at Meg.

"What's going on here?"

"We're pissing off the Border Patrol. Big time. If we can get away with it, we'll ride up into Maria Santísima del Carmen overlooking the border. By the time La Migra figures out whether to arrest us, Mari will have all the footage she needs."

By seven-thirty, the heat already felt like ninety-five degrees. After just a few miles of riding, we were all dripping with sweat, but the horses seemed okay.

"Hey!" Alex shouted. "Look."

Twin flashes of red and blue streaked among the trees east of and above us.

"Dirt bikes," Meg said disgustedly. "Oughta ban them in national forests."

We rode single file, the horses picking their way carefully on the sandstone shale as we moved down toward the Santa Cruz River bed. We'd unloaded the horses at Kino Springs, and Meg had deliberately left her GPS transponder inside the pickup. The horses saddled quickly, glad to be free of their aluminum trailer stalls. The river bed was dry in the July heat. Clumps of grass mingled with wands of white flowers bursting like horses' manes out of a stand of yucca.

Mari and Alex rode ahead of us, and Meg nodded confidently.

"Said they could ride all day," she told me. "You never know, but I warned them that down here we'd have to move quick. In and out. "

Meg's moods shifted like summer breezes. I enjoyed riding with her in the early morning because she'd rarely talk. Like a flywheel, she had a certain way of building up inertia for the day. Even when we rode side by side, her eyes stayed focused somewhere beyond the trees and hills, her face slightly tightened against personal contact. If I said anything, she'd nod or grunt but mostly withdraw further, as though she'd drifted into an emotional fog bank and found protection there. But now, with the sun in our faces, her pinto beside my Appaloosa, I could tell she'd dispelled the fog.

A hundred yards ahead of us, the dirt bikes suddenly burst out of a clump of cottonwoods, their four-stroke engines braying like chainsaws. One of the helmeted riders looked over his shoulder and saw us. Both bikes quickly slewed around and stopped to watch us. Alex reined her horse to a stop, dropped the reins, and worked the Sony with both hands. I could see the telephoto lens move out toward the bikers. One of them raced his engine *brrrrrrr brrrrrrrr*, and Meg pulled the Mossberg shotgun out of the leather sheath and pointed it above her head. The bikers abruptly turned away, tore along the river bed and around a curve and out of sight.

Ahead, Mari and Alex had stopped, waiting for us to catch up.

"Were they *coyotes?*" Alex asked.

"That wasn't cool," Meg finally said. "They saw you taking their picture."

"So, like, who *were* they? What kinda gun is that?"

"Look," I said to Mari. "I think we oughta turn back."

"No."

Mari took a topo map from her saddlebag, trying to steady her horse at the same time. Meg maneuvered next to her, holding the horses steady.

"The ranch is supposed to be here." She stabbed a spot on the map. "The Myron family. Just mom and pop, kids moved away. How far are we from the border? And what kind of security fences, or whatever, could I see there?"

"Two, three miles southwest."

"Can we get there along the river bed?"

"Yeah, but . . . look, Mari. This isn't smart, to keep going toward the border."

"Gotta do it. You want more money, just tell me."

"No. Money's not going to solve any trouble we get into."

"With the Border Patrol?"

"They're the least of my worries."

"Did those bikers weird you out?" Alex said.

Meg looked at the sky and east toward the distant tree line of Mount Washington, pivoting round and round in her saddle while she worked out an answer. She finally eased the Mossberg back into the saddle sheath and nodded to herself.

"Everything down here weirds me out," she said finally. "Any minute, one of the Border Patrol choppers is going to come along, and I'll really catch hell from them."

"Okay," Mari said. "Can we ride up onto the slope of that mountain? If the border's only two miles away, Alex can put in the long lens, get some shots. Then we'll head right for the ranch."

"Yeah. I'll settle for that. I know a trail that will take us up three or four hundred feet. You'll catch the border from there. Plus, when we take a dogleg back toward Duquesne Road, you'll see one of the ranch properties with the cyclone fences."

"Razor wire?" Alex said excitedly. "Cool."

She kneed her pinto, turned him toward the mountain, and Mari followed.

"Razor wire is *cool*," Meg said with resignation. "God, I am so glad I'm not a fifteen-year-old kid."

We rode high enough for a three-mile panorama of the Mexican border. But there was little to see from so far away. Alex fitted the long lens onto the video camera, but after panning back and forth, she snorted with disgust.

"Nothing," she said. "Just a stupid little three-wire fence. I thought there was this big concrete wall all along the border."

"You're thinking of Berlin, honey," Meg said.

"No. She's thinking of Tijuana," Mari said. "That's where we were last week." Far away, rising faintly on the wind, I could hear a helicopter. "Nice view up here. You can see forever."

"Okay," Meg said. "We leave now."

"You don't think it's a nice view?"

"So does the Border Patrol. This is the kind of place where they use night vision scopes. Two men up here can see twenty, thirty miles. When groups jump that wire and come across, the spotters can direct a dozen different vehicles."

"Night vision scopes? Like we used in Desert Storm?"

"Except when there's a full moon. The spotters like that even better. People who lead packs of people across the wire, they also have electronic scopes that pick up *our* scopes. So the Border Patrol loves a full moon. Great light for stalking *coyotes*."

A prong-horned antelope danced nimbly up the trail in front of us, bounded sideways out of sight as the horses nickered. Meg held her hand up quickly, motioning us all to stop and be quiet. I heard crunching noises from the other side of a rise and suddenly a flood of people ran across the path, one of them bouncing off of Meg's pinto. He reared on his hind legs, struggling to move sideways. Meg bent forward to lie against his mane, talking into his ear to gentle him while at the same time pulling out the Mossberg. Seeing the shotgun, most of the people immediately flattened to the ground, some kneeling, one woman running a rosary through her fingers.

"*Vamanos!*" Meg shouted. "Get outa here!"

She flicked her left hand at them, waving them away.

"We can go?" a man said, standing up slowly. "You're not La Migra?"

"No. *Ándale*. Alex, put that goddam camera *down*. Now!"

Alex shifted the video camera to her side, holding it by the handle, but I could see the red recording light on. The man motioned for everybody to get off the ground and then walked tentatively up the side of the rise, then everybody broke into a run, and I saw that they were all women.

"Yes," Mari said to herself, and worked her horse next to mine. "You notice anything about them?"

"You mean that they're all women?"

"What *kind* of women? You see anybody that looks Mexican?"

"No," I said shortly. "They seem kinda . . . I don't know, European?"

"Exactly."

I thought immediately of Xochitl Gálvez and the two murdered women with European names.

"I got a lot of it, Mom," Alex said. "The woman with the rosary, I focused right in on her hands."

Meg took her Uniden transceiver out of a saddlebag. Flicking the dialpad, she caught a burst of chatter and thumbed up the volume dial so we could all hear a border patrolman reporting angrily that he'd found the GPS transponder in Meg's pickup. She switched to another channel.

"Checking in, checking in, guys. Where y'all at?"

"Meg, where the hell are you?"

It was the voice from the BlackHawk helicopter.

"Got a little lost. Thought we were headed up Providencia Canyon."

"Lost, my ass. Where are you?"

"Coming down-slope off the Mount Washington foothills.

I'd say we're about a mile from Duquesne Road. Don't quite know *exact*ly where we are, though. But a few seekers of the better life just crossed the trail in front of us."

"Move your ass along, quick. There's *three* bunches in those foothills."

"Roger that, Jake."

"Stupid. Leaving your GPS in the truck."

"Roger that," she said again, randomly flicking the dial-pad. "You're fading out, but I'll keep my ears on for you."

"Fading out, my ass. You're gonna be restricted, lady, you're gonna be . . ."

She set the transceiver to autoscan ten Border Patrol frequencies.

"Okay. I promised you razor wire," she said to Mari. "But we're really going to have to move. The ranch is just over that rise."

She let Mari and Alex ride ahead.

"Listen, Laura," she said. "I'm going to be in a shitload of trouble because of this. When we get back and trailer up the horses, there'll probably be Border Patrol all around me. If you want, jump off before we get there and make your way out to the highway and hitch a ride."

"I'll be okay. Meg, tell me, what the hell are we doing down here? I get the distinct impression this isn't just some scenic ride."

"She's looking for water."

"Water? Here? In July?"

"Something about water. That's all she told me. That's what she paid me for, to take her any place in this valley where there might be a river, a creek, a spring. Water."

"How many trips have you made?" I asked.

"Eleven. Some of them we did by car."

"Did you find any water?"

"Here and there, but not really anything that interested her."

"Did she say anything about a water man?"

"Nope. Just wanted to see this particular ranch. Don't know why."

"I've got really bad feelings about all these Border Patrol types."

"You know what it's like down here. Relax, they're not after you."

Maybe, maybe not. I'd already thought about how I was going to avoid getting involved. My driver's license for Laura Cabeza would hold up in any legal check, but I didn't want any law enforcement people inquiring about me.

"Play it as it lays," I said. "Just tell them that I'm part of Mari's team."

I lagged behind while Meg explained things to Mari and Alex. Mari turned to give me a nod and a large wave. Alex gave me a thumbs up.

I've got it covered, I thought.

What I should have done is just ride in the other direction and make my own way out of the canyon. Shoulda, coulda, woulda. If I'd only known.

12

We rode slowly down the mountainside through a stand of saguaros and moved toward the razor wire fence. A light breeze was blowing, somewhat unusual for this time of the morning. Palo skittered sideways on a patch of loose shale, but Meg pulled beside me to steady the horses. We stopped several hundred yards away from the ranch compound.

"The bikes," Alex said, standing in her stirrups and pointing.

The main fence gate was slid back and wide open. Fifty feet inside, near the barn, the two dirt bikes were propped on their stands. I couldn't see anybody. Meg took out a pair of binoculars but shook her head twice.

"Nobody around."

Meg took out her radio and tried calling the Border Patrol.

"We're in a pocket," she said finally after several calls with no response. "The ground units can't hear us, and the chopper's not up high enough."

"Let's get outa here," I said.

Two men appeared. One came out of the ranch house, the other from the barn, both moving backward, bending, wiggling their arms, and shuffling. Meg studied them through her binoculars, her forehead screwed up in a frown.

"You've got the best eyes," she said to Alex. "What are they doing?"

"They've got plastic jugs," she said. "They're . . . waving the jugs, no, they're dumping water out of the jugs onto the porch, onto the ground."

We could see both men get on the dirt bikes and heard both engines snarl. One man rode to the gate, planting his left foot on the ground as he did a slow circle, scanning the canyon walls. He saw us immediately, and we heard him shout at the other rider, who threw away his plastic jug and reached inside his leather jacket.

"He's got a cigarette lighter," Alex said. "He's got . . . he's wadding up a bunch of paper."

"That's not water," I said. "That's gasoline. He's going to burn down the house."

The rider lit the paper, waited a moment until it burned vividly, and then frantically tried to separate the burning mass into two pieces. He'd not twisted the pages together tightly enough, and they fluttered around him, all of them burning so fast that he finally just flung the paper mass toward the trail of gasoline, and as it left his hands, it separated into sheets and sheets. One landed on his handlebars, and he whacked at it with his hands to get rid of it. Several pages blew into the gasoline and ignited it, causing a furious rush of flame across the ground, up the porch steps, and through the open front door. The entire front end of the house exploded in flame.

Riding to the gate, both riders stared at us for a moment, then roared along the roadway, disappearing around the first bend.

"Let's go down there," Mari urged. "Come on, there might be somebody trapped in the house."

She kneed her horse, riding ahead of us and through the gate. Meg shouted at her and motioned Mari back. We dismounted at the gate, where Meg quickly looped the reins through the chain links of the fence as Mari ran toward the house. Alex hesitated only for a moment, then followed her mother into the compound. Meg sighed and shucked a shell into the shotgun.

"Hello the house," she shouted when we got to the front porch.

Nobody answered.

"Look in the barn!"

Mari pulled back one of the heavy barn doors and disappeared inside with Alex.

"Gotta check the barn," Meg cried. "There may be animals in there."

But Mari and Alex came to the doorway, shaking their heads.

"Nothing in here," Mari shouted at us.

"Do you smell gasoline?"

"Yes!"

"Come on."

Meg shucked the shotgun slide, forgetting she'd already done that, and a shell flew out the port and just missed my forehead.

"I found a light switch," Alex shouted.

"Don't turn it on!" Meg cried. "The fumes are too strong. I don't want an electrical spark setting this place on fire."

Gasoline fumes filled the barn. Meg ran to the other end and slid open the back doors. A breeze whipped through the barnway, clearing out the fumes. Sniffing, she waved at Alex, who flipped the light switch. I expected normal barn lighting, but blinked at the heavy-wattage industrial lamps that came on in banks. Meg went quickly through the eight horse stalls, four on each side of the aisle.

"Nothing in these stalls for months," she said.

"Did you know these people?"

"Not really. I think it was a family named Anderson. Or Billings. I don't get down this far very often, and a lot of people have bought land in the past year. The old ranchers sold out. Too many *coyotes*, too many illegal immigrants begging or stealing food and water."

"Hey!" Alex shouted from the far end of the barn. "Come here."

She was struggling with a heavy door set into the concrete

floor. With two of us on either side, we slowly raised the six-by-eight wooden door and let it fall backward with a bang. I could see hydraulic pistons on either side of the door.

"Must be motor-controlled," I said. Meg went to her saddlebags and came back with a four-cell Maglite. Fifteen concrete steps down, and the gasoline stench rose out of the hatchway.

"You're not going down there!" I said.

"Got to make sure nobody's here," she cried, already at the bottom. "Here's a light switch." Fluorescent tubing hummed and buzzed into life down below. Mari and Alex quickly ran down the stairs, and I followed. It was a large, bunkerlike room with cinder-block walls and supporting beams holding up a seven-foot-high ceiling that ran back directly under the barn breezeway. On the left and right walls there were heavy steel doors, three on the left, three on the right. Gasoline had pooled on the unevenly poured concrete floor, and its cloying smell got stronger as we walked toward the other end.

"Don't turn on any more lights," Meg warned.

Alex went to the first metal door on the left and tugged on the handles. It slowly squeaked open. Meg ran the Maglite beam around inside, and we all stood silently in shock. The room was about twenty feet by thirty. Three-level bunk beds lined the left and right walls, and four chemical toilets stood at the far end. The walls were covered with graffiti, but the Maglite beam wasn't strong enough for us to read.

Impatient, Alex ran her fingers on one wall in the dim light, and then darted up the stairwell to return with her video camera. She attached the light and battery pack and turned it on. Meg started to protest, but the four of us quickly realized in the bright floodlight that the graffiti was all names.

Women's names.

In all shades and colors, some of them written in lipstick, some with ballpoints, a few just smudged lines as though written in mascara.

"What *is* this place?" I whispered.

"Get the names!" Mari shouted to Alex. "That's what we came for, the names."

Alex started shooting video of the walls, moving the camera slowly to capture as many of them as she could. As the lens zoomed in and out, Meg called from outside.

"There's gasoline all over this place."

"Steady, Alex. Laura, check the other rooms, see if there are names in there."

I opened the other metal doors.

Names, names, names.

Alex moved from one room to the next.

"Jesus!" Meg said, "We're not *think*ing. If the wind blows cinders from the burning house toward the barn, it could light the gasoline. *Run!*"

"Not yet," Mari shouted. "Alex?"

"In the last room, Mom."

"What are you doing?" Meg screamed as we heard a creaking noise from the barn above us. "Are you insane? We've got to leave *now!*"

We crowded in single file onto the stairs, Alex moving backward as she continued to shoot video until Mari grabbed the camera out of her hands. We ran out the front barn door. The horses were spooked and wild eyed, and Meg finally just freed the reins and urged them outside the main gate. The house was burning solidly, like in a disaster movie. Meg was shouting into her radio, but nobody responded. With a *whooomp* the barn exploded into fire. A burst of black smoke ballooned into the sky.

"Well, we don't need a radio now," Meg said. "By the time that reaches a hundred feet, the Border Patrol chopper will already be on its way."

"I don't want to wait," I said.

But it was too late. A BlackHawk appeared almost immediately and set down just inside the fencing. Three people leaped out of the chopper. Two wore Border Patrol uniforms, the third an immaculate western-style shirt with pearl buttons. About fifty years old, he walked with the confident stride of somebody twenty years younger, although his face and neck had the lizard leather look of people who've spent a lot of time in the Sonoran Desert sun. His boots were snakeskin, a gold band running around the tips. He studied our faces quickly and motioned one of the patrolmen over to us.

"Check their ID."

"Jake," Meg said. "You know who I am."

"Well, Meg, honey, I sure know that voice, but you're forgetting the dinky detail that we've never actually met. It's all routine. I just need to know you're really who you say you are. And you others. I need to know you too."

"Jake. We've met a dozen times. You bought me a beer once."

"Can't afford to say I remember that."

The patrolman held out his hand. Nasso moved off to the barn. Meg, Mari, and Alex dug out their wallets and began removing driver's licenses. I hesitated, uneasy at showing my fake license to anybody. Not that they'd spot it as a fake, it was too good. But once they saw it, the name Laura Cabeza would go into their databases. The patrolman turned to me, the other licenses in his hand. I couldn't afford to seem at all resistant, so I got out my wallet and gave him the license. He immediately started writing down names and addresses. Nasso came back.

"Jake," Meg said, "do you think you might remember me enough to radio somebody to drive my horse trailer up here?"

"We're not a limousine service."

"The horses are spooked by the fire. Besides, it's almost a hundred degrees. They'd never last the two-hour ride back to the trailer."

"For the horses, then," he said with a smile. "Where's the vehicle key?"

"It's on top of the rear inside tire. On the trailer."

"Cute. Dumb, but cute. Horses before women. I never used that line before."

He waved another patrolman over and told him to ride the chopper and drive back the horse trailer.

"So tell me, ladies, whatever are you doing up here?"

"These people are clients."

"I'm filming a documentary," Mari said. "About . . . about the ranchers, how their whole lives are changed by the waves of illegal immigrants."

"Uh huh. Keep talking to the hand, lady."

"What does *that* mean?"

"It's from rap music," Alex said. "Talk to the hand, cuz the face don't understand. He's saying he doesn't believe you. Who do you listen to, Jake?"

"My boys listen. I try not to, but in order to understand half what they say at breakfast, I've got to learn that language."

The patrolman finished writing down information and handed back our licenses. Nasso stuck out his hand, collecting the licenses and piling them like playing cards. He riffled through them slowly, finally putting one at the bottom while he scanned another. I could see he was memorizing the information.

"Mari? This your daughter?"

"Yes."

"And you live in Springfield, Illinois?"

"Yes."

"Laura Cabeza. Like the Cabeza Prieta Wildlife Refuge. And you live in Yuma?"

"Yes."

"Goddam *hot* over there."

"Yes."

"Nice woman like you, living in a goddam hot place like that."

He shook his head in obvious wonder at some private thought.

"Okay, ladies. That's all. I'm going to look over the property, and when the chopper gets back, I'm due in Nogales two hours ago. So it's *adios, amigas*, and we'll have to do this again sometime."

Hours later, sitting underneath my ramada, beer in my hand, I had nothing more on my mind than waiting for the AOL logfiles to be delivered.

Well, almost nothing more.

The fire was terrifying enough. But the underground rooms. All those names. I'd recognized that many of them were either Russian or Eastern European, just like the women we'd surprised while riding, just like the women who were murdered.

You *knew* about those names, I'd said to Mari.

No, she'd said, I was only told to look for . . . for whatever I could find.

Who told you that? I'd demanded, but she just shook her head in fatigue.

I don't like coincidences, I'd said. I don't believe in them. These things were connected, and you've got to tell me what I'm getting into because I'm thinking of getting out. I also didn't like the fact that the Border Patrol had recorded what was on my fake driver's license. For the first time in months I felt a flutter of anxiety as I realized that I wasn't quite so anonymous any more.

Another beer or two. I decided to soak in my spa. I heard an engine in the distance, not uncommon where I lived. The sound grew louder and louder until I realized it was the *whopwhopwhop* of a chopper.

It landed fifty feet from where I was sitting.

Two men climbed laboriously out of the chopper and came over to me.

"Hello, Laura."

A slow smile worked at the corners of his mouth. I didn't answer.

"I'm Jake. Jake Nasso. United States Marshal."

"So? I remember who you are."

"Well. I want *you* to remember something. Remember this moment, Laura."

"If you're all done toying with me, I'd like to take a bath, now that I'm home."

"And which home would that be? Back in Tucson? As Laura Marana? Or in Tuba City? Back to your life as Laura Winslow?"

That stunned me, just as he'd intended. My lips flattened against my teeth in despair, the loss of hope. Defeat. He saw it in my eyes and shook his head sadly, the smile melting away.

"Yeah. I know. You're somewhere between the first and second stages of denial. You're in a mixture of anger and defeat. But you'll remember this moment. I can't tell you why, not just yet. But trust me."

"Fuck you."

His cell phone chirped.

"Yeah?" He listened for a moment. "Yeah. Uncooperative."

"Damn you!" I shouted, and he smiled because he'd provoked me.

"See? Okay."

Switching off the cell, he clucked at me from the side of his mouth, the kind of noise I'd make when I wanted my horse to respond to a knee or hand signal. He punched in a number on the cell and waited.

"They want her in Tucson," he said into the phone. "But I don't think she's ready to cooperate yet. Uh huh. Uh huh. And you'll meet her there in the morning?"

He sighed, ended the call, and put away the cell. Inexplicably, he smiled and patted my arm as he waved an arm at the chopper. The pilot punched up ignition of the twin turbines, the prop blades jiggled and slowly started rotating. Nodding, smiling, he gestured at one of the border patrolmen behind me, who took out his handcuffs and gathered my arms behind me.

"Hook her up," Jake said. "But don't make them too tight."

He started walking back to the chopper.

"Hey!" I shouted. "Where are you taking me?"

"I'm going back to Nogales. Have some *cervezas*, microwave a burrito, watch a rerun on my dish TV of the 1982 Daytona 500."

"What about me?"

The cuffs bit into my wrists and as I twisted them to ease the pain, the border patrolman behind me gently put the palm of his hand on the small of my back and urged me toward a white, unmarked Jeep Cherokee Grand Laredo. He sat up front on buttery-smooth leather, driving in comfort, while I sat behind him on a stained Naugahyde bench seat, staring at a stainless steel mesh grille between us. There were no door handles, and the power window buttons had been disabled.

The next person who talked to me was the booking sergeant at the Florence Illegal Immigrant Detention Center.

13

Prisons vary from country clubs to fortresses, but they have one thing in common. They're built for inmates, convicted felons, whether for stock market swindlers or rapist murderers. Prisons have common and recognized routines.

Jails are the next degrading step down the institutional food chain. I'd been in jails seven times in my life, but nothing I'd ever experienced prepared me for the night I spent in the immigration detention center.

Six-woman cells, really nothing more than barred cages separated from the next cage, the line of them disappearing beyond what I could count. Across the hallway, about forty women were confined in a holding area, waiting to be processed.

Clean blankets. Guards who smiled. A counselor.

None of this mattered.

I wore a vivid orange, freshly laundered jumpsuit and clean underwear. The guards took particular care that each woman had clothes that were approximately the right size. No belts. No strings in the work boots.

At one point, a string of women filed down the corridor, chains fastened around their work boots with padlocks, all chains connected and not long enough, forcing the women to walk in that humiliating, shackled-prisoner shuffle.

I shared my cell with three women from San Luis Potosí who chattered in Spanish constantly and knew very little

English. Talking with a woman through bars, I learned that all of them had two things on their minds. Being sent back to Mexico, and contacting their families. Detainees came and went throughout the night. Sleep was improbable because of the constant noise, although all the women shared an unspoken agreement that sleep was necessary. The few who talked did so in whispers.

Breakfast arrived at five-thirty. Fresh scrambled eggs and toast. Real eggs, not the powdered crap most jails served. Cardboard knives and forks, stiff cardboard plates. A guard came by with a trolley containing small plastic cups. Some of these were given to the women for urine samples, a degrading experience, since the stainless steel toilets were completely in the open. Other women got medications.

Throughout the morning, women detainees continued to come and go. Most of them were processed in batches according to when and where they were taken into custody. The night shift guards addressed me twice as Miss Winslow. A counselor spent ten hurried minutes with me, informing me in an apologetic tone that I shouldn't be in the immigration detention center, that I'd be moved later the next day.

Moved where? I asked. The counselor shrugged. What were the charges against me? I asked. The counselor flipped through a folder, bit her upper lip, said nothing.

By eleven, I was entirely alone in my cell block.

Alone and staggeringly depressed.

Lunch was a tuna sandwich on whole wheat, Fritos, cranberry juice, and two individually packaged oatmeal cookies. Another batch of women were led in, processed, sorted into different cells. Throughout the afternoon, the women were taken away. I felt isolated, abandoned, wanting to be processed with them if only to experience some sense of change, of destiny, of knowing a possibility beyond the holding area.

At four o'clock I was again the only woman in the cell block. A shadow crossed my eyes, then another. Two women and a man stood outside the bars, backlit by the sunlight coming directly at me from a window in the holding area. They waited, motionless, for several moments, until a guard shuffled down the hallway, stopped outside the cell, and clanked keys in the door. One of the women and the man stayed outside, the man gripping the bars with one hand.

The other woman came into my cell.

"I'm the reason you're in here."

She spoke with that eloquent Castilian Spanish accent you seldom hear in Mexico. The slurred *dyou* for you, the elongated vowels. Standing against the cell door, the sunlight from windows across the hall backlit her hair, so all I could make out was a dark face surrounded by steel-wool kinky hair, a maze glowing with golden fibers. She wore a pale yellow suit of nubby silk, her jacked unbuttoned and loose over a darker yellow cotton blouse. She seemed anywhere from forty to sixty years old.

"Why *am* I here?"

"People . . . *some* people don't know quite what to do with you."

"And you?"

"My name is Pinau Beltrán de Medina," she said finally. "I am a judge from the Public Ministry of Mexico, the office of the Attorney General."

She motioned to the man, who leaned against the cell door, moving it open a few inches, then closing it. He seemed fascinated by the flutter of the door, shifting it several times, swaying his head as he moved the door.

"This is Hector Garza, an investigator from my office."

Garza pulled the door shut with a clang.

"Pinau," I said without thought. "That's a Hopi name."

"My mother. From Kykotsmovi. I lived there until I was seven, when she died. My father came from Chihuahua and took me back to Mexico. You're also half Hopi."

She looked at a sheet of paper in front of her.

"Kuwanyauma."

I was stunned and couldn't help showing it.

"So," I said with some irritation, "so . . . why am I here? With these immigrants, these illegals, these people without a country."

"Undocumented workers," Garza said.

"Excuse me?"

"That's the politically correct term. Undocumented workers."

"To us," Pinau said, "they're not illegal at all. Just hungry."

"Whatever," I said angrily. "Why am I here?"

"You were arrested."

"There are jails in Tucson for federal prisoners. Why here?"

"Uncooperative," Garza said. "Somebody wanted to teach you a lesson."

"Who?"

He shrugged. Pinau opened her briefcase and took out a blue-bound legal document. She tapped it with the French-manicured nails of both hands, a drumming sound in a particular rhythm. She took out another document, paused, and gestured at the woman standing outside the cell.

"That woman is a US Marshal."

The marshal wasn't in uniform, wearing instead a dark green jumpsuit. She was small, hardly five foot two, but large-breasted, with twin black braids doubled back and woven tightly. Across the left breast of the jumpsuit I could read the words *Tucson Expediter* stitched in looping blue italics.

"In a few minutes, she's going to take you to Tucson to meet a US Attorney. You can ask her who stuck you in this place."

"You're not together?"

"We're part of a joint task force to resolve border issues. Like illegal immigrant crossings, drug smuggling, crime."

"I have no idea what you're talking about."

She laid the document on my bunk, caressed its pages.

"This is a CIA report. Illegal Trafficking of Women into the United States. It's two years old, but has still got enough relevant statistics. All you really need to know is that there are major smuggling rings that deal only with women."

She hesitated, thinking she'd seen something in my eyes, but I sniffed and blinked and covered up my reaction to what she'd just said. Xochitl's stories made a bit more sense to me now.

"And not Latinas, but women from Eastern Europe. A few from Asia. Many from Russia. Most of them are tricked into thinking they've paid for guaranteed smuggling into the US, with citizenship papers and relocation to a major US city. Except it's all a hoax. They wind up as indentured servants, prostitutes, exotic dancers, you name it. The smuggling ring gets the women across the border, where they're sold."

"We know that the smuggling ring is based in the state of Sonora," Garza said. "We've intercepted cell phone calls, radio messages, tons of email."

"Yesterday, before you were arrested, the Border Patrol rounded up a group of forty-seven women from Russia and Eastern Europe. According to your friend Meg Arizana, you apparently saw these women."

"An accident."

"Surely an accident."

"Why are you here?"

"Exactly right," she said. "To the point. Officer Wheaton, could you please go process the paperwork. I won't be much longer."

"Wheatley."

"Officer Wheatley."

"You want me to leave?" the marshal said.

"If you don't mind. Just for a moment."

"Then ask me to leave. Don't bullshit me about going for paperwork."

She left the hallway, and the man came into the cell.

"Guard?" I shouted.

"They're all processing paperwork," Garza said. "I'm here for your protection."

I flattened against the wall.

"Exactly right," Pinau said. "Who is Bobby Gittes?"

"What?"

"Have you ever met him? Do you know where he's based?"

"No."

"How do you work with him, if you've never met him?" When I didn't answer, she began the fingernail-tapping, this time impatiently. "I'm the person who agreed to the contract about embezzled Mexican funds."

The first client!

"Because of the amount of money involved, Bobby Gittes told me the name of the woman who'd be handling the computer search for the money. In offshore banks. I can tell by your surprised look that you've never heard of me before."

"Guinness."

"What?"

"His name is Guinness. Jake Gittes was the detective in *Chinatown.*"

"Guinness. Gittes. Whoever. You've not heard of me?"

"Just the job. That's all Bobby passed on to me."

"There is nobody else? No partners? No couriers from Bobby? Nobody visiting you with messages, documents, details?"

"Nobody. Why are you telling me who you are?"

"When our task force heard about the underground bunkers at the ranch, the European women arrested, we also got identity packets on everybody involved. Your name, Laura Cabeza, got all my radar bells clanging."

"Why not work through Bobby?"

"I'd prefer that. But the Border Patrol arrested you. The US Attorney in Tucson has his own interest in you. I don't want you to forget *my* interests. So. I thought it over, decided that I'd have a better . . . how shall I put it, control, yes, that's the word. I want better control over what you're doing for me."

"For you? Or for the Mexican government?"

"For me. As an agent of the government."

No matter how well gamblers can hide expressions, all of them have a tell, to use Donald Ralph's expression. Pinau kept her eyes locked on mine, but as she said those last words, her tongue moved out between her teeth and then quickly darted back. She'd done this twice before as we were talking. Once, when she talked about being Hopi. The second time when she began asking about Bobby Guinness.

The thing about a person's tell, you can't give away that you've seen it.

You may need it at a critical time. If somebody's lied and you know how to mark the lie, believe me, you file that away for keeps.

"So," she said, "I know from your record, as Laura Marana, that you're very familiar with using computers to transfer money to offshore banks. And to hack into those banks to find out who's keeping what inside. Right?"

"I've done that," I said neutrally.

"Naura."

She took a single sheet of paper from her briefcase and handed it to me.

"One of those islands that don't have much money or principles. They literally sell you the right to set up your own bank."

"Are you saying that the money is in a virtual bank in Naura?"

"Maybe. There's a list of fifty known countries that allow private accounts. Bobby Guinness had asked me to highlight likely countries. I was going to send him this list, but you showed up. Knowing you is like knowing the devil. I'd rather that you know who is controlling you, and that you are known to me."

"Without a name, this list is useless. Even if I could hack into the bank records, I'd need somebody's name to verify that they have an account there."

"Hector."

"Yes?"

"Tell the lady your theory about King Kong."

"It's the wall," he said, sitting on one of the bunk beds. "You've seen the movie, right? You know about the big wall?"

"What are you talking about?"

"The natives. They're scared shitless of this monster ape. They build this huge wall to keep him in the jungle. You've seen the movie, right?"

"Yes."

It seemed to be what he wanted me to say.

"Right. So. They build this wall . . . which version did you see?"

"Jessica Lange. Jeff Bridges."

"I like the older one. Anyway, they've also built these big doors. Now this is an ape that climbs the Empire State Building, right? He climbs up that building, but he's not going to climb over a stupid fucking wall. No. He's not. Because the stupid fucking natives, they've made these doors. Why? That's the question. Why the doors? Somebody on that stupid fucking island wants to *open* the doors."

He went to the cell door and again swung it open and shut.

Open and shut.

Pinau handed me a long list of names.

"Check all of these doors. One hundred thirty-seven names."

"Tell me, Hector," I said. "What's your part in this? Are you the ape?"

After a moment, he exploded with astonished laughter.

"I've got to admit it. You're good," she said with a smile. "Sometimes, when Hector tells his theory about King Kong, people urinate in their pants."

But I was afraid. And they knew it.

"And he didn't even tell you his theory."

"The doors," he said. "You think they're built to keep him out. But *I* think that he's the one that opens the doors. Whenever he wants somebody in the village."

"Who are they?" I asked. "The people on this list?"

"Most of them are either politicians or law enforcement. From the Zedillo government. You have two days."

"To check one hundred thirty-seven names against bank accounts in fifty countries? You must think I'm God, that I can do the impossible in two days."

"On the third day, God created grass, herbs, fruit, the earth itself."

"I'm hardly a god."

"Just think of me as your god," she said sharply, as though lashing me with a whip. "I am your controller, the person who holds your future in my hands."

I thought of her as a terrifying person, and I had absolutely no idea why she was visiting me. But I've been in jail often enough to know not to say *any*thing when someone pulls a power trip. You do *not* talk back to guards and jailors and visitors in the night. You don't talk at all, especially when the ape holds the door shut.

You just listen and wait to get out of there.

She stood up.

"When you meet the US Attorney," she said as an afterthought, "remember that he knows *nothing* about this list. He knows nothing specifically about embezzled monies. This is strictly an affair of the Mexican government."

I nodded, not trusting myself to say anything. She handed me a business card with her name and title. On the back, she'd written a phone number.

"That's a cell phone. I will use it *only* to hear from you. I expect a report every twenty-four hours, or at any time you find out something about the money."

Hector swung the cell door open.

"You're free to go."

"Except I have to go with the US Marshal."

"Well. There is that. You can go with her, or stay here and wait for the ape."

She leaned suddenly toward me, her face just inches from mine.

"After all, they've got a dozen federal arrest warrants for you. And they'll want to control you even tighter than I do. But say nothing to them about our talk."

I nodded again.

She left with Garza, and Wheatley came back.

"Come with me," she said, and started walking away before I could even rise from the bunk. She carried a brown shopping bag. At the end of the hallway, the jailor let us through a set of doors, unlocking one at a time. For a moment I stood pressed close to the two of them, the jailor sweating and smelling of corn chips or Cheetos. The jailor unlocked a small conference room and left us alone.

"Get dressed."

Wheatley laid the shopping bag on the floor and leaned against a wall.

I thought the shopping bag held my own clothes, but inside were clean panties, a crosstrap running bra, and another dark green Tucson Expediter jumpsuit.

"Just put it on," she said. "Then we'll get out of here. But remember this."

She pressed a hand close against my stomach, her palm flat, the other hand underneath my chin.

"I'm a United States Marshal. I'm going to escort you to Tucson. I've got handcuffs and even leg chains, but I don't see much need for them. Do you?"

I shrugged off my underwear and dropped it on the floor.

"Nope," I said, pulling on the clothing from the bag. "That dog and pony show from Mexico. Are they really part of some task force?"

"Yes."

I waited, but she wasn't going to say anything more. I finished dressing and pulled on the leather work boots. Everything was my exact size. The boots were stiff, but comfortable. The jumpsuit was made of high-quality cotton, smooth against my skin. Finished, I looked around the cell and swore that nobody would ever find me again and put me in such a horrible place.

She saw the angry look in my eyes. She placed her hands on my shoulders as though she wanted to hug me.

"Where are you taking me?" I asked, shrugging off her hands.

"Out of this place. And if you're really as good with computers as I've heard, I'll give you a whole new life."

"I have a life," I said angrily. "Let me go back to it."

"Keep your anger," she said. "Feed it, nourish it. There is no shark like hatred. That will get you through the next few days, and then you'll be free."

But I *wasn't* free, not yet. She locked me into the back seat of an unmarked police car, the back door handles removed, the doors securely locked, and a solid steel mesh barrier between me and freedom.

14

"Laura Winslow," the man said. "Won't you please sit down?"

He stood at the far end of an oak conference table, across from Jake Nasso, who fiddled with the frayed cuffs of an old rodeo-cowboy's shirt. Wheatley leaned against a wall of built-in bookshelves.

"You've arrested the wrong person," I said.

He pointed at a chair.

"Please. Sit down. You've met Jake Nasso. Border Patrol Tactical Unit."

BORTAC. La Migra's SWAT team, the organization that pulled Elian González out of his relative's Miami home.

"I thought you were a US Marshal," I said to Wheatley.

"Wheatley is part of the Marshals' Special Operations Group," the man said. "An expert in Internet computer fraud. Identity theft. But back to you."

"If she's a US Marshal, why is she wearing that jumpsuit? Why am *I* wearing this stupid thing?"

"Later Taá is going to take you to a very private place. Show her the papers."

Taá stepped to my end of the table as the man slid a thick, rubber-banded folder toward her across the tabletop. They moved like a team, as though they'd rehearsed the bit with the papers. He stared at me, silent, a half-smile on his face, as he shrugged out of an expensive suit jacket and folded it meticulously before laying it across an empty chair. Inch-wide suspenders decorated with elephants lay taut against a crisply laundered pale blue shirt. He folded his hands in front of him and waited as Taá took out several clipped packets of paper, riffling through them until she found what she wanted.

"You've arrested the wrong person," I said again, although less convincingly as Taá began laying out sheets of paper. The man walked around the table and pulled out a chair for me.

"Look. I don't have time to be nice. It'll just be easier for all of us if you sit down. Because of the light. Some of these are old-fashioned photostats, hard to read. And I want you to be able to read them all. But I don't have much time, and if I have to, I'll be the sorriest hardass you've ever had to deal with."

I sat. Taá pushed a photograph in front of me. It was a jail photo of me taken in 1983 in the Yakima county jail. I was stunned, but tried not to show it.

"Who is this?"

Taá carefully placed an arrest record beside the photograph. Emily Gorowicz. I couldn't even remember using that name, and wondered what kind of drugs I was on to pick a name like Emily.

"Who are you?" I asked. "What am I doing here?"

"Ah! Who am I? A twenty-five-year-old Native American activist who turned left down a bad road and got arrested for shoplifting. Look at some more documents."

I swept the photo and arrest record off the table. Taá bent gracefully to pick them up and positioned them in exactly the same spot in front of me. I swept them off again. Taá started to kneel, but the man held out his right hand.

"Fair enough, if it will stop you from littering. My name is Michael Dance. I'm Assistant United States Attorney, head of the Tucson US Attorney's office. Let's cut to the chase."

"The bottom line," Nasso said with a smile. "The top of the flagpole."

Dance ignored him.

"Look at the last of my goodies."

Taá carefully placed a color copy of an Arizona driver's license in front of me.

"Laura Winslow," Dance said.

Taá positioned another driver's license copy, positioning it exactly so that the tops of the two pieces of paper lined up horizontally.

"Laura Winslow, meet Laura Marana."

My heart sank. My stomach shriveled so quickly I thought I was going to throw up. He must have understood my grimace, because he moved back two steps.

"And the last of the three," he said as Taá slid the two papers aside and meticulously put a third paper between them. "Laura Cabeza."

He moved quickly to my side, bending over, studying the three license photographs.

"Winslow. Longish light brown hair. Marana. Hair much darker, much longer. And Cabeza, well, were you wearing a blond wig for this photograph?"

"Three different women," I said.

Taá began laying out more papers in three piles above the licenses. Dance waited impatiently until she was done.

"We know who you are, Laura. Who you are and *what* you are."

He put his hands on the arms of my chair and in one swift motion wrenched it sideways to face him. He bent down and looked at my face. I kept my eyes on the table.

"Look at me. *Look* at me!"

I didn't move. He held out both hands: what can I do? Taá lined up seven pieces of paper below the licenses.

"These are federal arrest warrants. This first one, over here on the left, goes back to when you were fifteen. At Pine Ridge, where two FBI men were murdered. The next, well, you do see what I've got here, Laura?"

"What have you got?" I said faintly.

"Your life."

He leaned forward, as though he'd been waiting for this moment.

"Give it up, Laura," Jake said. "You don't remember me at all. But Rey once showed me your picture, told me your name was Laura Marana."

Nasso saw my startled look.

"What you don't know about Jake," Dance said, "is that before he joined the US Marshal service, he spent twenty years in the Border Patrol."

"Yeah. I also knew your friend Rey," he said to me. "Until eleven months ago."

"Do you know where he is now?"

"Somewhere in Mexico," Nasso said. "We worked together for about two months, just after he nearly killed two other officers and quit the Patrol. Before he met you and Miguel Zepeda."

"What is he doing in Mexico?"

"He comes north, three, four times a year. Runs SWAT team exercises for quick solutions to problems like, say, another Columbine High School."

"How long since you've seen him? How is he?"

Nasso thought for a moment, but decided not to say anything more.

"What do you want?" I asked Dance.

"Ah. What do I want? Do you think I have any interest in prosecuting you for those old, sad crimes?"

Actually, that's exactly what I thought. The only good piece of news so far was that none of these people knew where Rey lived.

"Yes. Of course. I *will* prosecute you. Taá is a US Marshal. She will take you into custody immediately, if I say so. Or not."

I took a deep breath and settled against the hard, curved back of the wooden chair. Dance saw this and clucked his tongue against the roof of his mouth.

"So what do you want?" I asked him again.

I looked at all the papers and slumped and nodded.

"How did you find me?"

"Ah!" He was delighted and moved quickly to the other end of the table. "Good. That part is settled. You're an expert at creating different identities. Not just an expert, a genius. You're as good as it gets with fake IDs. But Jesus Christ, Laura, why didn't you realize that almost all of them over the past ten years have the same first name?"

I smiled to myself, shaking my head.

"I thought of that once. To be honest, I just got tired of trying to learn different first names. How did you find me?"

"I work with computers," Taá said. "Just like you, I find people. When we recognized that you always used the same first name, Laura, I started running possibilities of what your new last name might be. One of the programs I ran suggested that you might be using names of Arizona cities. I set up a database of all the cities, the towns, the ghost towns, the crossroads, the last little bits of civilization in the state. I ran that database against social security numbers, driver's licenses, mortgages, credit cards, everything for a woman with the first name Laura. I had a master list ready for all law enforcement personnel."

"As it turns out," Dance said, "we didn't even need Taá's list. Jake knew he'd seen you before, when you were at the ranch. He just couldn't remember where."

"Had a senior moment," Nasso said. "You must have been living the big easy, down there on that ranch. Hated to give it up. From your records here, I'd say you've lost your touch at knowing when the wolf's at the door."

"So," I said. "What do you all want with me?"

Nasso pushed his chair back from the table as though he could no longer stand being confined against it.

"What do you know about smuggling?" he said.

He slouched in the chair and propped his legs on the table, ignoring Dance's frown. His scuffed and worn lizard boots had two-inch-high rodeo heels.

"You mean drugs? Across the border?"

"Not drugs. People."

"Illegals? Those people, the ones looking for work?"

"Illegal immigrants, yes," Nasso said. "But not somebody who'll clean your toilets, mow your lawn, wash and iron your clothes. We don't care about *those* people. God bless them if they want to come to the United States."

"So what do you want from me?"

"You're a computer expert," Dance said. "A hacker, a cracker, a whatever they call it these days. Taá is also an expert, but she's got a problem she can't solve. She doesn't want to do all the illegal stuff that you do. She's got morals, our Taá. So. To get right down to it, here's the deal. I need somebody with no morals when it comes to computers and the Internet. All those arrest warrants against you, I can make them go away. If you agree to work with our team."

"Go away?"

"They're in a federal database," Taá said. "We can expunge them. Totally."

"Irrevocably," Dance added. "Your record will be clean. *Can* be clean. If you agree to work with us."

"Doing what?"

"First you agree. Then we tell you what."

"Sure," I said. "Tell me what to do."

"I got a problem," Nasso said. "You change your identity more often than I buy new pickups. Personally, if I was sitting down there in your chair, I'd lie like hell, say anything, looking for an edge. And in a few days, a week or two, when I'm out buying milk and eggs at the supermarket, I just vamoose out the back door."

"Fake ID is a cinch for us computer people," Taá said. "If you've set up five, you've set up fifty."

Nasso pulled a crumpled wad of money from his left shirt pocket and tossed it onto the table without separating the bills.

"I'd bet whatever's in that poke that you've already got a bunch of fake IDs stashed away somewhere. And Jesus wept, have I looked everywhere! While you were stuck in that detention center, I spent five hours tearing your house apart. Nothing."

He flicked the wad of money halfway down the table at me.

"That, plus my bank account, says you've got 'em. I just couldn't find 'em."

"I don't get it," I said, ignoring him, but relieved that he hadn't found my hidey hole in Heather's stables. "You've got a woman here who knows exactly how to run identity searches with such sophistication that you found me. I don't buy your talk about morals. If she's good, what could I possibly do that she can't?"

"Deal?" Dance said.

I was about to say yes, but I saw the knuckles of his left hand whiten against the table rim. I pulled the arrest warrants close to me and took several minutes to read through them.

"Pass."

"Jake, hook her up again."

Jake hesitated, but reached behind his back and took out handcuffs. He shoved his chair back and stretched his legs out so that his boot heels lay just exactly on the edge of the table, all the while swinging the cuffs around his left index finger.

"These are old warrants," I said. "I was fifteen, seventeen, twenty-two. That was twenty years ago and more. I'm really not accused of anything in these warrants. I've got to tell you, I've been terrified for years that I could really get sent away. But after I've finally seen what's in them, I don't think you can do much to me. Pass."

"I told ya she'd pass," Nasso said to nobody in particular.

"We know that the smuggling ring is based in the state of Sonora," Dance said. "We've intercepted cell phone calls, radio messages, tons of email. That's where you come in. Most of this stuff is encrypted, plus it goes through some kind of anonymous Internet service. We've got people working for Taá, trying to intercept and decode the Internet traffic. We've got the best computer people in the Southwest.

But we need somebody who thinks different than we do, somebody who's used to going outside the law, finding things in a way that we might not think of doing."

"That's bullshit," I said. "Any hacker can do what I do. It's not the law that makes the rules, it's the technology. I'm not that good. You give me too much credit."

"Play your aces," Nasso said. "This woman is good."

"Aces," Dance said. "I've got three."

Taá fiddled with the papers.

"First there's this old friend of yours."

Taá placed a picture of Meg Arizana in front of me.

"She runs safe houses for abused women," I said. "What's that got to do with smuggling women?"

"Maybe nothing," Dance said. "I don't care. She's leverage. If you don't agree, I'll swear out warrants that state unequivocally that she *is* involved. I'll close her down. I'll send her to prison."

"You son of a bitch."

"I can be that. But hold off on your judgment for a bit. There's another old friend of yours that could be involved. Villaneuva."

Dance moved around to Nasso, put an arm under his legs, and lifted them off the table. He let them drop, but Nasso was ready for that and lowered his legs to the floor.

"The point is," Dance said, "if you found Villaneuva, you could get him to work angles in Mexico that we might not think of. Again, if you don't deal, I'll see to it that he never works in the US again. The next time he crosses the border, he'll be arrested."

"When this guy wants to be an asshole," Nasso said, "he's got no limits."

"But your old friends are minor league compared to this guy."

He shuffled through the stack of papers in front of him and found a single sheet. He brought it around and placed it in front of me.

"Remember him?"

It was an arrest warrant for Jonathan Begay. My ex-husband. Father of my only daughter, Spider. I'd been trying to find both of them for over twenty years.

"Would you still pass," Dance said, "if I told you I know where he is?"

"What has Jonathan done now?"

"We think—we *suspect* he might be connected to the smuggling ring. Not for the money. He's changed a lot from the person you once knew. Now he works for a Zapatista kind of organization for workers' rights. *Basta Ya*. We think he participates in the smuggling ring to get people into the US for a better life."

"Why would he want them to give up their own families?"

"He doesn't. The people who settle here make a lot of money, and they send most of it back to their families in Mexico. We think he gets a small percentage of that money which he turns right back into the smuggling ring."

"So what we're asking you," Dance said, "is to talk to your ex-husband and get him to describe the smuggling ring."

Ah!

There it was again.

One of those moments that mark before and after.

You go over the line, you can't go back.

"And let me be even *more* forthcoming," Dance said. "I not only will tell you where he is, I'll tell you that he's the very reason we thought you could help us."

I was totally conflicted.

Jonathan.

I wanted to find him so bad, for so long. But I also knew that these people would keep me on a very short leash, and I'd been *free* for so long, you see, free and private and un*known* in the world, I didn't know if I could give that up.

"You're conflicted," Dance said, as though he'd read my mind. "So am I. Finding you, offering you a deal, that wasn't my idea. Taá first brought it up, and Jake here said we'd never do what we need to do without you. But once I figured out who you are, I knew that you always work alone. If I tied you down to a team, made you work in a place where we kept close watch on you, you'd hate it like hell. But if I gave you some slack, you'd skip off with some other identity we know nothing about, and be damn sure you don't use the name Laura ever again. So you see, we've both got problems with this."

"Where is he?"

"In a dirty, cheap, cockroach-infested Mexican jail," Nasso said. "The very worst kind of jail, run by totally corrupt cops."

"Where is he?"

"Deal?"

Dance's tongue darted out and flicked to either side of his mouth. He looked at his watch, looked at Taá. She looked at her own watch.

"Seven minutes," she said.

"I've got to get your answer right away," Dance said.

"So I deal," I said finally. "How?"

Taá put a legal document in front of me and laid a ballpoint pen crosswise on the page.

"First," Dance said, "you sign that agreement."

"Agreeing to what?"

"You try to shuck us," Nasso said, "I come find you and we violate your ass directly to prison."

"If I agree, I want two things guaranteed."

"Depends," Dance said.

"My friends. Meg and Rey. No harassment, no arrests."

"That's possible."

"Write it on this paper. Guarantees that they'll never be bothered."

Dance didn't hesitate, standing behind me and leaning into my shoulder as he swiftly wrote out what I'd asked and signed it.

"Okay," Dance said. "Sign all of these papers."

He laid them on the table. They all looked at me in silence, waiting.

It's only paper, I thought. If signing my name gets me out

of here, I'll sign anything he puts in front of me. Once they let me go, I'd create a new identity, I'd get a new name, and I'd be *gone*.

Without reading the papers, I signed each one, dropping the ballpoint pen on the table. It rolled off the edge and clattered on the floor.

"Done," I said. "What now?"

"Let's talk about chat rooms."

15

Taá set a Sony Vaio laptop in front of me.

"Wireless," she said. "You and I can talk about that later."

The laptop was already logged into a Yahoo chat room. My heart sank. Yahoo, AOL, my god, how many major Internet portals have chat rooms. I'd just spent twenty thousand dollars to get AOL chat user names. But LUNA13 could be anywhere.

A chat window was open, the cursor blinking.

The user name was *MidnightChyna*.

"I watch wrestling," Taá said unapologetically. "Chyna's my idol."

"You're going to have to wing this," Dance said to me. "We were contacted by email, told to be online at this time in this place. The email was untraceable. It said we'd be given details of the two women who were murdered this week."

"Why are you having me chat with this person?"

"I'll explain that later."

The laptop chimed. LUNA13 was online, specifying a private chat room called Donette. I hesitated, not sure of what to do, and Taá quickly swiveled the laptop and typed something that created an overlapping window. She minimized the first window, and we all waited.

LUNA13: > who is there? names, please

Taá quickly swiveled the laptop and typed.

MidnightChyna: > Taá Wheatley. US Marshal. Michael Dance. US Attorney. Jacob Nasso. US Border Patrol.

LUNA13: > which are you?

The laptop in front of me again, I started to use my regular no-capitals minimal style, but realized quickly from Taá's first msg that I had to imitate her.

Capitals. Punctuation. Grammar.

MidnightChyna: > Wheatley. We already have the women's names.

LUNA13: > yes, i did that, i sent names to CNN

MidnightChyna: > How did you get the names? Did you know them?

LUNA13: > not important

Dance hurriedly scribbled a note and positioned it in front of me.

MidnightChyna: > VERY important to us. Do you know who killed them?

LUNA13: > not important

MidnightChyna: > Where are they?

LUNA13: > safe

MidnightChyna: > what does that mean, safe?

LUNA13: > out . . . free . . . not important

MidnightChyna: > Who are you?

LUNA13: > not important

MidnightChyna: > Again, VERY important to us.

LUNA13: > and who are you?

MidnightChyna: > What do you mean?

LUNA13: > you say wheatley, dance, nasso, you say you are wheatley but how do i trust all of you?

MidnightChyna: > You CAN trust us.

LUNA13: > you are police, you are prosecutors, you are la migra . . . you have never been in albania, what do you know about me trusting police?

"La Migra," Nasso said. "She's gotta be close to the border, using that term."

MidnightChyna: > WHERE are you? In Arizona? In Sonora?
LUNA13: > not important, where i am. i send you documents, where i send them?
MidnightChyna: > Why not email them?
LUNA13: > not possible, give me address,
MidnightChyna: > Bring them to our office
LUNA13: > <VBG>

"What the hell does that mean?" Dance asked.

"Very big grin. She's laughing at the idea of coming to your office."

MidnightChyna: > Who are you?
LUNA13: > you, wheatley, you are a woman, no?
MidnightChyna: > Yes.
LUNA13: > what is meaning, name? Taá? what country?
MidnightChyna: > I am Apache. Taá is my grandmother's name.
LUNA13: > american indian?
MidnightChyna: > Yes.
LUNA13: > outsider, like me, like all of us
MidnightChyna: > Please tell me, who are "all of us"?
LUNA13: > documents coming, where, please?

I turned to Dance and shrugged.

"Should I have her send them to my home?" Taá said.

Dance and Nasso exchanged glances, and Dance finally nodded. Taá wrote something on paper and showed it to me.

MidnightChyna: > send docs to 295 east 32nd street, tucson

Nothing happened for at least a minute. The cursor blinked, ticking off seconds.

"Did she disconnect?" Dance said.

"No," I answered. "Look at the top of the window. She's still connected."

LUNA13: > who are you now?
MidnightChyna: > What do you mean?
LUNA13: > you change style, you use lower case, who are you now?
MidnightChyna: > jake nasso
LUNA13: > i think . . . no, you are another woman.

"She's guessing," Dance said. I shook my head.

"Oh, Jesus Christ, Michael," Nasso said. "We're dealing with a pro here. You'd better be honest with her, or she's gone. Bye bye."

MidnightChyna: > i am laura. computer tech. these idiots, they don't know how to use computers, i'm sitting behind them in case they fuck up. wheatley just spilled coffee in her lap, nasso tried to take over, but he types with 2 thumbs.
LUNA13: > you are police, also?
MidnightChyna: > sergeant, us marshals service, computer division
LUNA13: > see what i mean, this thing, trust? you fuck with me, too bad
MidnightChyna: > don't leave
LUNA13: > why not? how i know, how many other policia in room?

"Policia!" Nasso said excitedly. "She's Mexican."

MidnightChyna: > none, i swear on my daughter
LUNA13: > what is her name?
MidnightChyna: > spider. I haven't seen her in twenty years
LUNA13: > ahhhhhhhhhh. i believe you, laura, you answer quick, from the heart. i have son, seventeen, daughters, eleven and nine. i have not seen them forever. so, not important. i send documents, you get them tomorrow. now, enough
MidnightChyna: > don't go
LUNA13: > turn monitor so dance man, so he can see

"Not a laptop," Taá said. "She's got a regular computer setup, she's working from either her home or a safe house."

MidnightChyna: > he can see
LUNA13: > warning, mister dancing man. i have NO trust
MidnightChyna: > you can trust me
LUNA13: > THEY HUNT ME, THEY WANT TO KILL ME

"Jesus," I murmured. "All caps. She's shouting at us, like we don't really understand the pressure she's under."

"Tell her we'll offer protection."

MidnightChyna: > come to us, we will protect you
LUNA13: > documents arrive wheatley tomorrow. dancing man, you see this screen now?
MidnightChyna: > he sees
LUNA13: > you read screen now?
MidnightChyna: > he's reading
LUNA13: > fuck you, dancer

Her login name disappeared from the top of the window.

"She's gone," I said to Dance. "You sure know how to piss off a girl."

"Summarize," Dance said to Nasso and Taá.

"Living near the border, maybe Mexico, maybe here. But my guess is Mexico. She's so tuned into corruption that she doesn't trust us in any way."

"There's another possibility," I said.

"What do you mean?" Dance asked.

"You're not a computer person. So you invest some trust in what you read on the screen. But that could be anybody. Anywhere. Faking the grammar, faking anything. She could be anywhere in the world. It could even be a man."

"Laura's right," Taá said.

"So what now?" Dance asked.

"I take only one thing as true," Taá said. "That she's sending some kind of documents. FedEx, she said. Could be anywhere in the world, as Laura said. But when the package comes, *if* it comes, we'll be able to track where it's shipped from."

"So tell me," I said. "Why did you have *me* talk with her?"

"She originally contacted us by email. We want you to track her email message backward. Find out where it came from."

"Wheatley can do that," Dance said.

"No, I can't," Taá said. "I do entirely different kinds of computer work."

"You see how you fell into our laps?" Nasso said. "You see why I told you that you'd remember the day I arrested you?"

"Can you find the source of the email?" Dance asked impatiently.

"Sure," I lied. "When do my arrest warrants get written out of your records?"

Dance looked at Nasso, who nodded. Dance motioned to Taá.

"Do it. Now."

"How do I trust you?" I said.

"Oh, you can trust him to get it done," Nasso said. "But there's one thing he didn't tell you. Once he's deleted the arrest warrants, he can turn right around and get them reissued. He's kept his word, but he's kept you on his leash."

"Jake, for Christ's sake," Dance complained, "why did you say that?"

"Because I know that's what you'd do. You're so much a lawyer, excuse me, you're so much an at*tor*ney, you're locked into legal-think. You guys are like the feebs. Well, that's an exaggeration. The FBI has no equal when it comes to screwing people."

"I'll need a few things," I said, to break the tension between the two men.

"What?" Taá asked.

"First, this chat was on Yahoo. But there are all kinds of major Internet portals. Yahoo. Netscape. Microsoft. AOL. Plus a few hundred smaller ones. I'm going to have to pay a hacker friend major money to get me data."

"Logfiles," Taá said.

"Right. To start, I'd say, focus on those four major portals. I'll need twenty thousand dollars for each of them."

"Lady," Nasso said. "My admiration for you just shot up two floors."

"I'm also going to need a dozen high-speed computers to process whatever information I get. Make that twenty computers. Multiple CPUs. Five twelve RAM."

Taá nodded, making notes.

"And I'll need a place to set it up."

"I'll show you that right now," Taá said.

"Tucson Outfitters?"

"Yes. It's really just a borrowed room in a very private electronic facility."

"Surveillance," Dance said. "Input from cameras at the Nogales border crossing. Satellite imaging. All kinds of surveillance intel that I know nothing about."

"About my friends," I said. "Meg Arizana. Rey Villaneuva. Don't violate our agreement about not harassing them. And I want to talk to Meg as soon as possible. If you know that she runs safe houses, you've probably got them staked out looking for foreign women who've escaped the smuggling ring. I'd like to talk to her about that. Chances are, if any of those women have gone through Meg's system, she'd never tell you about it."

"Granted," Dance said. "You got any ideas we haven't talked about?"

"Safe, she said. Safe and free."

"No," Taá interrupted. "That's not quite what she said."

She opened another window on the laptop, and I saw that she'd saved the entire chat conversation. Scrolling down toward the end of the chat, Taá dragged the mouse across three lines to highlight them.

LUNA13: > safe
MidnightChyna: > what does that mean, safe?
LUNA13: > out . . . free . . . not important

"Out," Taá said. "Not safe. Out."

"Out of Mexico?" Nasso asked. "Out of the US?"

"If these women are controlled by a smuggling ring," I said, "then she's telling us that there's a way to get free of that control. Get free. Get out."

"Out where?"

"Anywhere. West coast, east coast, anywhere. This workers' group you said my ex-husband worked with. *Basta Ya.* What if they were getting these women fake identities and helping them escape the smuggling ring?"

"What if some Mexicans want to find him?" Nasso said. "Somebody down there has a good thing going, smuggling these women. This guy screws it up, so they kill two women to send a message to him and to all the other women."

"Good!" Dance said. "I like it. Take her to the center."

16

All days should be bright, all skies so blue and clear, all freedom so desirable.

"There."

Taá pointed at a windowless one-story building east of US 10, just south of the airport. We entered an industrial park, new buildings sprouting as far as I could see.

"That's AZIC," she said, turning into the parking lot.

"Arizona Intel Center," Nasso said.

A fairly new building. No landscaping, no shrubs or flowers or cactus, just a black macadam parking lot with yellow spray-painted parking slots. The lot was half full of cars and trucks, all of them with private Arizona license plates.

Nasso held the front door open, and the three of us walked into a small entryway. To the left, a small room, fronted by sliding glass windows. Like a doctor's office. But nobody was inside the room. Nasso punched codes into a digital keypad and looked up at a video camera above the door. Taá also punched in a code, and the inside door swung open to a passageway lined both left and right with steel doors. Stopping at one of them, Taá swiped a passcard through an elaborate locking panel and punched in a code. The door swung inward on hissing hydraulic arms, and Taá walked through it. Nasso stretched an arm across the doorway, stopping me. Beyond him I could see forty or fifty computer monitors and a lot of people in cubicles.

"I leave you to all this technology," he said. "Just remember. I leave you, but I'll never leave you. Think of running away, I'm already there to stop you. We clear?"

"Sure," I said. "Whatever."

Raising his right index finger, he gently reached out to center it on my forehead.

"I'm the whatever. You fiddle with another identity, you think about leaving us, I'm the wrath of God, and my finger carries the gift of death."

Taá led me through the door and it hissed shut.

"Jesus Christ," I said. "He's certifiable."

"He's BORTAC. SWAT. All those crazy Mel Gibson types, with guns. You seriously do not want him tracking you down."

"And you?"

"I wouldn't hunt you down, if you decided to run. But I'd send him after you. We clear about that?"

"What am I doing here?" I said, mostly to myself, as I looked around the intel center. The maze of cubicles stretched out for a hundred feet. I could see at least thirty or forty people, half of them grouped around a central pod of computers arranged like the action room of a stock trader. Each person had at least three monitors, and high above them, like the wall of a television producers' booth, I counted over thirty large television monitors in a grid. Taá saw me frowning at the pictures on them.

"Satellite intel," she said. She pointed at one grouping. "Border crossings in the Tucson Sector. Nogales, Marshall, and Agua Prieta. Plus the smaller ones. Plus random sections of the fence. This room is a totally state of the art intel processing center. But using top secret government stuff, so we keep it quiet."

"Tucson Outfitters?" I asked.

"Why advertise? Better to be anonymous."

Suddenly, several of the TV screens flickered with static, then reformed into a large grouping eight monitors wide and six high to display a large area of desert. Several people cheered; somebody sharpened the image. Another grid of monitors showed a fixed picture and I could see that the two pictures were of the same place.

"Satcom images," Taá said excitedly. "They've matched up with the video of the two murdered women."

"How would you do that by satellite?"

"We digitized the entire video and mapped the terrain. Then we started comparing it with sections of the Sonoran Desert. And it looks like we have a match."

"Yeah," I said. "But it's just desert."

"I know. Where are the bodies? Now that we've found the spot, somebody will chopper a forensics team down there."

"What's this got to do with me?"

"Come on."

She led me to a large pod of cubicles near the back of the room.

"This is my group."

Six people were studying various computer monitors. Only two of them looked up at me, briefly, and went back to the monitors. I could see that two of them were writing lines of programming code, the rest running some kind of software that seemed to be processing email messages and comparing text and photographs against databases. Taá brought me close to one of the monitors.

"Every border crossing has digital video cameras that take single-frame shots of everybody who goes across. The frames are stored in a database, and we've got software that compares facial identity characteristics against known profiles stored in a database. You might remember the controversy at a Super Bowl two years ago in Florida. Everybody who entered the turnstiles at Tampa stadium had their faces shot, and the prototype of this software compared thousands of fans' photos against a database of known pickpockets, scam artists, whatever the Tampa police thought was relevant."

"I don't understand something," I said. "Why am I in this room? Why are you showing me all of this?"

"You're going to track LUNA13," she said. "You're going to find how they're connected to *Basta Ya*. You're going to see if your ex-husband is part of this smuggling ring, and most important, you're going to find out where he is."

"He's in Mexico."

"Exactly."

"You're asking me to go down into Mexico?"

"Oh no," Taá said. "You're not getting out of my sight. But you're going to track down his computer location. Where he logs onto the Internet. We'll coordinate that with GPS coordinates and use satcom to find out where he is."

"And then what?"

"Then your job is over."

It suddenly came to me. I gasped with astonishment at her request.

"You want me to rat out Jonathan Begay?"

"Didn't you understand that?"

"But why?" I protested. "If he's connected with *Basta Ya*, if he's involved in helping these women escape from the smuggling ring, that's a *good* thing."

"Sometimes," Nasso said from behind me, "morality just doesn't pay."

"Do your job," Taá said. "Find LUNA13. Find Begay."

"We'll take it from there," Nasso added. "Now. It's been a long day. You're tired, you want to get settled."

"But I need clean clothes. I need . . . I need . . ."

I needed to get away from them. Nasso smiled.

"Yeah. You just want to shuck us off your back."

"I've got clothes," Taá said.

"So," Nasso said. "Winslow, get started."

"That's not my name."

"Winslow, Cabeza, Marana, I don't care what you want to call yourself."

"Call me Ishmaela," I said with a smile, suddenly knowing how *I* would get out. "Let me get back to my house in Sonoita, let me get things started from there. I've got special software programs, all my hacker contacts."

"No. We let you off our leash, you'll get another set of identity papers and we'll never see you again. You're going to be living with Taá. She will babysit you twenty-four seven. "I've already brought up your computers from Sonoita. They're at Wheatley's place. I figure, anything else you want from Sonoita, I'll get it right away."

Nasso took out his handcuffs and laid them on the table.

"I like you," he said. "Whatever name you want to use, I like you a lot. But if I have to, I'll hook you up again, and this time you'll be so deep inside a jail somewhere they'll have to send an overnight messenger out to find a pay phone. *Comprende?*"

Yeah. I understood. Play the game.

Wait for my chance.

Women were smuggled from Mexico to the US by two different groups. One group treated them as sex slaves, the other group freed them from slavery. Who was who? I had no idea. Who was in the chat room? Who was LUNA13? I had no idea. Who were all of these law enforcement people that thought I was central to their investigation? I had no idea at all.

But what felt absolutely *terrific* was that I had little sense of despair, anger, depression, or anxiety. Just give me a few days, I thought. So, when I thought about Nasso saying *comprende*, yeah, I *did* understand. I'd just play my own game.

Wait for my chance.

Just give me time to find Jonathan, I thought. Forget about smugglers, money trails, US Marshals and Attorneys and all policemen.

If I find Jonathan, I can ask him where my daughter is.

Spider. She was the key, she was understanding, she was peace. I had a purpose now, I had a focus, I had the way out of my anxieties.

Find Jonathan.
Reinvent my identity again.
Then I'm gone.
Bye bye.

17

We turned left somewhere near 32nd Street, pulled onto 4th Avenue, and turned left again past more of the clustered, rundown homes I remembered from my South Tucson nights a year ago. But Wheatley's block somehow stood apart from other blocks. Since it was almost eleven, the neighborhood was very dark. But I could see that front yards were neatly groomed, a few with grass, most with rocks and some kind of cactus. None of the porches had dilapidated couches, there were no broken toys and swing sets visible, no abandoned and stripped cars at the curb.

We passed a house fenced on one side with a ten- or twelve-foot-high fence, topped with rolled razor wire. A sudden wall of rain came down the street toward us, the droplets fat as small pebbles and blurring the purple and green neon lights of a bar and dancehall two blocks in the distance. We sat in the car, watching the rain approach us, like entering a carwash and moving into the spray nozzles. Raindrops drummed and danced up and over the car, passing by so quick that the hood was clear as water gushed down the rear window.

Wheatley lived in a traditional stucco and frame South Tucson home, with faded aluminum siding on the east wall, bent aluminum awnings over the front windows. Taá pulled into her carport, and as we got out, the wall of water headed straight down 32nd Street for a block until it gradually veered into front yards and disappeared over roofs into the night. The night sky was clear and hot and dry again. The rain had no cooling effect at all, nor did it raise the humidity.

A flat-chested, older Mexican woman in cutoffs and an Arizona Diamondbacks tanktop waved at us from the yard next door. A large potbellied pig snuffled and snorted its way up to the fence dividing the two lots. Grayish-white, large jowls, a huge, round snout that poked at me through the fence.

"Hi, Sophie," Taá said to the pig.

"Are they raising it for food?" I asked as Taá unlocked her back door.

"Sophie's a pet. Started out a year ago no bigger than a Yorkshire terrier. Now Sophie weighs in somewhere around one twenty. She sleeps at the foot of the bed and dances to cumbia music."

"I'm surprised somebody doesn't take her, sell her to a butcher some night."

"It's a safe neighborhood," Taá said from the stove, putting on a kettle of water. "Two doors the other side of here, a family from Ghana had an idea of how we could group together against anybody who might break into the houses, steal whatever, threaten the people. We organized six houses like a compound. Three on this street, the three houses that back us towards 31st Street. We put in that tall fence you saw, some razor wire. Totally illegal, but one of the six houses belongs to a South Tucson cop, and then of course there's me. At least three people are in the compound at any given time. You like tea?"

"Can't stand it."

"Sorry. No coffee here."

I went down a short hallway, saw three computers lined up in one bedroom. A slab of foam lay on the floor, with sheets and a blanket flung to one side. Photographs covered almost every square inch of wall space. Black and white, color, some printed from computer files. Many photographs of Indians, probably Apaches. But other pictures of Hispanic men and women.

"You like my *vato* collection?"

She waved her palm over a group of photos of Hispanic men at parties, picnics, bars, playgrounds, and even schools. Some posed with their cars, some with their girlfriends or children or wives or parents.

"I was doing a job, trying to find a child pornographer operating out of Nogales. I had no trouble getting into the websites and downloading pictures of all the adult males. Something about the websites made me think they were in Nogales, so I spent two months down there. Even had a small apartment. Got to love the people. Even after I found the pornographer, I never forgot the people."

"And these are Apaches? Your family?"

"Apaches, yes. My family? I never knew them. They left me at a hospital when I was only a few hours old."

"And what's in all those?"

A row of four-drawer file cabinets against a wall.

"My data. All my cases, all my people. I have a terrible memory, so I keep data on everybody. Lots of files. Most of them from older cases. I don't even know what's in those drawers. I'm like that woman in that movie, something about living dangerous? In Malaysia?"

"*The Year of Living Dangerously?* The Linda Hunt character? Billy Kwan?"

"Yes. When I'm on a case, I'm . . . well, I'm obsessed. I get a lot of data."

I turned toward a group of pictures, all of the same woman, tacked up in the far corner of the room. Taá abruptly switched off the light and showed me her bedroom.

"You can have the regular bed. I pretty much sleep with my computers."

A standard double bed, the mattress stripped, but a set of pale green sheets and pillowcases laid out for me. I went into the living room, which had almost nothing in it.

"Where's your TV?"

"Haven't got one."

"I thought you said you watched wrestling on TV?"

"Sports bar."

"How about a stereo? CD player?"

"Nope. Got a radio for you, though. Open the carton."

I cracked open a cardboard box and took out a Grundig short-wave receiver. Great, I thought, no television, no music, just Radio Moscow. Backing into the kitchen, I watched her dip spoonfuls of Lapsang souchong tea into a wire mesh ball, drop it into a cracked ceramic teapot, and pour boiling water. She pulled out a three-by-five pink note card from underneath a refrigerator magnet and laid it in front of me.

"I've got a list of possible frequencies that your ex-husband might be using."

"Don't use that word."

"Husband? Sorry. Here's a list of different frequencies where we've monitored the pirate radio transmissions from *Basta Ya*. So, what do you think?"

"About him, not much."

"No. I meant, do you like my house?"

"Can I leave? Right now?"

To her credit, she blushed.

"I thought so," I said. "I guess the answer is that I don't much care about your house. Look, I'm tired. I just want to sleep."

"Take off the jumpsuit. What do you want to sleep in?"

"Usually a pair of running shorts. A loose tank."

While I shucked out of the jumpsuit, she rummaged through several cardboard boxes and finally held out some lime green Nike shorts and a faded tee with the arms cut away. She left me momentarily while I changed, and returned with what looked like two large wristwatches.

"Please lie back on the bed. I've got to strap these on your legs."

"Security anklets?"

"This one's a digital tracker."

Without apology she locked it onto my left ankle. The second device was heavier and she had to adjust the straps several times before I was comfortable.

"Like a pet collar. There's a security barrier buried in the lawn, right at the perimeter fence. Once I turn it on, this collar is active. You try to go past the security barrier, you get knocked on your butt. Works just like a stun gun."

"Do you mind," I said sarcastically.

"You didn't think I was just going to drift off asleep and let you roam the neighborhood. Now the house is yours."

"I need some shoes."

She laid two boxes on the bed. A pair of white and green Nike sneakers, a pair of black New Balance walking shoes.

"We matched up your shoe size. From what's in your closets."

"Wouldn't it have been easier to just bring up some of my clothes?"

"You can go into the backyard," she said, ignoring my question. "Just don't get too near the fence. The stun bracelet is set to start tingling at a distance of ten feet. Five feet, you'll get zapped. Okay. So. I'll be in my workroom. Good night."

She closed her workroom door.

I picked at both anklets, but they were fastened tightly. The straps were canvas braided with wire mesh.

You tell me, how do people deal with not having a television set? And if they've got one, how do they exist without being connected to cable TV?

I wandered Taá's house for half an hour before I realized what was wrong. TV is one of my major food groups, and I was starving.

Dragging out the carton, I opened it and took out the Grundig short-wave receiver. It needed batteries, but also had a power cord, and I got it operating quickly and figured out how to punch in digital frequencies.

I figured out how to work the automatic tuner—just like a car radio except here, instead of going through a limited number of AM or FM stations, I was going through the world. I heard a Muslim call to prayer, an Asian woman, probably Chinese from the sound of the different vocal tones, talking animatedly. Lots of languages, lots of voices, lots of stations. I switched to the seven-meter band and noticed that the auto-tuner found mostly Spanish-language stations.

I started to isolate those stations with male voices and set up a program that moved through the half-dozen frequencies on which at one time the *Basta Ya* radio station had operated. One voice sounded familiar, then another. I decided to concentrate on monitoring broadcasts on the hour and half-hour.

It was almost exactly two o'clock. A woman's voice streamed Spanish, her pace somewhat like an automatic machine gun, and then a three-note chord sounded and another woman's voice in English announced the daily broadcast of *Basta Ya*.

And there was Jonathan.

He spoke in Spanish. I understood none of it. Entranced, I listened instead to the modalities of his voice. The last time I'd seen him I was on my knees, my nose and mouth bleeding. He'd slung Spider under his left arm, his right fist around a Winchester .30-30. When I'd tried to get Spider away from him, he'd swung the rifle butt into my face. I touched my lips, remembering the moment, staggered that I felt no anger or hate. Through all my crazy years, I'd wondered if he was still alive, if Spider was alive, where was she, what did she look like.

The broadcast ended. I kept the radio on the same frequency, and a half-hour later the broadcast was repeated. Taped. Since it was in Spanish, I had no idea of dates or times, no idea if the broadcast was recent or something made months before. After listening to it again, and then again, I finally turned the radio off and lay on the bare mattress.

If he was alive, I would find him.

Once I found him, I'd learn how to find Spider. Nothing else mattered to me. I was willing to give up anything to find my daughter.

We convince ourselves of these truths, you see, without even knowing if they're true. How else do we survive the savage assaults from our memories?

18

I couldn't sleep.

An old song ran through my head.

Couldn't sleep, wouldn't sleep . . . I didn't remember the lyrics.

At some point during the night, Taá had dragged the foam pad from her workroom into the living room. She lay on her side, totally naked, her mouth half open, her lips and closed eyelids quivering to some dream. I turned my head away, embarrassed, and looked back at her body and realized how much younger she was than I. No wrinkles, her breasts falling gently down, no marks anywhere on her body.

I knelt beside her, listened to her steady breathing, watching veins in her throat and right breast throb with her heartbeat. No voyeuristic stuff, not me. I wanted to make sure she was sound asleep. I stood up, but kept watching her in the dim light coming in from the street. She sniffed, licked her lips, rolled onto her back, and began snoring. High on her left breast I could see two puckered scars and knew they were bullet holes.

I went immediately into her workroom.

Ignoring the file cabinets she said contained old data, I jimmied the lock on what looked like the newest of the lot. The drawers rolled out soundlessly, all of them filled with hanging folders, labels meticulously color-coded in some unknown scheme in tightly written, black-ink capitals. I flicked through an entire drawer of files and recognized nothing. Opening another drawer, and another, I looked at every file tab until I stopped short.

Meg Arizana.

I started to pull out the file, then remembered what had seemed vaguely familiar about the group of photos in the corner. Not daring to turn on a light, I moved a mouse, and one of her computer monitors came to life.

Before she'd gone to sleep, Taá had covered the entire corner with sheets of paper and other pictures, everything tacked up in a hasty, random pattern. I carefully unpinned all the new stuff and was stunned to see Meg.

Twenty photographs at least, maybe thirty.

Meg in every kind of clothes. Inside, outside, a school, a playground. No shots of her daughter, I noticed, and then froze. In three of the pictures, Meg was lying nude on a bed and smiling at the camera, one shot actually showing her with a beckoning finger. It was the bed I'd just been trying to sleep on.

I left the pictures uncovered and went back to the file cabinets, certain of what I'd find. I left all the file cabinets unlocked, the pictures of Meg uncovered. After an hour, I had two folders which I took into the bedroom.

Reymundo Villaneuva (aka Ramón Vargas)
Laura Winslow (aka Marana, et al)

The folders weren't new. The one on Rey was creased, stained, obviously older than the one on me, which contained copies of all the documents Dance had shown me.

I read everything.

For the first time ever, I was aware that my role had shifted.

For years, I'd hunted other people.

Now, people were hunting me.

I curled tightly on the mattress, clutching the files, and fell asleep.

Early next morning, I woke to the angry cries of mourning doves. It was already hot, the air inside the small bedroom smelling metallic and antiseptic. I'd started out sleeping in a tee and panties, but must have pulled them off while I slept.

The folders were gone.

Dressing, I walked barefoot past Taá's workroom. I could hear a clicking noise outside, from the rear of the house. Pouring myself a glass of water, I went out the side door and saw an automatic sprinkler ticking over in the backyard of the house behind me. It was quiet, hot, a cloudless sky marred only by vapor trails from two high-altitude jets, probably fighters from Montham Air Force Base. Her yard was small, but incredibly well gardened and groomed. A small aluminum work shed stood in a back corner, partially shielded by some bushes. I heard the toilet flush and went to confront Taá inside the house. She sat calmly at the kitchen table.

"So you saw the pictures," she said.

"Of Meg? In your bed?"

"Are you bothered by the pictures? By what you know?"

"I'm bothered by those files."

"I told you. I'm like Billy Kwan. When I work a case, I'm obsessed with whoever is involved. Nasso is always on me to not get so involved, but I can't help it. I met Meg four months ago when we were working an abuse case. Through her, I heard about Rey. I had to track him down. I do have some computer hacking skills, it wasn't hard. He really didn't try to hide the name change. I don't even think he meant to hide it, as though he decided he'd just play another role for a while, then maybe get back to his regular life. Whatever that was. I never met him. I never told Meg."

"And why do you have the file on me?"

"Meg once showed me your house. Where Meg killed that

woman. She mentioned your name, said you'd disappeared, could I help find you. I built a whole file of who you were but had no idea of who you'd become. If you read the file, you saw there's nothing in there about Laura Cabeza."

"So."

"So. Want some breakfast?"

She filled a teakettle and put it on the stove. Turning on a burner, the auto-pilot clicked and clicked, lit the flames, but she was lost in thought. I reached over and turned off the burner, and she jerked back into awareness of where she was.

"So. Now you know some things about me. What are you going to do about it?"

"Nothing. Are you still, um, still seeing Meg?"

"No. That's why her daughter ran away."

"She's changed her name from Loiza to Amada."

I could see her make the mental note. I knew she'd update her files later.

"Partly. She couldn't tolerate the idea that her mother was sleeping with another woman. Cared about another woman. Her daughter hoped that Meg and Rey would get back together. But then Meg stopped taking her medication. After six days, they both went nuts."

"I know what that's like. To go cold turkey with medication."

"Not pleasant."

"So where is Amada now?" I asked.

"Living with Rey."

"In Nogales?"

"No. At his father's old place, somewhere down in Sonora. I'm not sure she'll stay there much longer. He's got satellite TV, but you were there once, you know there's not a whole lot a fifteen-year-old girl wants to do in the middle of nowhere."

"I'd like to see Meg."

"Want to go this afternoon? For lunch?"

"I don't need lunch. I'd just like to see her."

"You know she does those weird things?" Taá said.

"Performance pieces."

"Yeah. Well. Her latest thing, she's running a restaurant."

"Meg doesn't have that kind of patience. Or cooking ability."

"Not a real restaurant. Well, she actually serves some food. Thai. She rented a space on 4th Avenue, not far from the women's bookstore. It's a fundraiser. To help abused women."

"Can you take me there?"

"Jake will come by, about noon. He's bringing some clothes for you to wear at dinner, but he'll also take you to see Meg."

"You're not coming?"

"It's difficult between us right now. I'm the law. I can't ever quite let that go when we're together. Plus . . . I still have this thing for her, but she's not interested. I was just an experience to her. Not a relationship."

"Why is Nasso taking me to see her?"

"We're using your friendship. Simple as that."

"Is there anything you people won't exploit?"

"Not with this."

"Ah," I said. "You want me to ask Meg if any of these smuggled women have gone through her safe houses. Is that it? Well, she's already told me they have. So spare me going anywhere with Nasso."

"He's really likable," she said. "Just takes a while for him to trust you."

"Why both lunch and dinner?"

"Meg's place only serves lunch. Tonight, Jake's taking you to dinner at Hacienda del Sol. Dance has the whole restaurant reserved. It's his fortieth birthday, and he's celebrating. And there'll be some interesting guests. Pinau Medina."

"And the ape?"

"Garza? I suppose so. Plus the third person in their own little team. Francisco Angel Zamora. Now, if I liked men, I'd move on him in a second."

"Who is he?"

"A businessman. In Sonora."

The doorbell rang and Nasso let himself in. He smiled at Taá, a look passing between them, a glance, a hint, a sparkle in his eyes. He crooked a finger, beckoned me to join him, but as we left the house I saw he'd checked out both my ankle bracelets.

19

"But I don't *need* a license," Meg cried. "It's not a restaurant."

"Are you serving food?"

"It's just friends, just people I know."

"Are you serving food?" the man asked again, less patient. He folded back the vinyl cover of his citation book and started to write.

"Well, sure. That's the whole idea of this piece."

"Piece?"

"It's a performance piece. Jesus, don't you ever go to the theater?"

"Not to eat," he said, walking over to one of the half-dozen tables. "Are you folks eating something here?"

A young couple looked up, startled, the woman with chopsticks full of noodles halfway to her mouth.

"It's *pad thai,*" she said, looking at Meg.

"It's food, then."

He started writing in his citation book.

"Wait a minute," Meg pleaded. "It's *theatre.* I'm only doing this for two weeks, but I've been preparing since January."

"Do you have a restaurant license? Is this place certified as a restaurant? Has your kitchen been inspected? Where are your food lockers, your refrigerators? Are your cooks certified? Are *you* certified?"

"Certified? What the hell for? Nobody ever has their play certified."

"Tell you what," the man said, flipping the cover of his citation book shut with a flourish. "I could be wrong about this. Look, it's almost one o'clock, and I've had a long morning. I'll just check with the Health Department this afternoon. If they've given me a bum steer, you're in the clear. Hey, that's theatre. At least, it's poetry. So you've got until tomorrow. My advice, though? You'd better close this place before I come back."

He brushed past me going out the front door. Meg watched him, exasperated, then cocked her head at me and stared in shock.

"Laura?"

Nasso stepped past me and nodded.

"Yeah. It's your old friend Laura. I'm Jake. We all met the other day, remember? What kind of food you got in here?"

He went to one of the tables and sat down to read the menu.

"Laura?"

Meg hugged me and whispered in my ear.

"What is he doing here?"

"I got arrested."

"By him?"

"And some other people. He knows all about your safe houses, and I wouldn't even be surprised if he knew there'd be a Health Department inspector here. In fact, he probably arranged it."

"Yup," Nasso said. "But let's keep this all friendly. I can't read this menu. Just bring me what they're eating."

"I've got to go to the bathroom," I said. "Where is it?"

"In back."

As I brushed past Nasso's table, he put up a hand to stop me.

"Tell me this isn't some twist on that scene from *The Godfather*. Where Pacino goes to the bathroom to get the gun, comes back, and kills Sollozzo and the crooked cop. McCluskey. Played by Sterling Hayden."

"You sound like Rey."

"Yeah. We liked the same movies. What I mean here, you're obviously not going into the back room to get a gun."

He eyed Meg, standing with her clenched fists on her hips.

"Well," he said, "I don't know about her. How do I trust that she's not going to let you slip out the back door?"

He followed me back through an improvised kitchen. A young Mexican woman was carefully slicing the skin off a papaya. Nasso stood against the back door, and I went into the bathroom. There was a small window with frosted glass, but the old wooden sash was painted shut, and I could see the shadow of iron bars on the other side of the glass. I slumped on the toilet seat and sobbed. I'd hoped there would be a way to shake Nasso.

I flushed the toilet and went into the kitchen. Nasso was talking with the Mexican woman, who was showing him how to julienne the peeled papaya. He paid no attention to me as I walked back into the restaurant, but I saw a Tucson policewoman standing outside, her foot upon a Ford Explorer front bumper as she wrote out a parking ticket. I sat beside Meg.

"What's going on?" she said quietly.

"In your safe houses, do you ever get women from Russia? Eastern Europe?"

"Never. Most of them now are Salvadoran, Honduran, some from Guatemala. But anyway, they're all women who've been living in Tucson. Laura, what is this about?"

"Have you ever heard of Russian or European women being smuggled across the border? Asians? Thai, Laos, Cambodia, Vietnam, any women from those places?"

"No."

"Have you ever heard of . . ."

"Whoa!" She put a finger on my lips. "This is weird shit you're asking. What's it got to do with that guy in there? And why did they arrest you?"

"For being Laura Winslow."

"But . . ."

"And for being Laura Marana."

Her shoulders sagged.

"For fifteen years I've run these safe houses. I knew that the police department had heard of them, maybe even knew where they were. But you're telling me the government knows all about me. What I do? What have you got me into, Laura?"

"I swear, Meg, until yesterday morning I wasn't involved in any of this. I went for a horse ride with you and got arrested. They humiliated me by making me spend a night in the immigration detention center at Florence. Today I had to make a deal to help these people with some computer stuff. In return they'll get rid of all those old federal arrest warrants from when I was a kid."

Nasso came in with the Mexican woman, each of them carrying plates of food. He sat at the table and began eating.

"Who is he?" Meg asked.

"Just one of them. He's my babysitter, he says."

"Mine too. Now."

"Meg, I'm sorry. But believe me, they knew all about you. I told them nothing. Only that I wanted to see you. That's all. And they showed me your life history."

"And what do you have to do for them?"

I explained what I knew about the smuggling ring.

"There's something else," I said. "Taá Wheatley."

"What about her?"

"I'm staying at her house. I saw her pictures of you."

"Well, Jesus Christ," she said. "Ain't this a frosty Friday. No wonder you showed up. You're working with them. And that fucking woman, she swore she'd never talk about my safe houses."

She clutched the back of a chair, rigid, muscle spasms running up and down her arms, rippling across her face as she breathed in and out so quickly I thought she was going to have a stroke or a heart attack. But just as quickly she relaxed.

"Laura, let me bash that fucking guy over the head. You'll get away from them."

"Except there's a cop standing outside, writing the same parking ticket for the last twenty minutes. And there's probably another one outside the back door. They put security anklets on me. I *can't* get away from them."

I pulled up my jeans, showed her the bracelets.

"Okay," she said finally. "This performance piece runs until Sunday. Unless that guy from the Health Department comes back."

"He won't," Nasso said from his table, *pad thai* noodles hanging from his fork.

I realized he'd been listening to us talk and wondered if he'd heard me give Rey's new name. But he picked up his empty plate and went to the kitchen for more.

"Meg," I whispered, "when you're sure nobody's watching you, go down to Sonoita. Ask for Heather Aguilar's ranch. Tell her I said she could trust you. She'll show you where my horse is stabled."

"You raise horses now?"

"He's coming back any minute, so just listen. Go to the stable. Once you're in the door, go to the far left corner. Two feet under the dirt floor you'll find a package wrapped in plastic baggies. Take the package, but make sure nobody sees you. There's liable to be police there. Or Border Patrol. Get Heather to go in with you, tell anybody who asks you're looking after my horse."

I noticed Nasso standing in the kitchen doorway, eating *pad thai* while keeping his eyes on us. I wondered if he could lip read, and in that instant knew that my sense of paranoia was coming back.

"Laura, how will I talk to you?"

"Give me an unlisted phone number. I'll call when I can."

She wrote out a phone number on a napkin and pressed it into my hands.

"When I get this mystery package, am I going to lose you again?"

"What do you mean?"

"It's got to be only one thing. Identity papers for a new Laura."

Not Laura, I thought. All three sets of ID were in completely different names, but none of them began with Laura. Subconsciously, I must have known that Laura Cabeza was the last time I'd use that first name.

I hated to let it go.

Your first name is like your first time for anything. You never forget it.

"Laura," Meg whispered as Nasso came to the table, "Laura, don't abandon me this time. Wherever you wind up after I get you those papers, don't just leave me twisting while I wait for that phone call that never comes."

"Find Mari Emerine and bring her to Tucson."

"You're asking a lot from me. You bring the wrath of the law down on me, but you want more favors. Why should I help you? No, no. Forget I said that. I'm wacky without my meds. I don't think straight."

"So start taking them, Meg."

"Not yet. Not yet. I have to find out . . ."

"Find out what?"

"I don't know, I don't know. Yet. It is what it is. Leave it that way. For me, just leave me as I am."

"Okay."

"This Mari. Why should I bring her to Tucson?"

"Can't tell you that. Just do this for me, okay? Think of her as another survivor. Like you and me."

She scrunched her eyes shut, waggling her head, contemplating.

We're all survivors, I thought, and she read my mind and smiled.

"To survive is to *live*. When will I see you next?"

"To survive is to *live*. Look. Laura, I know you don't understand why I quit my medications. Why I'm forcing myself into depression. But I *do* have a purpose, I *do* know what I'm doing, and I believe when I come out of this madness, I'll be able to better help some of the women and kids that come through my safe houses."

"I've been through depression," I said. "Anxiety, paranoia, panic attacks, depression. Good Christ, Meg, none of it is worth the trip."

"I'm really trying to hold onto my sanity. Trust me."

"Do you trust yourself?"

"You mean, will I know if I go over the edge? Maybe. Enough of this." She shook her head violently, like a dog emerging from a lake and flinging off water. "When will I see you next?"

"I'll call you when I can dump these police people."

"Taá? You'll never dump Taá. Once she's onto you, she's a second skin."

"Skin comes off. I'll call you."

"Ladies," Nasso said, "have you had your little chat?"

"Yes," Meg said. "Would you like some homemade mango ice cream?"

I thought Nasso was ogling her rear end, but he raised a hand to stop her.

"You're packing," he said.

Meg lifted her blouse and pulled her Glock from the holster that lay against the small of her back. Smiling, she held the Glock out to Nasso, who took it reluctantly, hefted it, flicked off the safety, and racked the slide. An unfired cartridge flew out of exhaust port and shattered a small china vase on one of the tables.

"Jesus Christ!" he said. "You keep a round in the chamber?"

"Got to be ready for anything," she said.

"You got a license for this piece?"

"Do you need to see it?"

He shook his head and handed the Glock back to her. She reholstered it and went to the kitchen to get the ice cream. Nasso turned to me with deep frown lines etched across his forehead.

"I found a baggie of coke back there. Somebody'd just snorted three lines laid out on a meat cleaver. I *hate* to see that kind of thing."

"Meg's having problems," I said. "That's why I wanted you and Dance to leave her alone."

"I'd never turn her in for using. I'm more worried that she's about to go over the edge. Right now, you need all the friends you can get."

"And you want to be my friend also?"

"Yeah," Nasso said slowly. "You're good people, you know how to work computers like nobody I've ever known, and you don't hesitate to bust my chops."

"You arrested me. You stuck me in that awful detention center. Friends? I don't think so."

"Give it time." He smiled. "I might surprise you yet."

20

Summarize. Plan. Act.

I slouched at Meg's kitchen table, deep in thought, mentally planning, looking for the logic in everything that had happened to me in the past few days, looking for a plan, looking for a final way out.

Isolating the threads of the thing.

First thread. Bobby Guinness, Donald Ralph, Mari Emerine.

Two clients, two contracts.

Smuggling people. Embezzling money.

Conclusions?

Forget about both contracts, forget about Mari, forget about LUNA13.

Second thread. Pinau Medina, Hector Garza.

No conclusions, except I couldn't forget about them, because I knew I'd be going into Mexico, where they controlled access to the police.

Conclusions?

On hold. Unpredictable. Don't waste time working on it.

Third thread. Taá Wheatley, Jake Nasso.

Michael Dance meant nothing. He just maneuvered his people, but whatever threats came from him would come through Taá and Nasso.

Conclusions?

Get out of the boat, I thought.

What Meg once said about Rey. Locked into his cycles of violence, he couldn't escape, he couldn't get out of the boat. But in the newly released version of *Apocalypse Now,* Martin Sheen *does* get out of the boat. He finds a French lady on a rubber plantation, he talks politics, and for a while he forgets going after Marlon Brando.

Conclusion. Get out of Taá's house.

Fourth thread.

Jonathan Begay.

Conclusions?

Forget about *Basta Ya,* forget about the smuggling rings, forget about everything except finding Jonathan. Then he'd tell me how to find Spider.

Wait. Fifth thread.

The water man.

Meaningless. Something in Mexico. Would have to wait until I met Rey.

I ran back and forth through all the threads and conclusions, not liking anything about them, but fixed on one thing only. I had to get out of the house and away from any kind of surveillance. Then I'd contact Rey, and we'd go looking for Jonathan.

At least it was a plan.

No, it was more.

A year ago, I'd have been wound so tight I'd have had a panic attack, I'd have been frozen and unable to do anything. Now I felt almost serene. Anxious about how I was going to follow through with my plan. But serene that I could do it.

Just a matter of finding the moment to start the ball rolling.

21

Nasso sat me in a wooden captain's chair, pulled up another one across from the round oak table. A young Mexican waiter in a tuxedo placed glasses of water on the table and lit a small candle inside a fluted, hand blown crystal bowl, tucked his left hand behind his back, and offered us menus.

"Two Negra Modelos," Nasso said to the waiter. "We'll order when you get our table inside the restaurant."

We sat outside the bar at one of a half-dozen tables set with yellow tablecloths, each surrounded by four elegant black chairs with cane-woven backing set into curved wooden frames. It was only twenty feet from the entrance to Hacienda del Sol, a circular driveway where harried attendants were parking cars.

"Sorry, *señor,* but the restaurant is closed. A private party."

"No problem. We're with that party. We just want to sit here at the bar for a while. Just leave the menus, bring the beer."

The server left us. People drifted steadily past us along the walkway toward the central fountain. Somebody turned on outdoor lighting, and a Mozart piano scherzo began on the sound system.

The server brought three plates of appetizers, laid them carefully on our table.

Twenty men and women were now chattering away near

the fountain. Men and women servers passed between them with full trays of margaritas. An extraordinarily handsome man came up from the parking lot. Passing our table, he looked back at Nasso and then down at the appetizers.

"Exquisite, these little *quesadillas,*" he said. "Tea-smoked duck, I'd say, wrapped up like holiday presents."

"Francisco," Nasso said. "How are you?"

"Well. Thank you. And who is this, Jake? Somebody from your office?"

"Madeleine Hunter. Not from the office. She sells Mercedes. In Scottsdale."

"Delighted."

"Who are you?" I asked.

"Francisco Angel Zamora."

He took one of my hands, raised it near his lips. His dark blue silken suit fit perfectly on his solid, well-muscled body. Unlike most of the men on the terrace, Zamora wore no tie, just a collarless white pima cotton shirt buttoned at the neck.

"I have an S5000. Fully armored. Not many of them around, I'm told."

"I sold three last week," I said, unable to resist.

"Well, you know what they say about Phoenix. LA without the beach. I'd rather drive my C Class convertible, but too many people in Nogales would love my head out in the open so they could get me in their sights and blow me to pieces."

He went out onto the terrace.

"The businessman."

"Right. Works with Medina. He also owns the biggest, newest, baddest maquiladora in Sonora. All kinds of electronic stuff. And he has the reputation of paying top wages, with health plans, frequent worker breaks, the whole nine yards. A model Mexican entrepreneur. All kinds of connections with the new Fox government. Public campaigns against the drug cartels."

"He's coming back."

This time, I noticed that he wore absolutely no rings, no jewelry of any kind, not even a wristwatch. He pulled another chair over and sat between us as a server hovered. A frosted margarita glass appeared quickly in front of him, but he left it untouched.

"Those women," Zamora said. "Are you working that case?"

"I'm thinking of working on the Atlantic salmon," Nasso said, tapping the menu. "But I can't rule out the Tomato, Polenta, and Mushroom Soufflé."

"If I can be of any help."

"Mr. Zamora," I said. "*Señor* Zamora. What *is* a maquiladora?"

"An assembly line. Parts come in, we put them together, we ship them out. Televisions, CD players, DVD players, MP3 players—well, you get the idea."

"When you said 'these women,' " Jake asked Zamora, "who did you mean?"

"The two who were murdered, of course."

"But nobody found their bodies," I said.

"It was on the news. You can't ignore CNN. Once they've shown dead bodies with no explanation, the entire United States news media is on the story all day, all night. Jake, aren't you working on that case?"

"Did the women's names mean anything to you?" Nasso asked.

"Hundreds of women work for me. I hardly know all their names, but I can certainly check our employment records."

"Please. That would be great."

"I'll have it done tomorrow." He stood up. "Jake. Good to see you. Miss Hunter, I'll visit you in Scottsdale when I'm ready for another Mercedes."

He went back out onto the terrace.

"Where did you come up with that name?" I asked. "Selling Mercedes?"

"From *The Sopranos*. That crazy woman, Gloria, the one Tony met at the Mercedes dealership."

In the crowd, I saw Xochitl Gálvez move behind an elderly lady in a large pink hat. Xochitl came back into view, and Zamora appeared behind her and placed a hand on her left arm. She shrugged it off and walked off the terrace, passing our table without a glance at me. Jake saw me watching her.

"Who's that?"

"A waitress," I said, not wanting to tell him about meeting Xochitl, or that I had another connection to LUNA13. "A server, I guess she's called. Some restaurant in Tucson, but I really don't remember where."

Dance appeared at the far end of the terrace, wearing a very pale blue tuxedo and a cranberry silk aviator's scarf around his neck. A woman bowed to him, whispered in his ear, and Dance began a soft-shoe routine. The crowd parted, and he swiveled to a moonwalk, headed toward the bar. The woman who had bowed turned. It was Pinau.

"Fuck," Nasso said.

"That's Pinau Medina."

"Pinau Beltrán de Medina. Courtesan to the Zedillo brothers, whore to Mexico City and the regions beyond."

"She told me that she's a judge."

"She is."

"Part of your task force, she told me."

"Let's go."

"Aren't we eating?"

"Why bother with dinner, when you've already had the appetizers."

In the parking lot, I saw Xochitl get into a taxi. We walked past Zamora's Mercedes, and Jake stroked the rooftop, drawing a finger down the heavily smoked glass of the driver's side window, which opened automatically.

"Yes?"

Zamora's driver had one hand resting on his throat, the fingertips moving just inside his suit jacket. Nasso rapped his knuckles on the rooftop, and the man's hand stopped moving.

"I know you," Nasso said. "Two years ago, I busted you over near Agua Prieta. You were a *coyote* then, and look at you now."

"America," the driver said, carefully placing his hands on the steering wheel. "A wonderful land of opportunity."

Nasso led me to his battered Honda Accord and drove out of the parking lot.

"Hungry?"

"Atlantic salmon sounded good."

"There's this place on Country Club. Ensenada. They make these gulf shrimp dishes smothered in onions and garlic. Nothing costs more than ten bucks."

"Are you buying?"

"America is buying. Tonight you get to wet your beak courtesy of my government expense account."

"I don't think so. Just take me home."

"Home? Sonoita? I don't think so. Back to Wheatley's and that pig. You saw the pig that lives next door? Imagine. What an incredible barbeque that pig would make."

"How was dinner?" Taá asked when I was inside her house.

"We barely ate. Listen. Why did he take me there?"

"He's got a thing for you."

"Oh, please."

"No. You're his ideal body type. Tall, thin, white teeth, great boobs, short hair."

"You're kidding me, right?"

"Nope."

"Taá. Tell him I'm not interested. And don't tell me that *you're* interested."

"You're not my type," she said with a smile. "I'll tell him."

"We met somebody there. A guy named Zamora. And Pinau Medina."

That got her attention immediately.

"They were there together?"

I couldn't remember if I'd actually seen them together or not.

"They hate each other," Meg said. "Hmmm. I'm going to have to find out why they were both there. Okay. I'm going to work, then to bed. Night."

"You expect me to sleep every night with these things on my legs?"

"I've got handcuffs. Take your choice."

Handcuffed to a bed while I slept. What a dreadful concept.

"I'm out of tampons," Taa said when I woke up. "I've got to go to Walgreen's."

"Okay."

Thinking I was too nonchalant, I started the tea kettle.

"You want anything?"

"Maybe some more Mountain Dew? A few Snickers?"

"Sure. What, uh, you're gonna be okay? I'll just be ten, fifteen minutes. Want to come with me?"

"No. I'll just be writing a program," I said. "Something to check chat room content. I was working it over last night, I've got too many lines of code in my head. If I leave, I'll forget what I was going to do."

"You're *sure* you'll be okay?"

She clearly didn't want to leave me alone, but clearly had to go out.

"Mountain Dew. And don't get the big bottles, it loses its fizz. A can or two. Half a dozen cans," I added quickly. Anything to make her think I needed caffeine.

"See you, then."

"See ya."

At my laptop keyboard, I began typing, running my left index finger over the screen to check the lines of programming code. She stood in the doorway for a moment, one hand resting on the frame, but I only saw her at the edge of my vision and kept focusing on the keyboard, frowning to make it look even more real. A few minutes later, I heard her car start up. I went to the front window, watched her unlock the gate, pull out onto the street, and get out to relock the gate. I stayed at the side of the window as she went down the street, stayed there for another five minutes, and coasted back, slowly, passing the front of the house. She tipped up her sunglasses and studied the house for at least a minute. Then she drove off again.

I hurried into the backyard.

The toolshed was locked with a padlock. Taa had created an obsessively neat border of stones around a bed of flowers. I took one of the stones and smashed at the padlock until it opened. Inside, I found the lopping shears I knew had to be there, since her hedges were as neatened as the row of stones.

It took fifteen minutes, but I finally cut through the tracker anklet. I carried it into the kitchen and laid it on the table on top of my file folder. But I had no luck with the stun anklet and didn't want to risk getting knocked out just a few feet away from freedom. I suddenly realized that there must be a signal activated by a transmitter, hidden somewhere in the house, and operated by electrical power.

Back outside again, I circled the house until I found the circuit breaker panel on the side of the house near the pig. Sophie snuffled at me through the fence, but the woman wasn't outside. Like the toolshed, the circuit breaker panel was secured by a padlock, which I also knocked open. I started turning off individual breakers and finally just threw the master power switch.

Hoping that the transmitter wasn't controlled by batteries, I walked slowly to the front gate, holding my breath for the last three feet. Nothing happened. I crossed over the dirt sidewalk area just as a FedEx truck pulled up.

"You Wheatley?" the driver said. I nodded. He gave me an envelope and had me sign his electronic tracker pad. While he drove off down the street, I headed the other way to collect my identity kits from Meg.

22

Walking to the first corner, as soon as I got onto the cross street, I began to run toward 6th Avenue, looking for a ride. Outside a bodega I saw a lowrider car, three *vatos* gathered around it as the driver worked his hydraulics to make the left side rock and roll. I had a twenty-dollar bill folded into my left palm. Without hesitating or talking to the *vatos* outside the car, I went straight to the driver's window and dropped the twenty on his lap.

"I need a ride," I said.

He stared at me through his sunglasses, not touching the bill.

"Just to a used car lot," I said. "Take me to one, I'll give you another twenty."

"What car lot?" he said, not sure how to read me. "Why should I do this?"

"I need to buy an older pickup truck."

"Ford? Chevy? What you talking, lady?"

"I don't care what kind. Just a truck. You find me the used car lot that's got one, let's say I give you another twenty. Sixty dollars, just to drive me there. Now."

"Cool," he said. "Show me the extra forty. How I know you got it? How I know you're not going to carjack me?"

He smiled at his own joke, nodding at his friends who drifted around behind me.

"Uh uh. You get me there, I get you the money."

"Reason I'm asking, why go to a car lot? Fernando there, that dude with the bandanna, he's looking to get rid of his '85 Chevy shortbed. You got the cash, you can deal with him direct. He signs over the registration slip. You got it, no dealer fees, no law, you're on your way free and clear."

"Fernando? You really got a pickup to sell?"

Fernando wore paint-stained coveralls over bare arms and shoulders. He nodded, shyly motioned his head towards a battered brown and gray pickup parked at the end of the lot. I walked straight to it, ignoring the *vatos* as I raised the hood.

"Start it up for me," I said to Fernando, who reached through the closed door and twisted a key ring. The engine ran smoothly, with not the slightest burr of trouble.

"I take care of it myself," he said. "It's got almost two hundred thousand miles on it, but I put in new valves, new rings, change the oil every three thousand."

"It's really yours?"

He got behind the wheel and opened the glove box, taking out the Arizona registration slip. "I'm a senior at the university. Sociology major. Need to sell this for fall tuition. Twenty-four hundred I'm asking."

"That's an honest price," I said.

"What do you think I am?" he said cynically. "Some street thug, some no good Mexican *vato* halfass car thief? You got the cash, or are you just jerking me around?"

"No. The money is real. You just have to drive me to get it."

"Yeah, right. I give you a ride, drop you off, you get a free taxi service, I'm stuck with nothing but a busted promise. How do I know you're not fucking with me?"

"That's a very good point. Well, the promise is real. But a promise is as good as it gets unless you take me there. I guess you'll just have to trust me."

"Okay. But they ride along behind us."

"Not a problem. I just need to make a phone call."

I suddenly realized I had no money and no cell phone, but noticed a public phone inside the bodega.

"Give me some change."

"Lady, you're really something. You're gonna give me twenty-four hundred dollars, but you want to borrow some small change?"

"Just enough to make a phone call."

He shrugged, fumbled in his jeans pocket, and dumped a handful of coins into my outstretched hand. I called Meg's private line.

"Ready," I said when she answered.

"Give me fifteen minutes to set it up," she said, giving me an address.

Meg had left my package at a house in central Tucson, an expensive area just north of the Arizona Inn, with large single-story houses of four- to five-thousand square feet.

Fernando navigated the complicated neighborhood street plan, his friends tailing us in the muscle car, until we found the address. The house was no different than its neighbors, the landscaping no different, no bars on any windows and no visible security precautions. I didn't even bother going to the front door.

A row of large clay *ollas* lined the gentle curve of the driveway, each *olla* filled with three-foot-high stalks of Mexican honeysuckle, the dirt underneath carefully groomed. Several hummingbirds flitted among the flowers, one swooping down to rest in the stretch of zebra aloe snaked between the *ollas*. A gardener came around the corner of the house, a bamboo rake over his shoulder, headphones on and plugged into a Walkman at his waist. He stopped to look us over, then idly raked underneath the aloe.

"Ah, come *on*!" Fernando said. "That dude's gonna make us *vamanos*."

The gardener seemed to be singing a few lyrics of the song he was listening to, but I saw a microphone clipped onto his blue denim work shirt collar and knew he was connected by cell phone to Meg. He moved slowly between the *ollas*, stopping briefly at the third from the end to wipe his neck before walking out of sight. I hurried to the *olla* and gently parted the greenish honeysuckle stalks. Some of the inch-long orange flowers flecked off as I twisted them this way and that until I saw the bright metal cap from a Dos Equis beer bottle. Scooping out dirt with my hands, I found a large Ziploc baggie, and inside that, another baggie that contained four manila envelopes.

Opening one of the envelopes, I counted out five five-hundred-dollar bills and took them back to the pickup, laying them on the hood and placing a small pebble to hold the bills secure against the slight morning breeze.

"Lady. I don't have a hundred to give back to you."

"Just sign the slip over to me. What are you studying?"

"Excuse me?"

"Why do you want to be a sociologist?"

"I actually want to be a lawyer. Want to work in Legal Aid, help these illegals that La Migra hassles all the time.

"That's cool."

"Let me clean the junk out of the pickup bed."

He motioned his three friends to help remove several old plastic milk crates and a large burlap bag full of empty paint cans, but I stopped them.

"No," I said, realizing it added to the image of a working-class pickup. "Leave it all in there, I'll dump it when I've got time.

"What game you running, lady?"

The four of them edged around me, boxing me against the step side box near the driver's side door. One of them raised a hand, and the gardener came around the other side of the house with a garden hose, the water running in a long, lazy three-foot arc as he watered some plants. Incredibly, one of the hummingbirds flew to the bottom of the arc of water and seemed to walk up the stream, drinking until he reached the nozzle of the hose. The gardener stood like a statue, but his eyes were on us, not the hummer.

"Wow," one of the *vatos* said, and in that instant all four of them stood transfixed, like six-year-old boys. "Did you see that?"

"Are we cool, Fernando?" I said, and the hummer flew away.

"Yeah." He stuffed the bills into his jeans. "So, like, how come you want a beatup old pickup like this?"

"I'm going on a sociology field trip."

"Oh yeah? What kinda people are you studying?"

"Single women who can't live a quiet life."

The *vato* with the funny car drifted over.

"Where's my forty?"

"Ask Fernando," I said, cranking the shift into first gear. "He's got an extra hundred."

I didn't want to drive along 4th Avenue to see if Meg was still running the restaurant, thinking that by now Taá had alerted Dance and Nasso, and they'd have people all over Meg. Instead, I drove along Broadway to the El Con mall. Parking in the front strip, I checked the ID packets and picked one, sliding the rest of the envelopes underneath the bench seat. Making sure that the pickup door actually locked, I went inside the Radio Shack, took out my new credit card, and ordered a cell phone account.

"Mary Stanley," the clerk said. "I've got a niece, same name, but spells it with an *ie* at the end. She pronounces it Mary, everybody wants to call her Marie. I'll need to see your driver's license, or some kind of ID."

I handed him the Arizona State driver's license.

"Pick out what kind of phone you want, and what kind of service. We've got some Nokias, plus the new StarTac digital. You want digital? Sprint?"

"Sure. Give me that top-of-the-line Nokia. Just put it on the card."

"Gee, you know what? I just realized, my niece is named Cherie, not Marie." He spelled Marie to himself. "Whoa, I think I'd better spend a little more time with the family. This job is turning into a twenty-four seven since I agreed to be the manager."

"Do you sell Palm Pilots?"

"Got to survive, got to carry what people are buying. Which model?"

"Wireless."

"Palm V. Um, that's a different wireless service. You want a contract with them also? Email, instant messaging, web browsing."

"Yes."

"I see these kids in the malls, they've got a cell phone with an earpiece, they're talking on it while they've got their Palm out, they're fingering the keypad. I kept wondering what they had so much to talk about."

He punched in my credit card number and started the activation process for both wireless services.

"Went up behind two girls, each talking on a cell phone. You know what they were talking about?"

"No. How much longer?"

" 'I'm in front of The Gap. Where are you?' Meaningless. Guess you've got to be a teenager to understand them. You got any kids?"

When he finally realized I wasn't going to talk, he concentrated on processing the wireless services. It took him fifteen minutes to activate the cell phone, then another five to activate the Palm.

I drove up to Speedway and headed east until I saw a taco truck on a side street. He apologized for how long it took to heat up a bean burrito and a *chile relleno* over his small sterno flame. I drove another two blocks, parked, left a message on Meg's voice mail, and ate while I opened the FedEx envelope.

A single sheet of paper with the address of an Internet website.

I drove back to the Radio Shack.

"Listen," I said to the clerk, "I just heard from my boss. The first call I got on my new cell phone, and it's my boss, chewing my ass because I haven't done something for him. Is there any chance you've got a computer in here I can use?"

"Not really. I can sell you a computer."

"I just need to look up a website. That's all."

He looked around the empty store and yawned.

"Sure. Why not. Keep me awake. Long as you don't mind if I sit at the computer and type in the address. That way, it's kosher all around."

Leading me into the back office, he sat at a keyboard and dialed up an ISP, shielding the keyboard as he typed in a user ID and password. He opened the Microsoft browser, looked at the sheet of paper from the FedEx envelope, and typed the URL.

www.moneytochihuahua.com

The website had only one page and simply asked for a user ID and a password.

"Do you have any idea what this means?" he said.

"Money. Mexico. I don't have a clue. Do you?"

"A guess, that's about it. You want to look at this website any more?"

"No. What's your guess?"

"Well," he said as shut down the computer. "Lots of these illegals send money back home. Really pisses me off. They come up here, get paid in cash, pay *zero* tax dollars, and then send a lot of the money home to their families."

"Through the Internet?"

"Mostly by Western Union. They're getting smarter. Used to be, they didn't trust any gringo banks or companies like Western Union. They go to money merchants, they'd pay twenty, thirty percent of their money just to get it sent to Mexico. Now, they just pay the standard Western Union wire charges. This website, could be somebody's found a new way to send that money."

"Thanks," I said. "Thanks a lot."

I sat in the El Con parking lot until Meg called and told me to meet her at Nonie.

23

"This is the last time you'll see me," Xochitl said. "I'm leaving today."

We sat in Nonie, the Cajun and Creole restaurant on Grant, the place where Xochitl worked. The restaurant was closed, but Xochitl let me in at the back door. She quickly introduced me to the owners, Chris Leonard and his wife Suzy, and we left them preparing pots of gumbo and jambalaya. When I asked if I could order something, Suzy brought me a bowl of each, plus some red beans and rice.

"Why are you leaving?" I asked.

"Because of Francisco Zamora. I saw you at Hacienda del Sol."

"And I saw Zamora put his hand on your shoulder, and right after that you quickly left by taxi. What were you doing there?"

"Serving. I make good money by working catered parties. Chris lets me have a night off here if I can provide a sub. He knows I need the money from catered jobs. But I didn't think Zamora would come up to Tucson, so I am leaving. Today. Chris and Suzy know that, they will miss me, but it cannot be helped. I have their love, support. I owe them much. You know me as Xochitl Gálvez. Not my name, not important to tell you my name. Not safe. Even you."

"Where are you going?"

"Out."

"But aren't you already free?"

Opening her handbag, she took out a newspaper clipping. A photograph from a Mexican newspaper. Seven people gathered around Zamora, who posed with one foot on a shovel.

"I can't read Spanish. What is this?"

"The groundbreaking ceremony for Zamora's maquiladora. Look at the women."

Pinau stood to Zamora's left, with a shorter haircut of streaked blond hair, but still recognizable. On the far right, a young woman's body was obscured by the man in front of her, but I thought I recognized the face.

"Ileanna. She was Zamora's bookkeeper. Veraslava, she was bookkeeper for another maquiladora. My friends."

"Those are the names on that videotape. The two murdered women."

"They had no faces, one news report said. Dragged through the cactus until the skin was ripped off most of their bodies. Off of their faces. That is a warning."

"To who?"

"Me. We did a foolish thing one night. We were working late one night. Zamora went outside for a cigarette. We made copies of some papers in his safe. His account books. For twenty minutes we copied papers. The next day, all three of us walked through the water tunnels to Arizona."

I had a sudden thought.

"Were you brought across by a *coyote?*"

"Everybody knows about the tunnels. We went by ourselves."

"This is important," I said. "Do you know of a *coyote* called the water man?"

"No. Why?"

"Never mind. How did you know those two women?"

"We were all accountants in Zamora's maquiladora. We made staplers, uh, no, staple guns. That's not important. How we got to Mexico, how we got to Nogales, *that* is what's important."

"You were smuggled into Mexico from Albania."

"Two years ago. The three of us, we paid thirty thousand United States dollars. In Albania, we also did accounting. For banks. When the Albanian mafia took over our banks, they replaced us with their own people. So. What future? What hope? America. But when we got off the boat in Vera Cruz, we had been promised identity papers, travel visas, passports, everything promised to us to come across the border safely. Instead, we were locked in a house. We are young women, we are all beautiful, we were raped over and over for three weeks. Instead of freedom, we were told that we'd been auctioned to a brothel in Las Vegas. That's the only way you'll get across the border, we were told. As whores. The next day, another man came. This one."

She pointed at another face in the newspaper photograph, almost hidden by Pinau. I could see it was Hector Garza. The King Kong man, the ape who'd been in the immigrant detention center with Pinau Medina.

"He needed three women to be accountants."

"Why did he want women?"

Xochitl shrugged.

"We are cheaper. We keep secrets. We are women. Who knows why? We didn't care. That afternoon we are riding in a Mercedes Benz to Nogales. We are given ten thousand pesos each and a house for the three of us."

"So if you had good jobs . . . I don't follow, why give them up?"

"Ileanna was the smartest of us three. The best bookkeeper, the best, how shall I say it, she had the best conscience. She started making a diary of how the women workers were being abused and underpaid. In Nogales, nobody of power is far away from knowing someone in the drug cartels. For people who learn secrets, a life of promise is quickly jeopardized. Assassins are cheap, easy to find. The three of us, we decided to get out. We contacted a friend in *Basta Ya.*"

"The Indian women's worker group? How could they help?"

"Many of them had worked with political prisoners from El Salvador and Nicaragua. Some of the escape routes into the US were still in place. There are still groups in Arizona that give sanctuary, give a new life."

"Does *Basta Ya* charge money?"

"No. If you have some, they will take it. But only to help others. So two months ago, the three of us copied Zamora's papers, and then we came across the border."

"Did you know anything about the papers you copied?" I asked.

"Nothing."

"Were they suspicious? Why did you copy them?"

"We thought he was connected to Garza, and if we left, Garza would come after us. So we copied the papers, thinking there might be something of value in them that we could trade for our safety. Something connected to the smuggling rings."

"Wait a minute. Let me get this straight. There are *two* smuggling cartels. The first brings women in from Albania. The second helps you escape the first."

"Exactly."

"And which one talks to you in the chat rooms."

"*Basta Ya.*"

"Can you connect to them right now?"

"Yes, but . . . they wouldn't talk to you. Why do you want to do this?"

"I know one of the people working for *Basta Ya.*"

"Who?"

"Jonathan Begay."

"Ah! *Señor* Johnny."

"He's my ex-husband. I haven't seen him for twenty years. Can you . . . do you have your Palm Pilot? Can you ask LUNA13 if I can contact Jonathan?"

Digging the last spoonfuls of gumbo from my cup, I avoided looking at her. She fidgeted in her chair. Chris abruptly turned off the cumbia music on the sound system, and I could hear Xochitl breathing. I kept avoiding her until she reached into her bag and took out the Palm. With relief,

I saw it was the same model and color as the one I'd just bought. Licking my lips at the last of the gumbo, I wiped my hands on my napkin and picked up my bag from the floor, rooting through it as though I was looking for tissues or makeup.

"We will do this," Xochitl said. "I will contact them, but I won't say you are here. I will ask about *Señor* Begay. Is that what you want?"

"Yes."

Removing the Palm pointer, she worked it rapidly through a series of screens.

"I am in the chat room."

She leaned sideways, holding the Palm between us so that I could read the tiny screen. The chat room user names were incredibly revealing.

LUNA13: > you are gone from Tucson?
LUNA5: > not yet
LUNA13: > this is no time to be foolish

If Xochitl was LUNA5, then LUNA was a network, not a single person.

LUNA13: > you have the money, the id package?
LUNA5: > i have everything
LUNA13: > kansas . . . it is a long ways off, my sister
LUNA5: > you are always in my heart.
LUNA13: > so . . . why are you not gone?
LUNA5: > senor johnny, i hear he is in jail

A long, long pause, the cursor blinking.

LUNA13: > i didn't know that
LUNA5: > can you find out where?
LUNA13: > maybe . . . do you know when he was taken?

Xochitl's eyebrows raised with the question. I shook my head.

LUNA5: > no
LUNA13: > we were wondering why his radio news has been the same tape msg for the last 4 days, so that must have been when it happened, 4 days ago
LUNA5: > see what you can find out
LUNA13: > yes, but you leave NOW
LUNA5: > agree to leave, but please find out which jail
LUNA13: > contact us when you get to kansas, dorothy
LUNA5: > i have my ruby slippers

Xochitl punched at the screen with the Palm pointer and logged out of the chat room. She slipped the Palm into its case and started to put it back in her bag.

"Can I see that?" She hesitated. "I've never used one of them."

She handed it to me. I knocked hard enough against the empty gumbo bowl to send it flying off the table. Her eyes followed the bowl's trajectory until it shattered on the floor. In that moment, I dropped her Palm into my lap and picked up the one I'd just bought and slipped it into her case.

"Everything all right?" Suzy said.

"I'm so clumsy," I said.

"Not a problem."

"Here," I said to Xochitl, handing her the Palm. "Take this before I break it too."

We went outside, where Luis Cabrera waited beside his pickup, his eyes anxiously quartering the neighborhood.

"If somebody is watching," I said to Xochitl, "he'll never see them."

"I know that. He doesn't, but he feels better because he's protecting me."

"Will I ever see you again?"

"How far is Kansas?"

"With ruby slippers, an instant away."

"Beam me up, Scotty."

She smiled, frowned, burst into tears, and hugged me fiercely.

"Goodbye, Ishmaela," I said.

"I am no longer Albanian. I am Dorothy America."

"Good luck."

"I hope you find *Señor* Johnny. I hope you find whatever you seek from him."

"If I go to Nogales," I asked, "is there anybody I can talk to? About the *Basta Ya* people who smuggle women out? About the maquiladoras?"

She hesitated a long, long time.

"Watch out for the man who drives the water truck."

That cryptic remark was the only thing she said. They drove away, headed west on Grant to US10. I watched the traffic on Grant for ten minutes, but finally realized that I had no idea if anybody was following them.

Too late, I realized that the phrase had two meanings. *Watch out* could mean *Look out*, be careful, don't go near him. But for somebody whose English was a second language, it could also mean *Find* the man with the water truck. I'd only know if I went to Nogales.

I called Meg and got no answer. Checking the voice mail box on my cell phone, I found a message from her telling me to go to Phoenix, to a safe house she operated in Scottsdale. She promised to bring Mari and Alex.

Working my way through heavy traffic on Grant, out to US10, I went over everything she'd said and realized I'd overlooked something vital.

The water man must be a man with a water truck.

No connection to the water tunnels? I didn't know, but I'd have to see them.

24

At the Casa Grande junction, US10 traffic slowed to a crawl and finally to stop and go. I could see bubblegum lights flashing a mile ahead, probably an accident. I tried calling Meg's cell phone again, but got no answer.

Twenty minutes later I'd barely gone a mile, but finally drew abreast of the accident scene. A brand new Saturn had been tailgated and crumpled. Nobody seemed injured, but a Casa Grande fire truck was parked across the right lane, and fireman were working with the Jaws of Life to open the passenger side door.

A tall, slim Hispanic woman strode back and forth beside the Saturn, yammering on a cell phone at the top of her voice. She'd obviously been the driver and was obviously angry. Tottering on her four-inch platform heels, with a head of riotous red hair and large breasts clamped tightly in a Julia Roberts *Erin Brockovich* Wonder Bra, she slowed every male driver in my lane. I passed the Saturn just as the firemen pulled the male passenger out of the car. He also didn't seem to be injured, but seeing him the redhead stretched out both her arms in anger and started berating him for switching the radio from salsa to country.

"But Sandy," I heard him start to complain.

I rolled up both pickup windows and turned the air-conditioning on full blast to drown out all the noise. Traffic picked up rapidly, and in no time I was back up to eighty miles an hour and pulling into the outskirts of Phoenix just as my cell rang.

"Laura," Meg said. "Don't go where I told you. Instead, go through Tempe and take the 101 loop north. Get off at Indian School and go west to Scottsdale. Turn right, make a quick turn right, park anywhere, and meet us in the atrium outside the Marriott Suites restaurant."

"Jesus, Laura," Meg said, sipping from a tall, very narrow and squarish glass. "You've got so much heat around you, I'm not sure how much I can see you."

We sat in the shade, although with the temperature nearly one hundred degrees, combined with the high humidity in Scottsdale, everybody was sweating. Mari slumped in her chair. Alex held Mari's hands, rubbing them briskly to warm them up.

"You've been seeing too many movies," Mari said.

We both were waiting for her to gather enough energy to talk.

"Oh yeah," Alex said enthusiastically. "That scene from *Heat*. You two are like Pacino and DeNiro, where they have coffee and talk over their macho lives. If the heat is around the corner, you've got to be ready to drop everything in thirty seconds and move on to a whole new life. Bullshit boys, that's all they are."

"Something like that," Meg admitted. "Except that's more like Rey and Laura. Not me. I don't want to be out of some movie plot, I don't want to be anonymous, I don't want to be an outsider these days. I can't even visit most of my safe houses since I started a public fundraising campaign. The Tucson heat is all over me. Tucson PD, state, federal, all kinds of different agencies have got me on their radar."

"Why did you cancel the meeting at your safe house here?"

"I always call before I visit a house. The woman on front door duty told me that two US Marshals had just been there, asking for you."

"Sorry I've got you into this mess."

"Yeah. So am I. Okay, what next?"

"Are you all right?" I asked Mari.

"Not really," Mari said. "But I can talk."

"Meg. Alex. Can you leave the two of us alone?"

"I don't leave my mom alone," Alex said defiantly.

"Unless I ask," Mari said with a wan smile. "And I'm asking. I really need to talk with this woman in private. So please go with Meg. Sit on the other side of the atrium or go into the restaurant and watch TV."

"They're tuned to the TV Land network," she said disgustedly. "I mean, who wants to watch a twenty-year-old dumb television rerun?"

They left.

"Are you okay?" I said.

"O*kay*. Isn't that just a typical happy-face phrase. You know I'm hurting, but you don't want to ask me straight out, so you slide around it by asking if I'm okay. Well, I'm not okay. Had my last chemo yesterday. Talked with the oncologist. I need a really, really big favor."

"I don't know that I'm much capable of that."

"Meg is right. You're getting ready to cut out."

"Yeah. She's right."

"Where you going?"

"Mexico."

"Take Alex with you."

"What?"

"I'm going back into the hospital."

"Oh, Mari. I'm so sorry."

"There's a 'but' in there."

"Tomorrow I might be in jail. I made a deal, I busted the deal. That's why the US Marshals are looking for me."

"So? You're still going to Mexico?"

"Yes."

"You're not worried they'll catch you at the border?"

"Not where I'm going to cross."

"Please. Take Alex with you."

"Can't do that."

"It would only be for a week. I'm going to have a bone marrow transplant. In a week, I'll be strong enough to have Alex back."

"She'd be furious with me trying to keep her from you."

"She'd be *more* furious at me for making her go."

"I can't make her come with me."

"No. You can't."

"Can't get around that one."

"But I will tell her to go."

"You'll tell her."

"Yes."

"To go with me."

"Yes."

"To Mexico. Even if I'm saying to you, I don't want her with me."

"Please. I have nobody else to ask. Meg is freaked out with all the police surveillance. And frankly, without taking her meds, she's really getting so unstable that I can't trust her to be responsible. There's nobody else. Don't you have a daughter?"

"Not the issue."

"Please. And to make it easier, I'll even tell you where to take Alex."

"You don't want her with me all the time?"

"Meg's daughter is at some ranch, out in the middle of nowhere in the Sonoran Desert. Take Alex to stay with Meg's daughter."

"Ranch!" I snorted. "You're talking about that run-down old place where Rey's father used to live. It's no ranch. Just a falling-down house full of holes."

"Rey said it would be all right."

"How do you know that?"

"He called Meg's cell phone. Meg wasn't there, I thought the call was for me, I talked with him. Their daughter, Amada, she's apparently going teenage nuts being all alone on that ranch. Rey thinks that Alex would be good company. He's got a TV satellite dish, he's rebuilt the house, he says

Amada would love another girl for company. If it's okay with Rey, if I make it okay with Alex, won't you take her?"

"That won't be possible."

"Why not? Jesus Christ, Laura, why not?"

"Because I think I'm headed back to jail."

Jake Nasso was loping across the atrium from the street. I got up to run into the Marriott restaurant, but Taá stood in the doorway. Both of them had holstered weapons, both had their hand on the holster. Two waitresses in the restaurant stood behind Taá, mouths open, too young to be anything but curious about what might happen. Jake gathered Meg and Alex, herding them to our table. I slumped into the chair as Jake pulled his handcuffs from behind his back and dropped them with a clank on the glass-topped table.

"Pull over those two chairs," he said to Taá. "Hellll-oooooo, Laura."

Taá sat next to me, her face flushed red with anger.

"And hello again. Um, Mari, was it?"

"Mari Emerine."

"And daughter Alice."

"Alex."

"And Thai food Meg."

"You don't need them," I said. "Let's just go, leave them here."

"Don't need them. But nobody's going anywhere, not just yet. How about some more iced tea, ladies? I need a cold beer."

"Jake!" Taá was exasperated. "Let's just take her. Now."

"Hey. You found her. Now I get to be in charge."

"How did you find me?"

"You still got that bracelet on."

I lifted my leg, pulling my jeans above the stun anklet.

"It's a stun thing," I said. "I cut off the digital tracker."

"Oh, Taá led you down the rabbit hole, Laura. Nobody's invented a stun anklet yet. It's just another tracker model, but she wanted you to think it was something else. We've got these map things? In the cars? Just like a James Bond movie.

We followed you everywhere. Taá wanted to grab you down in Tucson, but I said Hey, let's see what they got in Scottsdale. Always wanted to come sniff the money up here."

"I trusted you," I said to Taá, but she and Meg were staring at each other. Nasso followed their eyelocking and smiled. I realized he knew they'd been lovers.

"Uh uh. Honey?" He waved at one of the young waitresses. "Iced teas all around for the ladies. Draft beer for me."

I watched the waitress go to the bar and talk excitedly with a man who took her green apron and tied it on. A chef walked by and the man took the chef's hat and sunglasses, nestling the hat onto his curly black hair and tucking the sunglass temples above his ears onto the hat. The waitress hurriedly filled some glasses, put them on a tray, filled a glass with something out of a pressure spigot, and set that glass on the tray also. The man hoisted the tray up on his right hand and came out to us, setting the tray onto our table.

"Ah," Nasso said, reaching for the glass of beer. "I'm really thirsty."

"You can drink it when we leave," the man said, pulling a Glock out from underneath the apron and laying it alongside Nasso's left ear.

"Laura. Take their weapons."

"Rey?"

"Now!"

I was so dumbstruck I couldn't move. Alex jumped up, carefully approached both Nasso and Taá from behind, and removed their guns. Rey tucked both of them into his belt and waved into the restaurant. His old friend Manny lumbered out and sat down at the next table.

Manny. The Vietnam vet with the picture book of dead people. The man who'd babysat me a year before, content to eat and watch TV while keeping me safe.

"Y'all sit here a while," Rey said to Taá and Nasso. "Enjoy that beer. My friend over there, he's going to sit with you a while. He's got a chili dog coming."

"Three," Manny said.

"So he'll make sure you stay put while he eats all three chili dogs. And whatever else he wants. Laura, Alex, come on."

"Go with him," Mari said to Alex.

"Mom!"

"Sweetie, they can't do anything to me. I'm going in the hospital. For my last chemo treatment."

"But *Mom,* you can't ask me to leave you."

"Sure I can. Just for a few days. Go with Laura, go with this man."

"No way!"

"Way."

"Staying here."

"Not."

"Just for a day. Three days. Maybe four."

"Which hospital?"

"Right here in Phoenix. The cancer center."

"I can call you?"

"Every day."

"Promise?"

"Do I look strong enough to lie and risk bringing the wrath of teenage doom down on my head?"

"Come on," Rey said. "People saw the guns, they're making calls inside. I've got to believe 911 is a popular number."

Alex clutched my hand, clutched her mother's hand. I backed up, stretching her between myself and Mari. Their hands extended as I moved until only the fingertips touched, and then Alex and I turned and began running.

"Where's your pickup?" Rey shouted at me.

I couldn't believe he was that stupid, calling attention to my truck. It was parked across from the Marriott. Alex squeezed between us on the bench seat and Rey drove to Scottsdale Avenue, catching the light, and turning left. At Indian School he turned right, and then left again at Goldwater Boulevard. He pulled into a parking lot behind a building with fake Greek pillars and squeezed the pickup between two large SUVs. We walked past the back entrance of a mystery bookstore and then went through a boutique restaurant out onto Goldwater. A dirty brown Humvee was parked at the curb, three teenagers on skateboards looking in the front windows.

"I thought you didn't play with real guns any more," I said as he shooed away the skateboarders and got the aircon cranked high.

"Didn't say that. Said I didn't shoot guns any more."

"What if you'd had to shoot back there?"

He held up his Glock and pulled the trigger. It clicked. He thumbed the magazine release and showed it to me.

"No bullets."

"You braced two US Marshals with an unloaded gun?"

"They didn't know that. Seatbelts?"

We strapped in. The aircon started blowing cold air. He powered up all the windows and locked the three guns behind a secret panel.

"And Manny?"

"What about him?"

"What kind of gun does Manny have?"

"Nothing but a chili dog."

Four hours later we were at the Sasabe border crossing.

25

Sasabe. Tigger. House of death. The border.

Cross over into another world, another state, another life.

State of mind, state of grace, hail Mary and Joseph, I have sinned.

A year ago, when my life was steady and sane and safe, I worked with a bounty hunter named Tigist. She was Ethiopian, scarcely five feet tall, with luminous kohl-blackened eyelids, and intense ocean-green pupils, the eyes set deep over a long, slightly hooked nose in the exact middle of a thin face. Since few people remembered how to pronounce her name, she'd started calling herself Tigger after reading a Pooh book to her son. She always told me that she could handle herself in any situation, but I'd brought her into a case that took her to Sasabe, where she'd been murdered.

I'd live with that guilt for the rest of my life.

Driving through the small town, I looked for the spot.

An adobe house, six-foot fence, razor wire, Tigger.

But the house had vanished, scraped clean off the ground. At intervals, other vacant lots, houses destroyed, even the debris transported elsewhere.

"Guy who owns the town, he put it up for sale."

We drove past and took the loop down to the right, hay now eleven dollars a bale, curve up to the left and the inverted vee roofing of the border station.

"Three million, he first asked."

We waited behind an old Dodge Ram pickup, the bed so overloaded with hay that the weight bottomed out the worn springs and suspension, the rear wheels splayed outward like a *coyote* van overloaded with twenty hopeful illegals.

"When he got no takers, he picked half a dozen houses where some crime had been committed. Dope storage, rape, murder, maybe it was eight houses. Bulldozers came in, they wiped out the houses. Brought forty day workers over the border to carry away the debris. Picked the house sites clean. But still no takers."

The pickup was waved through by the US Customs agent, who slouched, bored, waiting for us to drive up to him.

"Don't know if the price dropped, or if the guy who owns Sasabe just took the town off the market. Couldn't say."

"Where are you headed?" the agent asked.

Rey flashed a fake Border Patrol badge. The agent nodded as soon as he saw the familiar shape and colors, waved us past without even reading the badge. At the Mexican side, Rey folded his left hand around his *policia* card and a twenty-dollar bill. The Mexican agent took the card and the money, palmed the money, and without looking at it, handed Rey back his card.

"We're in," he said, as the Humvee bounced off the US pavement onto a rough Mexican road. "You might as well try to sleep or something."

I took the identity card before he could stuff it into his pocket.

"Ramón Vargas," I read out loud.

"I told you. When I cross the border, I'm a different person."

The border. A statement of geography, a state of mind, a line. Like death. In one instant, you cross over the edge of your known world.

Approaching it on foot, you raise a leg and place it into another country before your body follows. Up in the four corners area, you can get down on hands and knees and have a different part of your body in four different states. Arizona, New Mexico, Utah, and Colorado.

A state of mind, state of grace, state of citizenship, state of escape.

You wake up feeling great, wonderful, life's a bonanza and cream. Go for a routine checkup, have tests, have a diagnosis and a follow-up chat and a second opinion, and then you're in for bone marrow transplants, knowing it's downhill, you're in another country, you've crossed the border.

Cruising at sixty kilometers per hour, the Humvee hit a stretch of dirt washboard. Before Rey could hit the brakes and slow down, the Humvee rattled violently, and because I'd taken off my seatbelt to try and sleep, the vibrations bounced me off the ceiling panel and against the door.

"Sorry," Rey said. "I didn't see that coming."

He slowed at a fork, chose the right track, accelerated when the dirt smoothed out for a long stretch.

"You know what you taught me?" he said.

"What?"

"There are conditions, options, rules. You taught me to question those rules. You weren't afraid to do that when I knew you a year ago. Question the rules, make changes, become somebody else."

"I just want to sleep, Rey."

"You want to know why I have these false identity cards? These Border Patrol badges? You taught me that. Be who you want to be."

"Please."

I looked over my shoulder at Alex, dead asleep across the rear seat.

"Just let us sleep."

The sun glowed full on the western horizon and dropped out of sight.

"Green," Rey shouted.

"What, what?" Alex said from the backseat.

I'd been asleep, but had awakened ten minutes before.

"Don't you remember telling me about the green wave?"

"Stare at the setting sun. Keep your mind on nothing else but the sun. Red, orange, big and fat, then *bop* it's gone and you see a green sun. You mind is totally betrayed. Your eyes have been taking in the color spectrum red through orange. And when those colors disappear, your mind tries so hard to compensate that it *over*compensates on the color scale and you see the exact opposite. Green."

"What are you guys talking about?"

"Go back to sleep, Alex."

"When do we get there?"

"A while," Rey said, "a while yet."

But she'd already fallen back asleep.

"Kids. Live for the moment. If they don't like that moment, they drop out of it."

"Rey, it's not that simple."

"Kids."

At Zacateca, nothing more than a junction in the road with three old houses, Rey pulled the Humvee to a stop.

"Need a beer. Want something?"

"Mmmnnn."

When he came back with four cans of beer, I popped the tab on one and drank thirstily.

Draining one beer, he popped open another.

"Talk to me about this job," he said.

"Smuggling people across the border.

"Two different . . . I'd guess I'd have to call them cartels. There's so much money behind one of the smuggling rings, it has to be related to drugs. They bring in foreign women, they sell them in the US. Whorehouses, strip joints, sweatshops, even as indentured servants. So I'm told. I don't really know this, I'm just told."

"People can say anything."

"You ever hear of *Basta Ya?*"

"Some kind of workers' union? For Indians? Mestizos?"

"I think so."

"Yeah. I've heard of it. Small change, I hear. When something is tolerated by the *policia*, when they let it continue, it's got to be small change. No money in it. No bribes, so let it happen until it shows a profit."

"It's run by my ex-husband."

Stunned, he let the Humvee drift off the road. We crashed down and over a small ditch and started ramming creosote bushes alongside the road until he regained control and took his foot off the accelerator. We drifted to a stop in the middle of a patch of jumping cholla.

"Jonathan Begay," I said."

"*Señor* Johnny. I've heard people talk about him. He's in jail."

"Where? Down here?"

"That's what I heard. But there are jails all over Sonora."

"Can you find out where he is?"

"I can make some calls."

I took out my cell phone, but he didn't see it, staring into the darkness beyond the cholla, thinking.

"Got a contact list. We'll look it over when we get to my place."

Fifty kilometers later, we suddenly came up to a paved highway and Rey turned west and drove much faster. Lights flickered in the distance behind us, slowly crept up.

"I want to call Mom." Alex sat up, her head silhouetted by the headlights. Then her head was in darkness as a Lexus convertible soared past at high speed.

"Here." I handed her my cell phone. "Use this."

She dialed several numbers, listened, handed me back the cell.

"We're out of roaming range. We're across the border."

"Down Mexico way," Rey sang.

"Don't worry, honey. We'll call her later."

"Stop at a gas station. I'll use a pay phone. I'll call collect."

"No gas station for two hundred kilometers," Rey said.

"No restaurants, no bars, no nothing. You can try calling from my place. I think my daughter's cell phone has calling privileges from Mexico."

"Okay."

She fell asleep again.

"How far are you into this?" Rey asked after a while.

"I really don't know."

"Those marshals. In Scottsdale. What's their beef?"

"My old arrest warrants."

"Wait a minute, wait a minute. You mean, back when you were with AIM?"

"Yeah."

"And that's your husband, that's the guy down here in jail?"

"Yeah."

"You really want to find this guy?"

"No. Not really. But if I do, then he can tell me where to find my daughter."

"Her name was . . . don't tell me, her name was . . . Spider. You think he knows? Where she is, I mean?"

"That's all I want to know."

"I'll make some calls. This smuggling thing—"

"Two different kinds of smuggling."

"One. Two. Whatever. You got anything invested in finding the smugglers?"

No, I thought, having thought about little else all night. No, I was through with all of that. Find Jonathan, find Spider. New life.

"Call me Dorothy," I said.

"What the hell does that mean?"

But I fell sound asleep.

26

"What's the most important thing in life?"

Rey and I at a trestle table, eating some granola and bananas for breakfast. He'd remodeled the main room of his father's house, and totally rebuilt the extended sun room. The screen mesh was new, with no evidence left of his father's habit of shooting holes through the screen while getting drunk. Rey had planted wide patches of vegetables, herbs, flowers, many things I couldn't even identify. A brand-new wooden building housed six electricity generators, some of them running with minimal noise because he'd taken time to soundproof the walls.

A large TV was up against one wall next to a desktop computer, both connected to a satellite dish on the roof. Brushed-chrome stovetop, oven, and refrigerator.

"Your computer's connected to the TV dish?"

"Christ, those girls. I'm not sure which they like best. The computer or the TV."

Alex and Amada sat cross-legged on the desert about thirty feet away, staring at various holes and depressions left by desert creatures.

"Being on my own," I said.

"No. I mean, for most people. What's most important?"

"Happiness? Money? Good sex?"

"Doing what's necessary."

I scraped my bowl clean of the granola and got up for more.

"Exactly right."

"You're talking about *you* again. What's most important for you."

"Sure. Why not? Right now, I want to find my ex-husband. I want to ask him where my daughter is. When he tells me, I'll go there. I'll leave all these jobs behind."

"Not that easy."

"So, what does that mean to you? Doing what's necessary?"

"It's got no specific answers. It's a plan. For living."

"Have you got a plan for today? For finding out where they jailed him?"

"Already know how to find that out."

"So?"

"Every town of a certain size has got something they call a jail. That's how *policia* make money. Throw somebody in jail, charge him to get out."

"You think I could buy Jonathan out of jail?"

"Maybe. Not the point."

"Rey! Come here!"

Amada shouted at him to look at something. Rey ambled outside, and I followed. The girls stood along the bank of a dry wash at the edge of a patch of jojoba and catclaw bushes. Underneath a twenty-foot mesquite tree, some creature had dug a shallow depression about two feet wide and four feet long. Rey knelt at the edge of the depression and picked up a clump of hair.

"Javelina."

"What's that?" Alex said, poking at a pile of scat.

"Pig shit. See those chunks of prickly pear cactus? And over there. Some hoofprints. You guys hear him snorting last night?"

"I was out," Alex said, and Amada nodded.

"Hey," Rey said quietly. "That saguaro off to the left. The one with four arms. You see that hole, almost near the top? You see what's peeking out at us?"

"Oh yeah! Yeah," Alex said. "It's an owl?"

"Pygmy owl. Hold on."

He walked slowly back to the house, returning with the spotting scope I'd given him at the Desert Museum.

"Check out the white streaks on his forehead."

"He's cute."

"He's fierce. Hunts birds, just like redtail hawks and eagles. He's smaller than raptors, but he's a tiger. Not many of pygmy owls left. An endangered species."

"Cool!"

"Why don't you girls see what other birds you can find?"

"Girls!" Amada snorted. "Like, we're only nine years old or something? Like, why don't you say what you really want, I mean, like, take a hike, leave you two alone."

"Yeah," Rey said. "That's about it."

"Oh Dad, you're so sick."

But they ran off happily.

"I'm glad they're getting along," I said.

"Come on. Back to what's necessary. I want you to run down everything for me. Why were we at the Desert Museum? Why do the US Marshals want your body? Why do you want to skip out on your life again?"

"I *don't* want to leave my life. But I have to."

"Have some more coffee. Tell me everything."

Where do I start? I thought. Where *do* I start?

"That woman at the Desert Museum. She's Albanian. I don't even know her real name. But she's part of a smuggling ring."

"Oh Christ. How do you get mixed up in shit like that?"

"It's not what you think."

"Smuggling people is now safer than smuggling drugs. Like the old days. Used to call them wetbacks, now they call them illegals."

"No, no. This is something totally different. It starts out the same."

"It *all* starts out with smuggling. People. Drugs."

"This Albanian woman was smuggled into Mexico with the promise of completely authentic US identity papers."

"An old racket. Get all the money they've got, take them across the border, say bye bye, dump them in the middle of the desert with no food or water."

"No. There's a difference with this ring. They smuggle only women. From Albania, Eastern Europe, some from Asia. They're promised US identities in a safe location. Once they get to the destination city—LA, Vegas, New York, wherever—they suddenly find out they're going to work off their fees in a strip joint, as whores, some of them as indentured servants."

"Ten years ago," Rey said. "Those deaf Mexicans in New York. They rode the subways selling junk, but they lived together."

"So. That's the first level. Smuggled into Mexico with false promises. But the woman you saw in the Desert Museum, she actually made contact with a *second* smuggling ring. The old sanctuary routes, used by people from Salvador and Nicaragua. It's run by *Basta Ya.*"

"Ah. Your ex. *Señor* Johnny."

"So that's what's necessary to me. Finding him."

"Not enough by half. Why the marshals?"

I told him about Bobby Guinness, about my work, about the horse ride and the arrest and night in the detention center. I told him about Dance, Wheatley, and Nasso. When I told him about Pinau Medina, his eyebrows shot up, but he said nothing. Then I told him about Zamora and showed him the fading newspaper picture.

"Zamora." He tapped the picture with a fingernail. "God's gift to Nogales, with his huge maquiladora. Treats his workers very well, I hear. Not like some of the hellholes. Medina. She's been in politics for decades. One of the PRI leaders, but now on the outs because Fox was elected. Interesting that she came to see you about recovering embezzled money. Makes you wonder, does she want to return it to the government? Does she want it for herself?"

"I don't care."

"Hey. You better care. You're in her country now."

He thrust the newspaper picture in front of me, pointing at Hector Garza.

"Death squads. Torture squads. The fact that Garza is Medina's bodyguard, that says enough just in itself."

"I only want to find my husband. Look. It's almost ten o'-clock. Can you make some calls, pull in some markers? Find out what jail he's in?"

"Maybe . . . I'm not sure, but at church a few months ago, I heard something."

"You go to church?"

"Part of the twelve-step program. Acknowledge the higher power."

"I can't believe you actually go to church."

"Not any more. I kinda got to believing that *I* was my own higher power. *I* had to take control of my drinking, set my limits, not cross over. Anyway, I used to go to Mass at the old Kino mission in Caborca. An hour and a half drive from here. One day, I saw this guy, this *Señor* Johnny."

"My husband."

"Your ex-husband, you said."

"Yes. Ex."

"He gave the sermon. Speaks absolutely fluent Spanish. There were a lot of women in the mission that day. I was surprised, at the time. Usually only twenty or thirty people for Sunday Mass. But that day there were easily a hundred, almost all of them women. He talked about *Basta Ya*, what the organization did for Indian and mestizo women. Especially those who worked in maquiladoras. Said to listen for his broadcasts on the radio. I don't know what he meant by that."

"A pirate radio station."

"Figures. Anyway, after the Mass, I had *café con leche* with the priest. A habit he got me into. Coffee instead of booze, he said. That's one way to do it. Plus, he got lonely down there, and he liked me because I once ran a coke peddler out of Caborca. Anyway, this priest said that *Señor* Johnny was in some danger from the government, so instead of having a fixed house, he lived in this van. Not the small kind, the ones the *coyotes* use. But more like a laundry van. Or a UPS truck. And he traveled pretty much on the circuit of the Kino missions. Pretty much down here in Sonora. From Caborca in the west all the way over to Cocospera in the east. Did you know that San Xavier was a Kino mission?"

The dogs, the dogs, I thought, the boy who burned in jet fuel, last year when Rey and I were searching Miguel Zepeda's office at the San Xavier mission. Rey saw the horror and sadness on my face and started talking hurriedly to dispel my memories.

"Anyway, I've got some calls out already. Wherever *Señor* Johnny spent the night before he was arrested, it's likely to be one of the missions. My friend the priest at Caborca is calling around."

"Thanks."

"This is important? Seeing your husband?"

"My ex."

"Your ex-husband?"

"Yes."

"You're not . . . the two of you, are you like, hoping, I mean, why do you want to see him again?"

"My god, Rey, you think I'm still in love with him?"

He blushed, turned to pour more coffee so I couldn't see his face.

"So. This daughter. How old is she?"

"Twenty-something. Twenty-five, maybe. I don't really know. We were on the run from the FBI at the time Jonathan took her from me when she was only two. I delivered. Had a Lakota midwife. We didn't even get a birth certificate."

"You don't even know your daughter's birthday? The year she was born?"

"It was a wild time for me."

"Yeah, but I know exactly when Amada was born. Three-fifteen in the morning."

"Rey. Enough of this. I don't remember, okay?"

"So you think your ex knows how to find her?"

"I'm hoping."

"So you're giving up everything, just to find your daughter?"

"Everything."

"What are you talking about, this . . . this *every*thing?"

I told him about how Bobby Guinness arranged scores, how each score I successfully pulled down was five to six figures.

"But you're going to shuck that whole life?"

"No. Just . . . just move on. Somewhere."

"Another state?"

"I was thinking, maybe Virginia."

"Ah, fuck," he said to himself. "Figures."

"You'll know where I am. I promise. I'll keep in touch."

"I don't trust you for that, Laura."

"So don't. Meanwhile. Once we get this phone call."

I'd been playing with Xochitl's Palm Pilot. I figured that she'd not check into any chat rooms while driving to Kansas. Plus when I'd bought my Palm Pilot, the one I'd switched for hers, I'd asked the Radio Shack clerk if he had any dead AA batteries.

He'd just thrown two away, and I'd put them into the Palm Pilot. If Xochitl did try to use it, the batteries wouldn't work, and she might just not bother to stop and replace them. It was a gamble, though, and I figured I had a window of a day, two at the outside, to use her Palm Pilot to get into the chat room as though I was her, as though I was LUNA5.

The downside of chat rooms is that when you use the same computer as somebody else, people out the other end have no real suspicion that you aren't who you say you are.

Working with the satellite dish system, I tried some hacks

I'd learned about from people in Canada, where some dish systems were illegal. Because they were declared "value-less" by the government, any attempts to hack into the systems to get free TV were not seen as a criminal action.

After two hours, I'd figured out that the chat rooms access by the Palm Pilot were on the MSN network. So much for the twenty thousand I'd spent for the AOL hack. I got as far as logging into the room and watching posts for twenty minutes. No LUNA13, no LUNAs with other numbers at the end. I had no idea how many people were involved, but I'd seen chat room talks by three different people. They'd all used different online grammar and syntax, the only sure giveaway to online identities.

I had no capability to set up a hack into the MSN computers and gather logfiles, so I decided not to post any message as LUNA5 until I had something specific to ask.

The priest called in midafternoon. *Señor* Johnny had been taken prisoner at the old mission in Cocospera. Since it was not a working mission, there was no priest there who might know what jail Jonathan had been taken to. We'd have to drive to Cocospera and talk with some of the workers who were rebuilding the facade of the old mission.

"Tell me more about that surveillance center," Rey asked.

I went over everything I could remember about the one time I'd been in the Arizona Intel Center.

"These government satellites. They take pictures how close to the ground?"

"Ten square feet."

"So they could recognize a car."

"The car, yes. If they're straight overhead, they usually can't get a license plate."

"And this woman, Wheatley. You say she had a file on me?"

"Yes."

"So she knows where we are now?"

"Not in the file. But . . . oh shit, she did know that you drove a Humvee."

"Glad I parked that in the barn. Okay, we can work around that."

"You'll get a car in Caborca?"

"Well. Maybe something else. You ever ride a motorcycle?"

27

"How much money we got to work with?"
"Don't worry about it."
"This mestizo, he only deals in Harleys. We're talking six- to eight-thousand dollars. You got that?"
"Yup."
"I'm in the wrong business."
"Are we going to Caborca?"
"That's a hundred miles out of the way, if we take the good roads. I figure we can take the Humvee to a place I know in Los Molinos. Then hire somebody to drive us to Tubutama. Tell me again about this surveillance."
"Satellites?"
"Whatever looks for digital transmitters."
"I don't have any of them since you cut off the second ankle bracelet."
"How do you know? Jewelry?"
"None."
"Pen? Any kind of writing instrument?"
"None."
"Belt? Shoes? What size are you?"
"Five seven."
"No, no, no. What size clothes? Like, dress size?"
"Four. Six when I feel fat."
"Amada is five seven. You go, what, a hundred thirty?"
"Thanks a lot."

"Just a little humor here. Okay, say, one ten?"
"One fifteen."
"Lo?"
Amada came outside from watching TV.
"Laura needs some of your clothes."
"Da*aad*. I hardly brought anything."
"I'll pay you," I said.
"No you won't," Rey shot back. "Tanktop and jeans. And sandals."
"I've got a wifebeater," she said.
"A *what*?"
"Tanktop. Like, you know, men's underwear shirt, like you wear."
"I'll take it," I said.
She ran to her bedroom.
"Jesus Christ," Rey said. "Can you imagine? A piece of underwear, like these skells were wearing when I used to arrest them for beating the shit out of their wives, and now my daughter thinks it's *cool* to wear something like that?"
"Laura," Amada shouted. "Come here."
"Hey, Stelllllllllaaaaaa!" Rey said.
"Marlon Brando?"
"From *Streetcar.*"
"Yeah. I think Amada wants to give you some underwear."
I went into her bedroom and changed into the tanktop, or underwear, I wasn't quite sure what to call it. We tried on two pairs of jeans, one fitting very tight in my hips, but the legs long enough.
I modeled it all to Rey's disgust.
"You're not gonna call that underwear by that name."
"Oh, Dad. Get real. Besides. It looks really sick on her?"
"Sick is right."
"No," I said. "She means cool."
"Cool. What was once called great. So we've gone from great to awesome to neat to cool to . . . what?"
"Bad," Alex said. "Phat. Now people say, like, sick."

"So what do you say if something's really bad?"

"It's gay."

"What!"

"Everybody says that. To be uncool is to be gay."

"Do you have any idea," Rey asked, "what you're saying?"

"Oh, come on," Amada said. "We don't mean *gay*. Like my mom. Leave it, Dad."

"You girls going to be okay here?" Rey asked. "A day, two days?"

"How much beer have you got?"

"Amada, don't start. And I don't want to see on my next month's dish TV bill that the two of you are watching adult movies."

"Oh Dad. We are *so* not going to have that conversation."

"Come on, Rey," I said. "Leave them. It's already three o'clock."

"Does she actually watch adult movies?" I asked Rey as we got into the Humvee. "Do you know that, for sure?"

"For sure."

The Tubutama mission rose on the horizon several miles before we dropped off the main road and headed due south. We drove slowly past the white facade and faded brick front entrance walkway, but Rey showed absolutely no interest in the mission.

"Look at the details," I said. "Look at those beautiful round windows on either side of the archway."

He whipped around a corner onto a dirt street. We passed a one-room adobe house so wrecked that only the walls were standing, covered with spray-painted gang graffiti. Inside I could see the coiled-spring remains of an old mattress. Through the doorway and across to the only window, a fourteen-inch aluminum car rim lay on its side atop the window ledge. Next to the house, a junkyard spread in all directions, an unusual sight in Mexico where cars rarely rusted and even totally-stripped frames were reusable. Rey parked near a mock teepee constructed of long mesquite ribs, the interlocking top of the teepee at least fourteen feet high.

An old man sat outside a garage built entirely of sheets of corrugated tin, nailed haphazardly to some internal structure. But it wasn't flimsy, and it wasn't unprotected. The sliding garage door was double-ribbed sheet metal, and the entire garage was surrounded by an eight-foot-high chain-link fence topped with a row of razor wire. Two pit bulls ran around excitedly inside the fence as we got out of the Humvee.

The old man said something in a quiet voice, and both dogs immediately dropped to the ground. As Rey approached the gateway, one dog raised up on his front haunches, a streak of white running diagonally from left to right down his face, but he dropped again when the man spoke to him.

"El Grandee," Rey said.

"Ehhh! Reymundo. Who's the *chiquita?* Is she for sale?"

"He's harmless," Rey said to me.

"His language isn't harmless."

"Oh, yeah. You get that old, that withered from decades in the sun, you see what it takes to get your blood rotating. Wiggle your hips for him."

"Rey!"

"Just do it."

I wiggled. El Grandee put his hand over his heart and sighed. He said something else to the dogs, and they ran around the corner of the garage out of sight.

"Come on in."

"I hate dogs," I said to Rey.

"Laura, meet El Grandee. Actually, it used to be just two words: Grand Dee."

"Dee for Dennis," the man whispered. I could see an oxygen bottle behind his chrome-legged chair. "You'll excuse me, you got me so excited, I've got to get a sniff here." He put a breathing tube around his head and turned on the valve of the oxygen cylinder. "Hey, so long," he announced as loud as he could to the open air.

"We just got here," I said.

"*Sí.* Seeing you, and then having to take this oxygen, I figured I'd better say goodbye to my hardon."

"You're awful, old man."

"El Grandee. Like those rich people, from the old days. Owned the big ranches, where you could ride for a week and still be on your own land. I walk so slow, pulling this oxygen tank, I get the same feeling just going around my garage."

"I need a bike," Rey said.

"Hoy. A bike. Are you in luck?"

"Depends."

"Got a girl's Harley for you. Five thousand. American."

He led us to the garage door and struggled with it before Rey put his shoulder against the edge and slid it back. Inside, there were no lights, but somebody had long ago cut rectangular skylights in the roof and laid plastic sheeting over the top. Seeing me look up, he laughed.

"Anybody get as far as the roof, they fall right through the plastic. First, they get by my fence, then they get by Rudolpho and Fernando. Anybody who can do that, they can steal anything in here. Of course, then they've got to get out. Here's the beauty.

"An '88 sportster, some call 'em huggers, I don't say hugger. Model eight eight three. Was gonna turn it into a chopper complete. Add a 1200cc upgrade kit, tons of chrome, some ape-hanger handlebars, an extended front fork. But money talks, Rey. You want it for five, it's yours."

Rey started to look it over and then saw another bike in the corner.

"Is that what I think it is?"

"Reymundo. What the hell you gonna do with a '79 Mexican *Policia* bike, eh?"

"Perfect," Rey said to me. "Everybody over twenty years old will know this is a police bike. They'll leave us alone. Grandee, this bike's got to be hot."

"Ay yi. I was going to send it to a guy in Arizona. Get it

across the border. Will sell for ten thousand up there. I don't know, I don't know . . ."

"Eight thousand," Rey said.

"Oh no. Even for you, even to get out of the trouble of getting it across the border, eight is nowhere near large enough."

Rey knelt to look the bike over.

"Pretty scratched up."

"Spray cans, wonderful inventions. Any color, just sand things down to bare metal, lay that good color straight on."

"Kinda dirty. Somebody obviously went down on it, just laid it on the dirt and let it slide until it stopped. One brake lever's bent but looks operational. Tires are weather-checked, still enough tread to get us where we want to go."

"Where's that?"

Rey took some tools, straightened the sissy bar behind the seat, and checked for anything else that might be loose from the slide. When Rey tried to crank the engine, El Grandee checked around for a battery, since the one in the bike was dead. After several attempts, the engine started. Rey got the carburetor adjusted with some fiddling.

"Pipes are loud."

"It's a Harley, Rey. What Harley isn't loud."

The headlight and brake lights worked, and even though it was burning oil, Rey was satisfied. I held out eight thousand dollars in hundred-dollar bills.

"There it is."

"It's not enough."

"It is what it is."

"Eight isn't enough. Go nine. Look. It's got a hand shift. That was rare, back in '79, you didn't see no hand shift."

"Grandee, this is no fucking cow auction."

"Tell you what," El Grandee said. "Sweeten the pot here."

He dug into an old cigarillo box and removed an unsealed packed of decals that said *Policia de San Luis Potosí.*

"Put them on the saddle bags, that make you look like

what you want? I've even got a whip antenna. 'Course there's no radio, but hell, you got that antenna. And look. A police foot siren. Police odometer. Eight seven. That's the bottom.

I counted out the money and we left.

The Cocospera mission was sixty kilometers from Imuris, the road winding back and forth up a mountainside and frequently crisscrossing the Magdalena River. Down below the bridges I could see the old tracks, where travelers had to ford the Magdalena.

With both of us riding on a totally unfamiliar vehicle, Rey had some trouble balancing the Harley for at least twenty kilometers. Then he rapidly grew familiar with the clutch and throttle and remembered how to lean into a curve while compensating for my weight. By the time we hit the mountain road, he was averaging sixty kilometers an hour, at times reaching one hundred. He also learned to ignore my panic as I wrapped my arms tighter around him.

Nuestra Señora del Pilar y Santiago de Cocospera.

Years ago, a continent away, I'd seen the Sphinx. I barely remember the long body, the head, the broken-off nose. My strongest impression was that it reminded me of the wind-eroded sandstone wonders of Utah. The Cocospera mission had that same look. A massive building fallen into disrepair, abandoned a century and a half earlier when Apache raiding parties finally drove out the last of the Franciscan fathers.

"Horses," Rey said, as we dismounted from the Harley and wobbled a bit on unsteady legs. "That's what killed this mission. Horses."

"Wind," I said. "If we'd ridden another fifty kilometers, I'd be worn down also."

"Spanish conquistadors. Brought horses. Apaches learned how to ride, learned how to raid from their strongholds all over Sonora."

"Forget the history lesson. Let's find Jonathan's van."

But despite holding no services, the mission was far from deserted. The nearby desert floor was crammed with a tour caravan of some fifty Airstream trailers, and nearly a hundred people were gathered in front of the mission. Piped scaffolding rose over forty feet, protecting the facade.

"Father Kino and the Jesuits built a simple mission in the seventeenth century," a tour guide was saying into a bullhorn. "What you're looking at was added by the Franciscans another century later. This scaffolding was erected in the '80s by the Instituto Nacional de Antropologia e Historia."

"The van," I said. "Let's find the van and get away from these people."

"Let me ask you," the guide shouted. "Anybody have a corn tortilla around here? Not so likely. You see those women by the side of the road, making the large, paper-thin flour tortillas? They're using flour. Not corn. Father Kino taught people to plant wheat. They've been doing that for centuries. Wheat and livestock, that's one of Father Kino's legacies to the people of the Sonoran Desert."

"Over there." Rey pointed. "That bluish van, looks like a delivery van."

Behind the Airstream trailers I could make out the tail end of the van. We got back on the Harley, circled the crowd and their Airstreams, and parked out of sight.

"Locked," he said.

I picked up a large stone and flung it through the windshield.

"Jesus, Laura."

"I just want to get in there."

"Yeah, but why not through the door. It's a helluva lot easier."

He raised a triangular slab of sandstone and slammed the pointed end into the driver's side window. Running the rock around the window frame to scrape away the remaining glass, he reached inside and opened the door.

The back of the van had been converted into a camper.

Two narrow bunk beds ran along the passenger side, unmade beds, with green sheets and lightweight cotton blankets lying about haphazardly. A drop-down table was set into the opposite wall, with two Naugahyde seats built to face the table. In the back I could see a combination shower and toilet stall.

"What are we looking for?"

"One thing I *don't* see. Whoever lived in this van."

"You go back to the mission. See if there's a caretaker. If you can, find out where they took Jonathan. When they took him."

"And you?"

"I don't know."

"You think there's something in here that can help us?"

I slumped into one of the chairs, fingering odd bits of paper taped to the wall. After a few moments, Rey left me alone. Nothing I could see had any relevance to me. Workers' broadsides, union announcements, all in Spanish, told their activist tales without my even being able to comprehend them. Every square inch of available floor and shelf space was filled with stacks and stacks of Xeroxed handouts, fliers, booklets, pamphlets.

Just in front of the toilet and shower combination, a small tabletop folded down from the van wall. A journal lay open, all entries in Spanish, the last entry from five days before. I kicked something under the tabletop and pulled out a small wooden box. Sitting on the lower bunk bed, I opened the box top and dumped the contents on the mattress.

My past spilled out.

A copy of the picture of my father on a rodeo bronc. Right arm ready to swing like a machete. From the depths of my memory came the *Life* magazine photograph of the beheaded Indonesian guerrilla.

I turned the picture over.

Jesus Christ!

And there I was with Jonathan in front of his stolen pickup.

I couldn't even remember when the picture was taken. Barely fifteen, I looked so impossibly young and innocent I could not, I tell you, I could *not* remember ever being that way.

Newspaper clippings of AIM events. Pine Ridge. Pictures of the dead FBI men.

Everything I looked at I turned face down. I didn't ask for and did not want the memories, but had to look at everything. And then I found them.

Two pictures of Spider.

One when she was six or seven weeks old. We'd been running from BIA police, somewhere in South Dakota or Minnesota, *no*, it was the Badlands. Some guy from Iowa was playing with his new Polaroid, posing his wife until she got annoyed, and so he asked us to pose and gave us the picture.

At least I'd seen that one. The other picture was of a woman in her early twenties. On the back, Jonathan's almost unreadable scrawl with a red ballpoint pen.

spider—22nd birthday
4488 Lexington Avenue
West Hollywood

Underneath this in pencil, he'd written something else.

La Pintoresca (?)
Pasadena (?)

Tall, model-slim, model-beautiful, brown hair cut very short and neat. I couldn't make out the color of her eyes, but I could trace the shape of her cheekbones, her mouth, her nose, her neck. I just couldn't make out how this woman could be Spider.

How she could be my daughter.

Clutching the picture, I climbed out of the van and went looking for Rey.

He saw me, started to say something, and noticed the picture.

"That her?"

"Yes."

"Let me see."

He did the same thing I'd done, running his index finger over the face.

"Beautiful."

"Hardly looks like me."

"Got your eyes, your neck. Even got the slope of your nose, the way your face indents below the forehead and comes out onto the nose."

He handed back the picture.

"Did you find a caretaker?" I asked. "Anybody who knew about Jonathan?"

He nodded, looking troubled.

"And? And?"

"The worst possible thing for us."

"They took him a long ways away? To the US? To Mexico City?"

"Not that simple."

"For god's sakes, *where?*"

"The central Nogales jail. It'll be a nightmare just getting in to talk to him."

28

"*Quién es?*" the man said, stumbling into the filthy interrogation room. By habit, he looked down, not wanting to confront anybody, not wanting to be beaten again. Rivulets of partially dried blood ran from his left temple down the side of his face.

"Jonathan?"

He started to look up, but couldn't raise his eyes above the boot level of the two *policia* standing against the door at full attention. Trying to stand, he grimaced, holding his ribcage and sinking painfully to the stained concrete floor.

"How much to leave us alone?" I asked the guards.

"One hundred," one said.

At the same instant the other said, "Two hundred."

"Here's two hundred each. Go outside."

They hesitated.

"You gave them the money too quick," Jonathan murmured. "You didn't bargain. Now they want more."

"Fifty dollars each," I said, "when you come back in half an hour."

"Fifty dollars is worth only ten minutes."

"Half an hour. If you make no noise, if you don't *once* open the door, I'll make it seventy-five each. That's all I've got."

One of them extended his hand, and I put four hundred-dollar bills in his palm. They left. I heard each of the three deadlocks turn, then a metal bar slam into place across the outside of the door.

"Jonathan?"

Without moving his head, he raised his eyes to look at me, frowning.

"Who are you?"

"You don't remember me?"

Something in my voice caught his attention. His whole head came up.

"I can't focus. Can you wipe the blood out of my left eye?"

One of the guards had left a half-empty bottle of spring water. I moistened a piece of my tee and gently blotted around his eye socket. He rotated his arms and legs as well as he could against the restraints, twisted his torso and neck back and forth.

"Nothing broken?" I said.

"Not yet. Who are you?"

I finished cleaning him up and stood back, then lowered myself until I could look him straight in the eye. Recognition came very slowly, as though he was forcing himself backward in time, year by year, but just hadn't quite imagined he'd have to go that far back.

"Kauwanyauma?"

"Yes."

"Butterfly? Is that you?"

"Yes."

"I forget . . . what's your other name?"

"Laura."

"My god. Did they arrest you too?"

"No, Jonathan. I found out you were here, I came to see you."

"Bad move. You'll never get out of here once they find out who you are."

"They *won't* find out. I told them I was an immigrant legal aid lawyer from Tucson. Told them I was making a tour of Sonoran jails to talk to American prisoners. Actually, I don't think they cared about that. I bribed my way in here."

"Leave. Now. Before *he* comes."

"Who?"

"One of those guards is calling him now."

"Who?"

"Don't know his name. A man from Mexico City."

He tried to sit up straighter and grimaced with pain, grasping his ribs.

"I think they broke something in here. Do you know why I'm in here?"

"For smuggling. That's what I thought."

"Smuggling? I don't do drugs, I don't smuggle drugs."

"Women."

"I've helped a few women. *Basta Ya* has sent some women into safety with the sanctuary movement. Is that why you think I'm in here?"

"Yes."

He smiled to himself.

"Well. I'm glad some of them made it across. Got out. Got free."

"You don't know about LUNA?"

"Luna? The moon? Is that a code word I'm supposed to know?"

"The chat rooms? You don't know about that."

The steel bar on the other side of the door crashed back. The deadbolts were unlocked. One of the guards stuck his head inside.

"You got a few minutes, *gringita*. Then watch your ass. He's coming."

"Who?"

The door slammed shut.

"Listen. Jonathan." I took out the photo of Spider. "Where is she?"

"That's why you came here?"

"Yes. Where is she?"

He croaked with laughter, one of his lips splitting open as he tried to grin.

"Turn." Licking blood from his lip, grimacing. "Turn picture over. Date?"

"It just says 22nd birthday. No date. Two addresses."

"Two years ago, I think. No. Three. Somewhere in LA, I think."

"West Hollywood and Pasadena."

"Oh. Yeah. I went there. West Hollywood. Lots of Russian immigrants."

"You know about the smuggled Albanian women?"

"Yeah. Helped them, I think. Hard to think back that far."

I took out my Palm Pilot.

"You don't talk in chat rooms?"

"What's that? Some computer thing?"

"You're not LUNA?"

"You keep asking me if I'm the moon. I'm not. Just . . . I'm just . . ."

The door flew back with a crash, and Hector Garza entered, arms akimbo, dressed in full military cammies and wearing a visored hat with the insignia of the Mexican National Police.

"You're a fool," he said to me. "Come."

"Jonathan!"

The guards pulled me toward the door.

"How do you know this man?" Garza said to me.

"Sanctuary," I answered.

"Fools. Smugglers of dissatisfied women. Come out of there."

"Jonathan!" I cried again, but the guards wrenched me through the door and one of them slammed it shut and locked it.

"He's an assassin," Garza said. "Are you here to get him out?"

"Yes."

"Not possible. Not with the charges against him."

"What charges?"

"That's *Señor* Johnny. *Basta Ya.* That stupid fool, he put out a bounty on the drug cartel. Payment of ten thousand dollars to anyone who killed a cartel leader."

"Which drug cartel? I don't know what you're talking about."

"Any cartel. There are three here in Nogales."

"He'd never do that, never pay for somebody to be killed."

Garza waved to the guards to release me. Placing a hand firmly on my upper left arm, he steered me out of the jail onto the dusty street. A white Chevy Suburban with heavily tinted windows was parked at the curb, the motor idling to keep the aircon going. A uniformed officer opened the rear door, and Garza motioned me inside.

"Where are you taking me?"

"You won't be harmed."

"Am I under arrest?"

"If I arrested you, if I threw you into one of our jails like that man in there, how would you ever find the money for *Señora* Medina?"

"Then where are we going?"

"To school. Get in."

"I don't want to get in."

"Don't beg for your life, woman. Just get in."

"My *life*? You want me to get into a car with you and you're talking about my life? I won't go."

I tried to kick him, but he swerved aside effortlessly, struck my extended leg, and knocked me to the ground, and in the same fluid motion bent to offer a hand to help me get off the dirty sidewalk.

"Get in. It's time for a learning experience."

We climbed into the Suburban and settled on the middle row of seats. Behind me another uniformed officer sat next to a terrified Mexican woman, a handcuff on one wrist with the other end of the handcuffs locked onto a metal D-ring bolted to the floor.

"Where are we going? What school?"

As we pulled away from the curb, I saw Rey on the motorcycle, arguing with a women selling snow cones from a pushcart.

We drove into a huge dump.

Mounds of trash, with people picking through everything. The Suburban drove to the far end of the dump, where a bulldozer was covering trash with dirt. Nobody was there. The bulldozer moved back and forth, creating a shallow depression about fifteen feet long and the width of the dozer blade.

We stopped. Everybody got out. Garza held a handkerchief over his nose.

The other woman was led twenty feet away from the Suburban, next to the bulldozer. Without any warning, the officer holding her arm drew his pistol and blew off the back of her head. She fell gracelessly into the rubble. The bulldozer operator maneuvered his machine behind her, hooked a chain from the back of the dozer, and wrapped it around her legs. He dragged the body into the bottom of the depression, streaking the rubble and desert sand with a wide swath of blackening blood. Unhooking the chain from her legs, he ran the dozer out of the depression and immediately began covering her body with dirt and trash.

"School's over," Garza said.

We got back into the Suburban and left the dump. Halfway through a slum area, I could hear a motorcycle revving its engine, but couldn't see if it was Rey. In ten minutes we were back near the jail. The officer got out and opened my door.

"You're not finding the money," Garza said. "You're down here in Nogales, you're visiting some American, but you're not at your computer. Finding the money. Who is that American, by the way? That *Señor* Johnny, is he DEA? Some kind of secret agent, down here to expose corruption?"

They all laughed.

"Or does he just run that silly little workers' group so he

gets all the women he needs. Mestizos, Indians, foreigners. You'd think a man would have better women on his mind, but as they say, once your cock is inside where it's wet and you're going to come, you don't really care who you're fucking."

"Why did you kill that woman?"

"A learning experience."

"Who was she?"

"She assembled printed circuit boards. For high definition television sets."

"You killed her for that?"

"Get out." He handed me a piece of paper. "Call this number at midnight tonight. Tell whoever answers that you've found some of the money. Or tomorrow, we'll find you, and we'll go back to school. *Comprende, señorita?*"

I sat on the broken concrete curb, sobbing. A man came down the street, leading a donkey and carrying an old Speed Graphic camera.

"Souvenir pictures," he cried. "Memories of Nogales."

Passing me, he stopped and leaned over to me.

"Twenty minutes, walk two blocks down, look for the place where they sell bread. Go inside, go out the back door. Your friend is waiting there."

"What friend?"

"The one on the old police bike."

29

"Bobby. Donald, Don, what the hell do I call you?"

"*Why* are you calling, Laura?"

"Don. That's what Mari calls you, isn't it?"

"Don is fine."

"I need serious help."

"Wait, just wait a minute."

"Money and information."

"Laura, slow down, listen to me for a minute."

"I've got no time to listen."

"Mari is dying."

"For Christ's sake, I *know* she's dying, I just saw her yesterday and she was going in to the hospital to get a bone marrow transplant so she could *stop* dying."

"No," Don said very carefully. "Listen to me. She never got the transplant. She's in a coma. She'll probably not last another day."

Rey caught me as I swayed at the pay phone. He lowered me to the concrete sidewalk. I could hear Don's voice shouting in the phone, but the shock was too great, and my guilt even greater. I didn't care so much that Mari was really dying. I cared more that she couldn't help me. Rey didn't know what to do, but he recognized my panic attack and laid me on the ground. He picked up the phone, told Don I'd just fainted because of whatever he had told me, what the *Christ* did he say, anyhow, how could he goddam well say something that threw me into shock.

"Don't hang up," I screamed.

Rey froze, his hand on the phone, inches from the cutoff plate. He listened, shook his head.

"He's there."

"Help me up. No. Just hand me the phone."

"Where are you?" Don said with alarm. "Ah, I see the trace. Nogales? Mexico?"

"About Mari," I said. "Is there any way I can talk with her?"

"Yeah. I know what you're feeling. But no. She's in the operating room. They don't expect to be able to do anything for her. Did an MRI yesterday and found tumors all over her body."

"Can't they operate?"

"No. Today, they're trying exploratory surgery, but the lead doctor told me that they'd probably just close her up without doing anything. I need to find Alex."

"I'll call her. Tell her to contact you."

"No. Have her call the hospital," he said urgently and gave me a number.

"What do I do now? Please help me, Don."

"We take down the score."

"Don, believe me. I don't even know who the clients are any more."

"So keep it simple. One thing at a time. What do you need from me?"

"How much money can I get?"

"How much do you have, wherever you have it? I mean, I can transfer funds from your bank account to Nogales."

"Doesn't Mari have some? I mean, can't you do what you always do, get money to me from Mari's accounts?"

"She closed them all two days ago."

"What?"

"She must have known. About the cancer. How little time she had."

"Where did all her money go?" I said.

"Actually, she's been draining off her accounts steadily in the past six months. Some of it is in an irrevocable account. Trust fund for Alex. The rest, I can't trace it. Have no idea what she did. A guess, I'd say, she's transferred almost four hundred thousand dollars that I have no information about."

"Where? For who?"

"Can't say. Back to the basics, Laura. First things first. I looked in your main Tucson bank account. You've got sixty-five thousand dollars. If you need it immediately, you'll have to cross back over the border. No Mexican bank can quickly process that much money."

"Okay, okay. I'll come to Tucson."

"What information do you need?" he asked.

"Everything on these names. Pinau Beltrán de Medina. Office of the Mexican Attorney General. Hector Garza. Colonel of Federal Mexican *Policia* and also works for Medina as her chief investigator. Michael Dance. Assistant US Attorney for Arizona. Jake Nasso. US Marshal. And while you're at that, look up Taá Wheatley. Another US Marshal."

"I'll get on it right away. But I can't promise how quick I can get background."

"There's a guy, a score Mari set up two years ago. Belgian. Opium smuggling."

"I remember. He flipped, gave us major resources."

"Look back through his file, Don. He gave us a name, somebody in Guatemala or Nicaragua, somewhere in Central America. Had files on all top Mexican officials."

"I'm on that. What else?"

"Francisco Angel Zamora. Runs a large maquiladora down here in Nogales. Find out his US connections, what product lines he does, the size of his NAFTA contracts, if there's any complaints logged against him."

"Got it."

"Xochitl Gálvez. This is purely a hunch. I don't think that's her real name, and I'm not even sure she's using Xochitl any more. On her way to Kansas, so you might strike out with her. Oh, and run two addresses in California. 12 La Pintoresca, Pasadena. 4488 Lexington Avenue, West Hollywood."

"Am I looking for an Albania connection?"

"No," I said without explaining. "The addresses are personal."

"What else?"

"One last thing. Try to find out where Mari's money went."

"I promised her I'd never do anything like that."

"Do it. For her."

"Will it help you take down her score?"

"How the hell do I know, Don!"

I was shouting into the phone, and Rey put a hand on my shoulder, trying to steady me, trying to get me to move back from my anxiety attack.

"I'm assuming I can't call you?"

"No. If you can believe it, I gave my cell phone to Mari's daughter."

"Why didn't you tell me that when I just asked you how to find her?"

"I'm really confused, Don. It's a bad, bad time down here."

"So. Where is Alex?"

"Safe." I gave him the cell number. "Out of the action."

"Not if I know Alex. When are you coming back across the border?"

"There's something I have to do here."

"Laura, when you call me remember our phone code number?"

From my refrigerator magnet.

"Use this code. Minus six. Plus five. I'm dumping *all* my cell numbers. This line may not even be safe. My scanners are showing intense traffic trying to read my encrypted stuff. I may have to move somewhere."

"Don't leave me hanging, Don."

"If I move, you'll be able to get me with absolutely no delay."

"Why are you talking about moving?"

"Tell you later. Let me get cranking on these names."

He hung up. Rey wrapped an arm around me and led me to the Harley.

"Let's go back to my place," he said. "Let's just get you away from all of this."

"No!"

"Well, at least let's get out of the center of town."

We sat outside a Pizza Hut on the southern edge of Nogales. I'd gone through three Diet Cokes but had barely touched the pizza. My shoulders ached, my back was on fire, so I'd made Rey take me to a *pharmacia* where I bought a hundred tablets of Vicodin and another hundred Percosets. I'd now swallowed two of each, but my body vibrated like piano wires, wrapped too tight, and I couldn't feel any buzz from the pills.

"You're sure the woman died."

"He shot her. She fell. The bulldozer started to bury her."

"Could have been staged."

I hadn't thought of that possibility, considered it, nodded.

"Death squads. Americans have been hearing about them for decades. Sure. It could've been, except . . . no. Dead. The chains. Remember the video? On CNN? Death by dragging across the desert? I'm telling you, Rey, when that bulldozer dragged the woman's body into that hole, it left this—this—Jesus, it was a bloody streak."

"So are you saying that the videotapes were made by Garza?"

"Maybe. But why?"

"He works for the Medina woman. What do they gain by murder?"

"Not just murder, Rey. The publicity. Videotapes of the murder."

"Warnings, okay, sure. But warning *who*? And *why*?"

"I don't know."

"So. Please. Let's go back to my place."

I took out my money pouch and spread the bills on the stained plastic table.

"Laura. People can see what you're doing."

A quick count. I had almost fifteen thousand dollars left.

"I've got to go back to the jail. I've got to get Jonathan out of there. Do you think this is enough money to buy his way out?"

"Those guards, they're probably terrified of Garza."

"With this kind of money, Rey, they could walk away from their lives here. They could just go somewhere else in Mexico."

"Garza would find them."

"I don't *care* if Garza finds them. I don't care if he kills them tomorrow morning. By then we'll have Jonathan out of the jail."

"No room for three on the Harley," Rey said.

"Dump it. Trade it for an old pickup truck, the older the better."

"Could do that."

"We'll take Jonathan back to your place. Give him the pickup, tell him to disappear into Mexico. Then we'll take the Humvee back to Tucson.

"Gotta do one more thing before we get Jonathan."

"There's no time."

"Trust me, Rey. There's one thing we can do that may unravel all of this."

"Okay," he sighed. "What are we going to do?"

"We've got to find the water man."

30

Away from the downtown streets, away from the tourist sprawl, passing through middle-class neighborhoods, we soon found the shadowlands of life on the margins in Nogales. Huge shantytowns sprawled unchecked in the ravines and atop the rocky desert mesas south and east of Nogales.

An hour later we found the entrance to the water tunnels, guarded by five men in brown uniforms with M-16s.

"Police?" I asked Rey.

"They're taking money just to get into the tunnels. Could be *policia,* could just be guys dressed in a uniform and out to earn a living."

A long line of people straggled behind them, disappearing up over a hillside. Almost all of them carried lightweight white supermarket plastic bags. Singly or in groups they approached the armed men. Negotiations were swift and entirely dependent on who had money and who hadn't. Some bargained with stacks of *pesos*, some tried to barter with items wrapped in cloth, bags, or even woven baskets.

Far off in the distance a siren cranked up. The armed men disappeared quickly and the people scattered. Those close enough to the tunnel entrance ran inside. The rest disappeared over the hill as two police jeeps drove up, one pulling a U-Haul trailer. Men from both jeeps removed a portable generator and several light stands from the trailer. In ten minutes a dozen floodlights lit the tunnel entrances.

"It's still daylight," I said. "Why are they putting up the spotlights?"

"A warning. Who knows?"

"This can't be what I'm looking for," I said.

"You got any other ideas?" Rey asked.

We drove around aimlessly for half an hour until Rey pulled off the dirt road.

"You notice anything about these neighborhoods?" he said.

"Shantytowns."

"You see any electricity?"

"They're too poor."

"Right. You see the open sewers?"

"I see them and I smell them."

"So there's no running water either. What do you suppose they do up here for bathing? Washing clothes? Drinking?"

"No idea. Drive up there."

He carefully worked the pickup along a rutted dirt track between rows of shanty houses constructed up the side of a waterless ravine. Some of the shanties were connected, others stood precariously alone. Some were constructed of concrete blocks, showing a certain degree of either wealth or luck in scavenging or stealing from a building site. Most of the shanties were built from cardboard packing crates, chunks of tin siding materials, mesquite ribs, old tires, anything usable and free.

It was early evening, but still incredibly hot and almost intolerably foul with the stench of industrial and human waste. Shallow channels of watery sludge ran between houses, alongside the dirt track, all of it headed downhill.

"Good Christ," I said angrily. "Mexico's border cities, land of NAFTA opportunities. How can people live like this?"

"Ten dollars a day in wages at a maquiladora. If they're lucky."

We passed a family of nine clearing a spot of land, using

an old pair of kitchen scissors and a paring knife to cut off creosote bushes and everything else that grew above ground. Rey stopped and got out of the pickup. The family drew together protectively, the woman and children huddled behind the man. Rey talked to them in gentle, apologetic tones, and when I heard him say *agua,* the woman nodded fiercely and pointed uphill.

"That's what she needs most. Water. Forget plumbing. They just need enough to drink and cook. Every day, it's a struggle up here to get water."

"So where are we going?"

He pointed to the top of the hill. I could see a tank truck.

"Pedro. The water man."

"Good. We found him."

"Not really. That woman told me that every shantytown has a water man. There may be fifty, a hundred men with old tank trucks, delivering water to places like this."

"I don't see a hundred trucks. One will have to do."

Pedro cut his eyes toward us as he filled a woman's plastic liter jugs. Fifteen people stood in line, waiting with pans, buckets, jugs, anything of plastic or metal that would hold water. Pedro patiently filled them all.

We could tell that he wasn't charging exorbitant fees, because everybody seemed to be able to afford the water. Finally his truck ran dry with three people left in line. We heard him apologizing, showing them that no water ran from his taps. They trudged away, disconsolate. He closed up the taps and hoses, stood at the door of his truck.

"A moment of your time?" Rey asked politely.

"I have no more water."

He looked us over carefully, a sense of fear in his eyes. He kept one hand on the door handle, getting inside his cab being his only escape route.

"Policia? Traficantes?"

"He thinks we're with a drug cartel. He's afraid."

"Habla ingles?"

"Yes, *señora*."

"We're from Tucson. We're not police of any kind. We're not involved with any kind of drugs."

"Begging your pardon, but why should I believe you?"

I took his boldness as a sign that in fact he did believe me to some degree, but didn't much trust us, and mainly wanted us to go away.

"There are women up here that work in the maquiladoras?"

"If they're lucky, *sí*."

"About these women, have you heard about those who want to go north?"

"Ahhh. So you are *coyotes,*" he said with disgust.

"No! We have *nothing* to do with smuggling women across the border. But there are stories in Tucson. In the sanctuary groups, among women who are in safe houses, women who have survived the *coyotes* and now have a good life."

"There are stories everywhere."

"They talk about the water man."

"I am a water man," he said, puzzled. "There are many like me. But we just do what we do. Bring water."

"Where do you get it?"

"Anywhere I can afford it."

"No. I mean, in Nogales."

"Nogales, sometimes. But water is expensive there. And it is not safe to drink. All the maquiladoras, they have chemicals, they dump whatever filth they want into the rivers, the water supply. Me, I live south of here. In Caborca. Every morning, I get fresh water from a spring. Nobody else knows about it. But the spring moves slowly. It takes me three hours to fill my truck. Then I drive up here."

"You do that every day?"

"People need good water."

"And you've never heard about a water man who also smuggles women across the border?"

"Never. I stay out of that kind of talk. Most people here, they know about the *coyotes,* they dream of crossing, of going north. It's not safe to talk about such things unless you have a lot of money. And sometimes, only if you have protection."

"Wait a minute," Rey said. "Do all of you water men get your water in Mexico?"

"If I went north, it would be so expensive, these women could not afford to buy any from me."

"Do you know anybody who *does* get water from the north?"

"No. Why would they do that?"

"Thank you," Rey said. "Thank you very much."

We left him by his truck, watching us to make sure we drove away.

"I just don't understand where you're going with this," Rey said, winding his way carefully down the side of the ravine and trying to ignore the hosts of children who ran alongside the pickup, their hands out to beg.

"Me neither."

"Then let's get ready to spring your ex-husband from that jail."

At midnight, new guards appeared at the jail, three of them visible from the street. Rey took ten thousand dollars of my money, saying he'd start bargaining at seven and work his way up.

Rey had traded the Harley for a '59 Ford stepside with empty chicken crates stacked four deep in the short bed. Although he'd parked three blocks away, I'd walked to the main street, looking down to the jail. If the guards called Garza, if other police cars rushed up, I would drive away. But in less than ten minutes Rey came out of the jail, a supporting arm wrapped around Jonathan. Nobody followed them for the first block, then one by one the three jail guards came out of the jail and ran in different directions. We got back into the truck.

Rey turned off the street, down an alley. As we got nearly through the alley, a green Land Rover pulled across the alleyway, blocking our pickup. Rey rammed the gearshift into reverse and stomped on the gas pedal. A woman got out of the Land Rover and waved at us.

"Stop!" I shouted.

"Jesus Christ, Laura! That's the *policia.*"

"No. Stop."

He put the shift into park, goosing the engine. I opened my door to get out.

"Who is that?" he asked.

"You met her in Scottsdale," I said.

It was Taá Wheatley.

"Take off your shoes," she said.

"What?"

She held out a black plastic trash bag.

"Give me your shoes."

"Why?" I said, but sat on the broken pavement to pull off the shoes.

"Now your bra."

Rey came up to us, watched as I wiggled my bra out from underneath the wifebeater shirt. She tossed it into the bag.

"Now I know you," he said slowly. "I wasn't sure in Scottsdale, things were happening so fast. But you're that woman."

"Yes. I'm *that* woman. Laura, give me your wristwatch."

"What's going on? Taá, why are you here?"

"Wristwatch."

I hesitated, but Rey grabbed my arm and unstrapped the watch.

"Anything else?" he asked Taá.

"I don't think so. But I've got a sweep."

Setting down the trash bag, she took an electronic sweeper wand from her back pocket and started running it along my body.

"Hold up your arms."

"There were transmitters in my shoes? My watch? I thought you told me that those two anklets were the way you people would do surveillance on me?"

"We lied."

"Even my bra?"

"We had to try everything we could. That's why we didn't get your clothes from Sonoita, so you'd wear whatever I gave you."

"I changed some of them," I said.

"Yeah. But not your bra, not those Nike sneakers. Turn around."

She swept up and down my back, hips, along my thighs.

"I think you're okay now."

"How about me?" Rey said.

"We bugged your Humvee only. But that's sitting back with that crazy old biker. I saw your house, though."

"How the hell did you *see* my house?"

Taá pointed up.

"Intel satellites. Everywhere that Laura went, the satellites did go. Poetic, no?"

"Poetry my ass. So who else knows about my house?"

"Nobody."

"Not possible," I said. "I've seen your intel center. I know how many people work there. I don't believe that Dance, or Nasso, doesn't know about Rey's house."

"Well. Nasso. I've been having some problems with him lately. As for Dance, he wouldn't know one satellite photo from another. I was working alone at AZIC when you crossed at Sasabe. I saw you drive south. Then the satellite orbit took it out of range for ninety minutes. Nasso had some interviews, so I was all alone again when the satellite did its next pass. I fiddled the data. It happens, sometimes. The shots don't work because of cloud cover, smog, forest fires."

"Nasso," I said. "What kind of problems?"

"Personal."

"So he doesn't go for dykes," Rey said. "Neither do I, really."

"Actually," Taá said with disgust, "it wasn't about sex at all. All my arguments with him are about power and control."

"But truth is," Rey said, "without you, I'd never have been able to spend time with my daughter."

"She's at your house."

"I can't believe you put a tracking device in my bra!" I complained.

"You're a fool to think we'd give you the chance to get away from my house without taking a lot of precautions to run digital surveillance."

"You let me go?"

"Sure. The tampon thing was convenient, but I'd have thought of another excuse to leave you alone, to let you get out of the house and think you were getting away from me. From us. I've got another surprise for you."

"Nothing you can tell me will be a surprise," I said. "Not after the bra thing."

"Luna."

That staggered me. She pulled a sheaf of papers from her bag, showed me printouts of all kinds of LUNA chat room materials.

"We used Carnivore," Taá said. "At the Phoenix switch hotel."

"I thought you couldn't legally set Carnivore to pick up specific traffic."

"Legally? Don't you understand, Laura? *Nothing* about this whole operation is legal. Even the threats of executing the federal arrest warrants against you. Those warrants would be thrown out by any respectable federal judge."

"Are you telling me that you didn't even delete them from the system?"

"You're catching on. Dance will lie about anything if he thinks he can crack this smuggling ring."

"So," Rey said. "Why are you telling us all this?"

"I'm not sure."

"You're protecting Meg, aren't you?"

"In a way."

"And protecting my daughter?"

"In the same way. It's more than that, but I can't tell you. Yet."

She looked at the pickup, cut her eyes between us and the truck bed.

"You got him in the back?" Taá asked.

"Who? Nobody's with us."

"I just watched you take Laura's ex-husband out of that jail."

"Good Christ," Rey said. "What *don't* you know?"

"I'll leave you with just this one question. Who is Luna?"

"It's a lot of people," I said, separating the sheets of paper. "I mean, look at the different ways that LUNA13 writes. Some messages use capitals, some don't. I'd say there are at last five different people here, all with access to the same user name."

"Ah. But who's behind all this?" Taá asked.

"I thought Jonathan would tell me."

"I've seen his camper. He doesn't even have a bank account that I know of. No. It's not him. Somebody's spending major money to help these women. Who is it? Dance doesn't really care. Once he decided that there were *two* smuggling rings, he eliminated any desire to go after Luna. He's after whoever is making millions of dollars smuggling in these foreign women and then selling them in the US for prostitution, slavery, whatever."

"Does he know who's behind it all?" I said.

"Nope. But Jake . . . Jake knows something he's not talking about. I'm going. Anything else you want to tell me, about what you're doing on your own?"

"Nothing," Rey said quickly before I could open my mouth.

"Don't trust dykes, do you." Taá was both bitter and resigned.

"Don't trust federal law agencies. And whoever works for them."

"Fair enough. One last thing. I'd leave that Humvee parked right where it is. As things stand, nobody knows the location of your house. For your daughter's sake, I'd like to keep it that way."

"Thanks," I said. "And if I need to talk to you? I mean, to *you* only. Give me a cell number, an email address, anything that only you will read."

"On the papers I gave you. The last sheet."

Taá took a half-step toward the pickup, but Rey jumped in front of her.

"Not a chance," he said.

"I was only curious. I wanted to see what the man looked like who set up *Basta Ya,* the man who's helped so many Indian women down here."

"Another time, maybe."

"Just keep him alive. Better yet, tell him to disappear deep into Mexico."

31

Interlude. Late night, shading into early morning, shading into false dawn.

Jonathan and I talked and didn't talk. Intervals of each. Alex and Amada slept like babies, like teenagers, like young people who think it's going to last forever. Rey came into the sun room twice, first claiming that he was hungry, two hours later that he had just woken up and couldn't go back to sleep. We banished him both times.

It was like a foreign movie. Italian. No. Almodóvar. *Women on the Verge.*

You watch movies, he'd said at one point.

Don't you? I'd said. Doesn't everybody?

It's Hollywood, he'd answered. It's make believe. Down here, life is raw.

I thought of the woman I'd seen executed right in front of my eyes. I realized I'd pushed that unpleasant memory so far down into my subconscious that it was painful just to probe in there, trying to recall her face. All I could remember was the bulldozer.

They say when you have a bad accident, you can't remember any of the details. For days, for weeks, sometimes you'll never remember.

I thought of a scene from *Schindler's List*. The Jewish woman architect, who tells Ralph Fiennes that the foundations have been poured badly, that the whole building is wrong, that it will collapse. He orders her shot. The blood bursts sideways from her head, her body flops.

Good God, that's only a movie, I thought. What's wrong here?

Are my memories of happiness just a few days ago, memories of being happy on Heather's ranch, are those memories as false as a movie?

The first conversation was really, really short.

"Tell me," he said. "Back then, what did we see in each other?"

"Sex."

"Be serious."

"I am. No woman forgets her first lover."

"What did we have?" he said, as though it was a mystery seen dimly from the distance of so many years.

"You had a pickup truck. You took me away from the Hopi mesas. We went out anywhere to be alone."

"Together, I mean."

"We made love in your pickup."

"That's all we had? Sex?"

"No. Sex was just the opening act."

"For what?"

"Freedom."

"From what?"

"You don't remember?"

"I don't even remember the sex."

"I don't expect anything from you," he said. "For getting me out of jail."

"You owe me nothing."

"I mean, I expect nothing. No favors. No kindness."

"Forget it."

"What did it cost?"

"Cost?"

"To bribe the guards. To get me out."

"You don't need to know that."

"Had to be in the thousands. US thousands."

"Doesn't matter."

"Had to be a good chunk of money to buy me out of that jail. Ten thousand minimum."

"Don't get on with this. It doesn't really concern you, what it cost."

"Easy for you to say. Ever spend a night in a Mexican jail?"

"Not a Mexican jail," I said. "There was a jail in South Dakota . . . maybe Iowa. The graveyard shift jailer tried to rape me."

"Guess I was long gone by then."

I nodded.

"What do you do, to make so much money?"

"I work on the edge."

"On the edge."

"Yes."

"Edge of what?"

"Between a little money and a lot."

"Is it legal? What you do?"

"I work on the edge," I said again. "I'm not even sure where that edge is any more. Not about what's legal and what isn't. About who I am. What I'm doing."

"Ah," he said with a smile. "Identity. Who are we, anyway? Listen. Did you ever get back up to the rez?"

"I lived there for a year."

"In Hopi?"

He seemed incredulous that I'd have ever gone back.

"No. In Tuba City."

"Want to tell me about it?"

"No," I said after a long time. "That part of me I don't want to talk about."

"So what's left to talk about?" he asked.

"Our daughter."

"Ahhhh," he sighed. "That."

"Who is Luna?" I asked him later.

"Nobody."

"Come on, Jonathan. It's too late for games. I know that it's not a single person. I know it's the way women talk to each other, once they're out."

"Once they're free."

"That too."

"Luna. It's a password. It's . . . a recognition thing."

I took out Xochitl's Palm Pilot and re-created the chat room. I showed him the prompt, asked if he ever joined in.

"No. Believe it or not, I've never owned a computer. Never turned one on. No idea what this thing is you're showing me."

I thought for a moment of joining the chat, but I wasn't ready for that yet, didn't quite have the one question formed that I had to ask. I turned the Palm off.

"But you do know about Luna?"

"It's . . . what do I say, it's an escape route. They talk, offer advice, tell each other about jobs, money, cities, hairstyles."

"How did you get involved, Jonathan?"

It was the first time I'd said his name, and I stumbled over it.

"Johnny," he said. "Down here, they call me Johnny. Or Juan. As for when . . . a woman approached me about a year ago."

"You met her?"

"Never. First, I got a letter. Then a man came to see me."

"And?"

"The man gave me a cell phone. After that, I talked to the woman."

"Who was she?" I asked, thinking that it had to be Mari Emerine.

"She said she was called Luna. She knew there were women being smuggled into Mexico, then sold in the US as sex slaves, strippers, servants. Things like that. She said she could help with false identity papers, money, travel. A lot of things."

"But you never met her."

"No."

"What happened to the women who got out?"

"I don't know," he admitted.

"You ever hear from them?"

"Never. That was part of the deal. So they wouldn't compromise me. Compromise the network."

"Luna."

"Yes."

"Was it a code word?" I asked. "Or her real name?"

"I never knew. She helped over a hundred women. That's all I know."

"Did you ever know Xochitl?"

"Xochitl Gálvez?"

"Yes. So you did know her."

"Know *of* her. Met Subcommandante Marcos once at a workers' strike. But Xochitl wasn't at that rally."

"No, no, no. This woman I know named Xochitl, she worked at a maquiladora."

"Can't be the same woman. Xochitl Gálvez is the name of the Commissioner of Indian Affairs in the Vicente Fox government."

And so one more little thing was explained. I told him about the Xochitl I knew. But he wouldn't talk about the only real thing I wanted from him. After another hour, I finally had to ask him, straight out.

"Where's our daughter?"

"I don't know where Spider lives now," he admitted.

"This picture. Did you take it?"

"Nope. She sent it to me. Said she was living in West Hollywood."

"You really don't know where she lives?"

"No."

Jonathan had showered and was now eating his fourth bean and chile burrito. He wore an old tanktop and jeans that Rey had given him. Almost totally bald, his scraggy untrimmed beard had grown below his Adam's apple. I'd seen him in just the jeans, seen scars all over his torso. I figured he was just over fifty years old but totally without the paunch and love handles of men his age.

Looking at his face . . . weird.

Think of your first lovers, I mean, do you really remember what they looked like? Do you really recognize people you haven't seen for decades? Do you even know who they are?

Weird.

"About Spider," he said. "When she was, I don't know, sixteen, seventeen. I got a postcard from Alabama. She knew where I was back then."

"Where was that?"

"Prison. I was doing three to seven, up in Florence. A bar fight, somebody hit somebody hit somebody, I was the only drunken person left when the cops got there. Had blood on my knuckles. DNA match showed my blood on a dead guy. So she sent me this postcard, said she was coming west from Alabama. Moving to California. Stopped by, actually stayed in a motel in Florence for a week and visited me every day."

"What was she like? What did she look like?"

"Um."

"I haven't seen her since you took her from me."

"Hey, Laura, I'm sorry. That was totally wrong for me to do that."

"We were young, we were . . . on the edge back then. Wild. Crazy. I hardly remember those days."

"Me either. I'd eaten some peyote that day, that's all I remember. You were ragging me about leaving a jar of honey open, and there was this long trail of ants across the kitchen floor and up onto the tabletop and into the honey. You were ragging me, hell, I don't remember anything more than picking up Spider and a box of Pampers and getting into my pickup and driving until I ran out of gas in an Iowa cornfield. I tried to call you, at that camp we'd broken into, where we were living. But you'd already gone."

"Looking for you, Jonathan."

"Even I didn't know where I was. Family took me in, told me how to feed Spider. I was high almost every day, so I left Spider with that family for a year. Went back, got her, moved to Minneapolis, got a day job as a trucker, we drove all over the country for ten years. Been in every state except Oregon. I loved that girl."

"So did I."

"I loved you, Kauwanyauma."

"Who knew what love was, back then. We were so young. The picture, Jonathan. How did you get her picture? Tell me how she knew where to send it."

"She said she looked me up on the Internet. Said she found two hundred and seventy-three guys named Jonathan Begay, and she was contacting all of them in Arizona first, and if that didn't work, she'd start in other states. I was working in Yuma back then. Front desk clerk. Hardware store. I sold a lot of dynamite to those militia crazies. I guess I got mixed up with them, for a while. Hard to forget my crazy AIM years, protesting the government. So that's when I got the picture. I drove right out to LA without stopping. Went to the address in West Hollywood, but they said they didn't know her there. Still got that address."

From memory, he wrote it down for me.

"Listen, there's something you've got to know about her. From that week she stayed in Florence. Came to visit every day. By the third day, she was telling me a lot of stories, a lot of . . . um, a lot of stuff she did."

"Like, what stories?"

"Why she called herself Begay. Said she admired my life with AIM. Like my way of dealing with the law, which as I remember was pretty much telling them to kiss my ass."

"She still call herself Spider?"

"Hated that name, she told me. Hated spiders, actually. She was calling herself Ashley. Or Kimberly. One of those yuppie names. Heather, maybe. Amber. I don't remember, except that she didn't ever want to be called Spider. Didn't want to have people think she'd turned into something creepy."

"And what kind of girl did she turn out to be?"

"I don't know whether to tell you, Laura."

"Tell me what?"

"She's a grifter."

"What?"

"Told me all the cons she'd pulled. Her partners, her lovers. Toward the end of that week, she was flinging her whole life at me, like it was my fault, except she was proud of it, proud of what she could do."

"Had she been arrested?"

"Don't know. I think so, I think maybe that was why she left Alabama."

"A grifter. Like, who did she con? How?"

"She never told me those things. Just the money she'd conned. People with money. That's who she went after."

"Well. Maybe she's changed."

"One thing I learned from living down here. People are what they are. You try to change them, they've got traditions, they've got family histories, they've got the class of people they were born into."

"Even so. Maybe she's changed."

"I hope you find her," Jonathan said after a long time. "I hope you do."

He fell asleep for a time.

A grifter. A con woman. I hated knowing that about her. Partly because I wanted her to be *nice*, to be *civilized*, I don't know, something at least different from me. In a way, with some of the scores I took down, I was also a grifter, a con woman. I'd sometimes do anything to get the digital information I needed.

But my daughter a grifter?

Unpleasant.

I wished I didn't know that. But the flipside of that wish was the gratitude to know at least something about her.

About three or four o'clock, Rey came out one last time, watched Jonathan's mouth open and close, snoring very lightly.

"You know he's not sleeping either."

"I know."

"Who?" Jonathan asked, awake and instantly alert.

"Garza." I said. "Hector Garza."

"Which one was that?"

"The man who took me away. The first time."

"That guy. I'd never seen him before."

"You don't ever want to see him again."

"He wanted something from you," Jonathan said to us. "What?"

"It was only about money. Not about you at all."

"Just money?"

"That's right. But a lot of money, he said. He knew about *Basta Ya* helping women get across the border. Maybe he thought we were doing it for profit. But he was talking about millions of US dollars, and I think he knew I wasn't anywhere near that kind of money."

"Garza's not sleeping," Rey said. "He wants *us*, wants something from us."

"What does he want? That's what I'd like to hear more about. I'm going to do some computer work."

I logged into the chat room. Five differently numbered LUNA users were logged in, but as soon as my LUNA5 prompt appeared, they all disappeared but one.

LUNA5: > this is laura
LUNA13: > i've been waiting for you
LUNA5: > good, and i've been waiting to ask you a question
LUNA13: > stay away from us
LUNA5: > who are you?
LUNA13: > we are many people
LUNA5: > yes, i know why you use this chat room, but who are **you**
LUNA13: > we are many women
LUNA5: > **you** are the woman who runs things
LUNA13: > not important who any of us are

LUNA5: > but who are **you**
LUNA13: > what does it matter, you know what we do
LUNA5: > yes, you help women get out
LUNA13: > so our names are of no importance
LUNA5: > jonathan begay is sitting two feet from me

A long, long pause.

LUNA13: > is he safe?
LUNA5: > safe from what?
LUNA13: > Garza
LUNA5: > how do you know about that?
LUNA13: > is he safe?
LUNA5: > yes, and he will head south into Sonora this morning
LUNA13: > i have prayed for his safety—thank you, Laura
LUNA5: > he was my husband
LUNA13: > i know
LUNA5: > WHO ARE YOU, THAT YOU KNOW SO MUCH?
LUNA13: > not important
LUNA5: > it is to me—listen, this chat room is being monitored by the us attorney's office, by some very powerful and sophisticated tracking software in Phoenix
LUNA13: > you mean Carnivore
LUNA5: > yes
LUNA13: > i told you that i've been waiting for you, in this chat room
LUNA5: > why?
LUNA13: > to say goodbye
LUNA5: > don't go
LUNA13: > it's time to go, it's time for me to be free
LUNA5: > i want to meet you

LUNA13: > in a day or two, that will no longer be possible—btw, don't worry about feds and their carnivore

LUNA5: > why?

LUNA13: > they know little about us and understand less

LUNA5: > please, don't go, i want to meet you

LUNA13: > you already know me

LUNA5: > who ARE you?

LUNA13: > goodbye, laura

The LUNA13 prompt disappeared.

And I suddenly realized who it was.

Alex stumbled outside before sunrise.

"My mom's dying," she announced. "I need to get to Phoenix today."

She went back inside to get dressed.

Rey was wearing his cammies.

"You can stay here as long as you want," he said to Jonathan. "I'm leaving you that old pickup."

"Thank you."

"But I'd advise you to move on. These people, they have ways of knowing about us. There'll be visitors here today. Tomorrow at the latest. Probably in the middle of the night. So take what you need. Leave as soon as you can."

"Today we've got to cross the border," Rey said to me privately.

"North," I said.

"Let's go east."

"East? Why?"

"I was thinking—Florida."

"No, Rey. I am *not* running away from this."

"You're the one who told me about Garza executing that woman. You think he wouldn't hesitate putting a bullet in *your* head?"

"North," I said.

"It's foolish to go to Tucson."

"Actually, further north than that. Back to Hopi. Back to the reservation. I want to talk to a policeman."

32

Once he recognized who I was, Floyd Seumptewa stared at me with amazement.

"Return of the prodigal Hopi," I said.

He glanced at some papers on his desk and turned them over.

"Aren't you going to say hello?"

"Laura Winslow. I didn't think I'd ever see you again."

He wasn't wearing a uniform. His office in the Hopi Tribal Center was down the hall from the Tribal Police.

"Are you still Captain Seumptewa?"

"Had to leave that. Broke my leg in the rodeo last year. Just can't much get around, couldn't go on patrol."

"So what do you do here?"

"Special information officer. Miss Winslow, what are you doing here?"

"I need some special information."

He grasped the edge of his desk and levered himself upright, clicking locks on a full-length brace on his right leg. Stumping over to the window, he pretended to look out onto the main street of Kykotsmovi.

"Did they ever find her?" I said.

"Who?"

"Judy Pavatea."

One of the lost butterfly maidens.

"No. Didn't find her body. Didn't find any of the other

missing Hopi girls. That was a sad business back then. I heard that you'd found the man who killed them, up in Cheyenne. But then you just . . . vanished."

Rows of kachina dolls stood in a glass-fronted bookcase. Many of them were clowns. One looked like the Joker character from *Batman* movies. On the opposite wall was a tapestry about three feet high and five feet long with vertical lines in red and blue and gold and bordered on the left and right with tasseled fringing.

"Gold embroidery threads in there," he said. "From Japan. My daughter-in-law made that one."

An alabaster carving stood on his desk next to a pen set. Butterfly hairdo.

"Sewa," he said, and went to sit down again. "Little sister. I keep it here to remind myself of Judy Pavatea."

He thrummed his fingers against the desk, squinted at me, finally turned over the papers he'd been reading when I first walked into the room.

"Laura Marana."

He held up both hands, palms toward me. I must have looked in panic at the door I'd shut behind me.

"Nobody up here cares about this notice. I picked it up from this morning's duty pile after I saw that the officers had no interest in it. It's a notice from the US Attorney's Office in Phoenix. Be on the lookout, that kinda thing. Who'd've thought I'd look up and see you right in front of me."

"I can explain all of that."

"You don't have to."

"I don't?"

"Whatever you've done, there's got to be an explanation. But in my heart, you helped us when nobody else wanted to. So to me, you're just a tourist in here looking for some kind of information about the Hopi villages."

"Thank you. I can explain. But I don't have time."

"So what do you want from me, Laura?"

"I need to know about somebody who claims she was brought up here."

"How long ago?"

"She's about sixty years old. Says she lived here in Kykotsmovi until she was eleven. So that would make it . . . back in the '40s."

"You don't want much, do you. Nobody kept records in those days."

"Not written records. No. But there have to be people here of the same age. People who'd remember clans, families, names."

"What's this woman's name?" he finally asked.

"Pinau."

"That's a pretty unusual name. She said it was Hopi?"

"Yes. Insisted on it."

"Full name?"

"I only know what she calls herself now. She says she moved to Mexico City when she was eleven. I have no idea if she married, but her full name is Pinau Beltrán de Medina."

"Got to be either a husband's name, or the family that took her from here. But Pinau. You sure that's her Hopi name?"

"Yes."

"And she lived in Kykotsmovi? In the '40s?"

"That's what she said."

"I know two women I can ask," he said. "They're down the hall in the craft preservation office. But maybe you can tell me why the person you're asking *me* about is the same person that signed this notification from the US Attorney's Office."

"What are you talking about?"

"If you're identified by any law enforcement agent, do not apprehend, it says here. Notify Pinau Beltrán de Medina. Half a dozen phone and fax numbers, some of them in Phoenix, some in Tucson, some in Mexico."

He stood up again, grabbed an elaborately carved oak cane, and went down the hall. I read the papers, saw her name, understood nothing about it. Medina identified herself as part of a joint US and Mexican task force.

I poured a cup of coffee, wandered out in the hallway. He was gone for nearly half an hour, and returned with a frown.

"Didn't live here," he said.

"You're sure?"

"Part of the new Tribal Chairman's mandate. Compile a record of everybody living on the mesas. Since we're in Kykotsmovi, the women started here. Nobody ever heard of this Pinau. In fact, everybody I talked to insisted that it's not a Hopi name. That doesn't mean it's not a family name, a clan name. My guess, it could be a private name. But my opinion? She never lived here."

"So why would she tell me that she did?"

"Was she trying to gain your confidence? Get you to trust her?"

"Yes."

"Where were you at the time?"

"In an illegal immigrant detention center."

He laughed out loud.

"I don't know about you, Laura. You sure got a knack for getting into trouble. Listen. You staying the night? Wife and I got a spare bedroom."

"No. I've got to get back to Phoenix."

"A long day's driving, if you just came up from there."

"I came up from Mexico."

"What kind of trouble are you into, Laura?"

"Me? I'm not *in* trouble, I'm about to cause trouble."

Rey drove me back south through the Apache reservation. In Globe we stopped for some Big Macs, and I called Don. I could tell by the clicks and signal shifts that the phone was rolling over from one number to another.

"Hostess Catering," he said.

"Don?"

"Ah, finally. I've been waiting to hear from you."

"Why is this phone number rolling over?"

"I thought you wouldn't have time to clone your cell phone to the new number."

"Don, I'm sorry. I should have told you I had no access to the cloning software."

"Realized that. Doesn't matter. Look. I've got all the information you wanted. What do I do with it?"

"I don't know if I'm on a secure phone any more."

"Assume you're not. But I'll give you the info myself."

"What do you mean?"

"Can't tell you that on an unsecure phone."

He hung up.

Rey continued on into Phoenix, into Scottsdale, and to the Mayo Clinic Hospital.

33

"There's nobody here by that name."

The information desk of the Mayo Clinic Hospital.

"Mari Emerine? You're certain?"

"Perhaps she wishes privacy?"

"You mean, she might be using another name?"

"Some patients do."

I thought about that for a few minutes while I went to the Coke machine, but while the can of Diet Coke was thunking its way down the chute, I suddenly realized who to ask for.

"Hey, lady," a teenaged girl shouted after me. "You all done left your Diet Coke in the machine."

"Take it if you want."

Somewhat breathless from running back to the information desk, I smiled at the clerk and patted my breastbone and shook my head.

"Silly me," I said. "Of course she's using her married name. Mrs. Bobby Guinnness. She's divorced, but she still uses that name at times."

"Yes. Mrs. Guinness. Oh. Family only, I'm afraid."

"That's okay. I'm her sister Elizabeth. I just flew in from Des Moines. Her ex-husband called me and said to hurry."

The clerk was crestfallen, but recovered immediately. She took a map of the hospital, circled a specific floor and wing, and wrote down the room number.

"How is she?"

"I can't really say." She avoided my eyes for a moment, then looked directly at me. "I do apologize. I've not been here more than three weeks. When you get to the floor, please check with the nurses' station. I'll tell them you're coming up."

"How is she?" I asked again.

"In good care. The nurse will page the doctor, you'll get a consultation. Oh. And the ex-husband is there also."

"What husband?" I said without thinking.

"Mr. Guinness, of course. In his wheelchair."

"You found me," Mari whispered.

"Yes."

I barely recognized her. In a week she'd lost another twenty pounds, her face haggard, tubes and monitors attached everywhere to her body.

"I'm Don," said the man in the wheelchair at the other side of the bed.

"He's Bobby," Mari whispered with a large smile.

I pulled a plastic chair next to the bed and stroked Mari's cheeks.

"Are you in pain?"

"No. Plenty of drugs for pain, when you're dying. But actually, yes, I'm in pain that I won't see Alex again."

"Rey left to get her."

"How . . . long?"

"She tires out after a few sentences," Don said. "And I was just going over some things with her, so she's already at the point where we have to leave her alone."

"Don't . . . go. How long?"

"From here, almost four hours each way."

"I'll wait. Talk . . . talk . . . to . . . Don."

"Why don't we go outside?" he said.

"No. In . . . here," Mari said.

"Okay. Laura, why don't you bring your chair over here?"

"Who are you, Don? Really, who are you?"

"Captain, US Army. Served with Mari, went through

Desert Storm as a tank commander. One of the few lucky hits by an Iraqi tank, jammed me inside mine, broke my back. Mari and I, both casualties of George Bush's war. I'm thirty-two years old, I'm single, I have an MBA from Wharton and a Ph.D. in Computer Science from MIT."

"All that while you were in the army?"

"Before. One of those child prodigies. Finished the Ph.D. when I was twenty-two, decided on a whim I'd join the army, thought I'd make a difference. A foolish notion, but we're all fools at one time or another. Here."

He handed me a stack of envelopes, each with a name in tiny, neat black ink written on the envelope flap.

"I'll look at them later."

"Oh? I thought there was a specific thing you wanted about each of these people. Perhaps you've already learned what you wanted to know?"

"Some of it."

"Don. Tell . . . her . . . about . . . the water."

"Yes," I said. "That's what I *don't* know."

"Water. Specifically, the water man."

"Xochitl, well, the woman who called herself Xochitl, she told me to watch out for the water man. I realized later that could be taken several different ways."

"And made more difficult by her imprecise English. Well. Water. We're actually talking about water trucks. Tank trucks."

"I saw some of them. In Nogales. The men who bring water up into the slum areas. Is that what you mean?"

"Not quite. As you probably know, Mexico has a bad problem with polluted water. Nogales, Juárez, the border towns, the problem is even more severe because of the less worthy maquiladoras. So some maquiladoras, the ones with enough money and good reputations, they bring in water from the US. In Nogales, there are several maquiladoras that regularly send tank trucks into Arizona."

"Wait, wait. I'm having trouble following this. Can you

go back to why Mari went on all those horseback rides, looking for water in the San Rafael Valley?"

"Of course. But let me jump sideways here." He laughed. "I can't really jump, but I still like the memory of jumping. So. Bobby Guinness. I think Mari told you that we were cutting back on the number of jobs we took on. Her reputation was world famous, well, Bobby Guinness was world famous. But two things happened. Two problems. Her cancer, of course. We decided to scale back, work only with you. Did you know that I'm also a hacker, that I pretty much do the same things you do?"

"I guessed that."

"Don't need much sleep, since I doze in my chair between computer tasks. So I've been working pretty much inside this big circle. More like two horseshoe-shaped desks with an aisle on each side large enough for my chair. I've got a dozen workstations, but then, I don't need to tell you how I worked."

"I'd like to see your setup."

"When I'm set up again, you will."

"Again?"

"I've had to move my operational base. I told you we had two problems. The second thing that happened to us was that after we took on this job of finding the embezzled Mexican money, we started getting all kinds of probes directed at our computers. I had enough cutouts, firewalls, that kind of thing. Nobody got within three jumps of my computers. But they were clumsier, and I could trace most of the attacks to Chechnya. Then we heard about the new, increased trafficking in women into Mexico and on to the US. When we agreed to take on that job, trying to find who ran the smuggling cartel, the probes increased. Not just in number, but in sophistication. One probe got just a jump away from me. I knew it was only a matter of time."

A nurse came in to adjust the morphine drip.

"Can I bring you anything to eat?" she said.

"I've never been in a hospital where they gave you food," I said.

"We're different. Most hospitals figure that only the patients need special care. We know that family and friends suffer in their own way. Food? Something to drink?"

"How about a beer?" Don asked.

"I'll see what's in the fridge. And you, miss?"

"Some Vicodin," I said with a laugh, but she took me seriously.

"Are you in pain?"

"Actually, yes. I fell off a horse a while back, really screwed up my shoulder."

"I'll have the doctor write you a scrip, I'll make sure it gets to you. The doctor would like to have a consultation with you, Mr. Guinness, when you're free."

"Ten minutes," Don said. "I'll ring the call button."

When she left, I flipped through the envelopes and opened the one labeled ZAMORA. Don let me glance over the pages.

"Nothing there that rang any of my bells. What were you looking for?"

"Can't say."

"How about this one?"

He nudged the MEDINA folder.

"Not yet. You need to wrap things up for me. I see three separate threads here, I don't yet see how they connect."

"Four threads, actually. Smuggling. Water. Money. *Basta Ya.*"

"How are they connected?"

"I don't know, Laura. Do you?"

"Not entirely."

"Okay. Two last things you should know. Water. Zamora's maquiladora is one of the Nogales corporations that sends tank trucks into Arizona for water. He has five trucks. I did some sophisticated math. Gallons of water, number of workers. One truck a day would take care of all needs inside his maquiladora. Including worker's showers."

"So? Five trucks, a different truck goes up every day."

"By hacking into the US Customs database, I found out that as many as three trucks a day come across at the Nogales border station. The database also shows the time they go back into Mexico, so I can make a rough calculation of how long they're in the US. Average time, sixteen to twenty hours. My guess? The trucks are smuggling women. If I had the time, I'd access whatever computers stored digital satellite information, mapping the most popular smuggling routes of the *coyotes*. My guess? We'd see a lot of those trucks up into the ranching areas of the San Rafael Valley. Wait, wait, hold that question, I may have the answer. I'm having somebody do a search right now of ownership of all ranches. I want to find out how many have been purchased over the past two years by some front organization that I can trace to Zamora."

"God, you're a busy boy, Don."

"Don't you love it?"

"What's the other thing you want to tell me?"

"*Basta Ya* and Luna. What did you find out?"

"I know my ex-husband was heavily financed to get women authentic identity kits and then help them relocate in the US."

"Exactly."

"He was only the conduit. He never knew who provided the money."

"Mari is Luna. Luna is Mari."

We both looked at her. She was still unconscious.

"But there are so many people involved."

"At least twenty in different cities, helping the women get settled. But it was all Mari's idea. Her money, her connections."

"So I was talking to her. In the chat room."

"She was doing that when I first got here. Amazing that she had the strength to focus on operating that Palm Pilot. There's one thing more."

He took a thick list from his briefcase. Page after page of names, some with addresses or other information, most of them blank.

"Do you recognize these?"

I ran my finger down several pages, finally stopped and shook my head.

"It's all the names in those underground bunkers. The names from the videotape that Alex shot. That's why Mari was up in that area on that day you rode with her. She'd gotten something from Xochitl. I don't know what, but she'd told Mari to look at that specific ranch."

"Jesus Christ. I can't deal with all of this."

"I'm sorry. We didn't think for a moment that you'd get so . . . so involved. Your arrest was a major surprise. Mari was heartsick."

A doctor appeared in the doorway. She looked at Mari, looked at the computer monitors, and flipped quickly through her charts.

"Mr. Guinness. I'm Dr. Nancy Miller. Could we have a talk?"

"Sure. Dr. Miller, this is Mari's sister, Laura."

"Laura. Please, you're welcome to join us. Can we talk in my office? Do you need help with your wheelchair?"

"Can you please give us another ten minutes?" I said.

"We need to talk now."

My cell phone rang.

"Mom?" Alex said.

"No. It's Laura. But I'm in her room. Let me see if she can talk."

Mari's eyes flickered open. She looked vaguely around the room until she fixed on the cell phone in my hand. She tried to reach for it.

"Hold on, Alex."

I put the phone to Mari's ear, intending to hold it there. But she slowly maneuvered her hand to the phone.

"Leave me with Alex," she said.

Don wheeled his chair to the doorway, and the three of us left. As the door swooshed shut behind us, I looked through the window and saw Mari smiling.

"It's her daughter," I said. "She's on her way here."

"How long will it take?" Dr. Miller asked, her lips a tight line—not a good sign, not at all what I wanted to see.

"She's in Mexico. She's just leaving. She'll be here in four hours."

"I'm really sorry, Laura. Your sister probably won't live another ten minutes."

"We've got to be inside," Don said, about to ram the door open with his chair.

"No."

I held back his chair.

"Let go, Goddamnit! Let me in there. I want to be with her."

I put my hands on his shoulders, knelt, leaned against him, put my head against his neck, and hugged him.

"She's saying goodbye to Alex."

The three of us watched through the glass, Don pressing against the chair's armrests to raise his body high enough. Mari's lips moved slowly, deliberately, her chest rising and falling every so slightly as she tried to keep enough oxygen in her lungs to propel yet another word, yet one more.

Finally, I couldn't bear to watch her face and turned to the heart rate and blood pressure monitor. Her vital signs ebbed and flowed, falling off.

"I love you," Don said, his lips pressed against the glass as we saw Mari make an extraordinary effort to say the same words into the cell phone. Her head settled into the pillow, the hand with the cell phone relaxed away from her ear, and she died.

Dr. Miller pushed the door open, and I picked up the cell phone.

"Alex," I said, but she wouldn't stop screaming. "Alex. She's gone."

34

I drove Don to Tucson, arranged a room for him at Lodge on the Desert, and set about unpacking his aluminum work cases. In an hour we had all three of his laptops connected through Qualcomm SatPhones into the Globalstar Stratos network.

"You know what I want?" I asked him.

"Gonna take a while. But when you called last night, I started crunching the financial data. I used the IRS databases, some from the Justice Department, other stuff that I've collected on my own. Here's where we are so far."

He handed me a list of fifteen countries, eleven of which were printed in a purple font, one in yellow, and the other three in red.

"Purple means they're clear. Yellow means not likely, but the data's not all in. Red means I've found at least one of your names, and the computers are looking for more names, plus getting me details of the accounts in the one name identified."

I'd faxed him a copy of the newspaper photo of the groundbreaking at Zamora's maquiladora. He spread it on top of one of the laptop keyboards.

"Major financial players. Zamora and Garza."

"Medina?"

"Nothing yet. As expected, nothing for Xochitl, whose real name, by the way, is Svetlana Peshkova. From a small village in the Caucasus, with known ties to Chechnya rebels, according to Russian Intel files."

"I thought she was Albanian."

"Laura, there's a lot of people here using fake IDs."

"Kinda like you and me," I said.

"Right. Okay. These other two people in the newspaper photo were harder to identity. I had to scan their faces, digitally enhance them, then run them through the face identification software and compare them to officials in the Zedillo government. This one's name is Carlos Ibarra. Ministry of Tourism. This other one is more interesting. Luis Ocampo. He was once in the Public Ministry, which operates under the Office of the Attorney General. Medina's inner circle. Ocampo was bounced when Fox got elected and appointed a new public security chief. Alejandro Gertz Manero. Manero cleaned house with a vengeance."

"I don't really want all this detail."

"Okay. Let's switch to the offshore bank accounts. Here's a summary of money trails for Ocampo, Zamora, and Garza, who, by the way, was once a major player in the Mexican drug cartel headed by El Chapo. Real name, Joaquin Guzman, who made major headlines a year ago when he bought his way out of Puente Grande prison. Toughest in all of Mexico."

"Don, way too many details I'm not interested in."

"Believe me, you want to know about El Chapo. Along with some of his top lieutenants, he's wanted by the US feds. Warrants have been issued. If El Chapo or any of his guys are found and arrested, they could be extradited across the border. Guess who's in charge of the task force, waiting to process the extradition?"

"Michael Dance."

"Bingo bongo."

He pushed off from the laptop, gliding his chair across the room to a stack of bound documents with red covers.

"I'm assembling all the backup data. You'll get summary printouts. Each folder is for a different country."

"What are we looking at?"

"Well. There's the usual suspects of offshore secret banking accounts. Bahamas, Caymans, Panama, a lot of little Caribbean islands that have tighter morals and are really not worth looking at. Then there's Lebanon, Israel, Russia, and Liechtenstein. But I struck gold when I started looking at banks on Niue and other Pacific Island accounts. Major tax havens. *But* last year the US government declared sanctions against transfers of money to Niue."

"Please, Don. Skip the lectures, okay? I don't have time."

"You'll never succeed in a government job."

"Thank God for that," I said.

"But you need to know this much. There's an agency called the Financial Action Task Force on Money Laundering. FATF. It's an inter-governmental group, develops and promotes policies to defeat money laundering schemes. Not just in the US, but internationally. As far as we're concerned, FATF is the group that sets up money laundering countermeasures in *non*-member countries. So. Niue. This dinky island money laundering paradise. Nobody can move money in, and it's getting increasingly difficult to move money *out*. So that's what I looked at. Not what might have gone in, but what's going out."

"And that's how you came up with this list of players?"

"Yup. But . . ."

"You've got one hell of a lot of buts today, Don."

"One last thing. A lot of Mexicans working in the US send money home to their families. Conservative estimate, six billion a year. One of my sidelines in this office is to see if any of the drug cartels are trying to expand into this money transfer business. Take it over, take a percentage, whatever. So when I cross-reference every bit of financial stuff I've got here from all these sources, this name wins the lottery."

"Garza."

"I'd guess that he's really Zamora's man."

"But that doesn't mean that Zamora is involved."

"Doesn't mean he isn't. Mexican drug cartels have many layers of cutouts to protect the top players."

"But no direct connection to Zamora?"

"No."

"Medina?" I asked.

"No."

"And Michael Dance? How does he fit into this nasty business?"

"You'll have to ask him yourself."

"Why me?"

"He's powerful, Laura."

"What about Jake Nasso? Taá Wheatley?"

"Just haven't had time to get to them. I thought the Mexicans were most important, so I ran all their data first."

"Well, I'm going to have to talk to Dance."

"You're going to brace an Assistant US Attorney?"

"Today," I said. "You just keep working on the rest of the financial data."

"When are you meeting him?"

"His birthday party. Tonight, at his house down in Tubac."

"Seeing as how you escaped from his custody, I don't think a birthday present would be appropriate."

"I'm bringing him a big cake," I said. "He just won't like what pops out of it."

"Well, it's going to rain down there. Don't get wet."

Don't get wet, I thought. Don't get water. Don't get the water man.

"Trucks," I said excitedly. "Godammit, how could I be so stupid."

"What are you talking about?"

"Can you hack into the Border Patrol's satellite imaging programs?"

"I can arrange it. What do you need?"

I told him, he made three phone calls, and we waited until one of the laptops pinged. He made another phone call and held the cell phone out to me.

"Tell him what you want."

"The Nogales border crossing," I said.

Nobody answered, but I watched images flicking across the laptop screen.

"Not the main crossing," I said. "Switch to the newer one, where the trucks go."

A high shot appeared on the laptop covering an area of at least fifty square miles.

"Tighten in," I said. "North of the truck crossing, tighter, tighter . . . there. Just leave that up for a while. And thanks, whoever you are."

"Laura, what am I looking at?" Don said.

"Trucks. Hundreds of trucks."

"So?"

"There's a new border agreement for long-haul truckers. *Cruzadores*, they're called. Crossers. Before the US signed this agreement, the Mexican *cruzadores* had to park their rigs in these lots and wait to transfer the goods to another truck. Now they just stay there a few hours until all their paperwork is checked. They can take the cargo directly to US cities. It's all sealed electronically, so the trucks can pass with a minimum of hassle by US Customs."

"I don't get it."

"Most of these trucks are bringing goods *out* of Mexico. But one of the things they need desperately in Nogales is good water. So some of these trucks are certified as empty when they cross north to pick up cargos of bottled water."

"And even the empty trucks are electronically sealed?" Don said excitedly.

"Right."

"But they're not? What are they bringing in? Narcotics?"

"In a diesel semi-trailer? Nobody would take a chance loading something that big with narcotics. No. They're smuggling people."

"Human cargo."

"Women."

"Somebody's paid money," Don said, already working at

another laptop. "Bribes to tamper with the process of electronic sealing."

"The women are put inside, then the truck is sealed. US Customs must have a database of all *cruzadores* that have the necessary papers. All the trucks, with license plates, plus all the international paperwork."

"I'm on it," Don said.

"How long will it take?"

"In one sense, not long. It's just a matter of money. Like the satellite images. Once I find a hacker who has up-to-date copies of the Customs database, I can get listings of whatever trucks you want. But that's the easy part. What trucking company? What dates? If you don't give me some specific filters, I could be crunching that database forever without knowing what I was looking at."

I wrote out a name and a date.

"Look for this," I said.

"Where will you be?"

"I'll wait outside."

A wedding was taking place in the grassy main square of the Lodge, with a *chuppa* positioned in front of the wall behind the swimming pool. The ceremony had just finished, and the bride and groom were kissing to wild hoots and applause.

The bride wore a white wedding gown, off the shoulders, and the groom grinned proudly in a traditional tuxedo. With a shock I realized the bride was Joanna, who worked the front desk.

"Laura?"

One of the guests stood in front of me, wearing a powder blue two-piece periwinkle dress, holding a champagne flute. She pulled off her sunglasses and I saw it was Donna, one of the servers at the restaurant.

"Laura?" she said again. "Is that really you?"

I shrank back against a sumac, nodding. The eighty or ninety guests were all dressed so well, they were so elegant, so perfect that I felt sloppy and out of place.

"Hi, Donna," I said.

"Are you staying here? I didn't see your name on the guest list for breakfast."

"No," I said. "I mean, I'm just visiting a friend. In room nineteen."

"Isn't this grand, this wedding? Don't they look happy?"

"Grand," I said. "Um, look, I've got to leave. Nice to see you, Donna."

"Okay. Sorry to bother you."

"It's not a bother."

But she stepped away from me, put her sunglasses on, and turned back to the party. I stared at the party, the bride, fascinated by the happiness of the wedding, wondering what it would be like to get married again.

A fantasy, I thought.

I went back to Don's room just as paper finished chugging out of his printer.

"You'll love this," he said.

I read what he'd found.

"What are you going to do now?"

"Going to a dinner party," I said.

Don frowned at my wrinkled jeans and yellow tee.

"You'd better dress up."

"No time," I said. "Besides, I won't be staying there very long."

35

Driving into Tubac after sunset, I saw the first monsoon of the summer working its rainy way up from Nogales. Still forty miles away, the monsoon dominated the southwestern sky. Dark, gunmetal-black clouds, webbed with yellowish-white veins of lightning.

South of the Tubac art colony, Dance's house stood off-road from US 19. After two miles of a smoothly graded dirt road, I crossed over a cattle guard and onto a paved surface. His entire property was surrounded by high fencing, with video cameras stationed every hundred feet. Double-parked cars filled his circular driveway. I parked my rented Ford Escort between a Ferrari and a Lamborghini.

The house looked glass-sheeted and framed in steel, much of which had rusted to a burnished yellow color. The front door stood open. Live jazz came from a central room, which was surrounded by a three-story atrium walled on two sides entirely with glass. One wall looked east, where the sky was still clear and spectacularly cobalt blue. The other wall directly faced the monsoon, already much closer, although I couldn't tell if it would move west of the house or flood us with rain.

I had no idea how many people were at the party, nor did I recognize anybody. The servers were dressed in rodeo cowboy clothing and extraordinary red boots by Paul Bond, the Nogales boot maker. Some women wore diaphanous sheaths, others strapless gowns, some just jeans and tees. A very mixed crowd, except all of them looked rich.

"Laura, honey."

Jake Nasso pushed a glass of red wine into my hand.

"What are you doing here, Laura?"

"I need to talk with Dance."

"Don't think he's much in the mood for that."

Setting the wineglass on the carpet beside my feet, I hoisted my briefcase a few inches and ducked my head toward it. A young couple tangoed by, the woman kicking the wineglass over without realizing what she'd done. The reddish stain blossomed on the carpet, but Nasso didn't even bother to look at it.

"He will be."

"What have you found out, honey?"

"I know it all," I said, looking up at the balcony two floors above the atrium. "I'm going up there. Away from the noise. Tell him to look for me in one of the rooms."

"Okay. I'll bring him."

"No. Him only. I want to look over that railing and see you standing in the middle of this floor. Stand right on the wine stain, so I can find you. Clear?"

"You got some *plastique* in that briefcase?"

"Just paper."

"You don't mind if I have a peeksee?"

"Not a chance."

"Why are you here?"

Nasso was intensely serious, troubled, wary. I saw the stairway up and turned toward it.

"Tell Dance I'm upstairs."

Nasso watched me climb to the second balcony, but when I got to the top floor, he'd disappeared. I opened doors at random. Master bedroom. Guest bedroom. Guest bath. Office. On the wall facing the monsoon. I sat in his antique Eames chair. The desktop was cluttered with documents of all sizes and colors, but I didn't bother to even glance at them. A gold pocket watch sat on a jade stand, next to the hooded green library lamp. I turned it on, walked over to turn off the two floor lamps.

Thunder echoed in the distance.

I waited.

Dance stopped at the doorway, leaning against the jamb, holding a squarish glass of what looked like bourbon. He wore a dark blue blazer over an off-white pleated cotton shirt, the neck band buttoned. Designer jeans tapering into a fabulous pair of boots, the uppers colored dark red with elaborate tooling, the bottoms a faded-leaf yellow. He saw me looking at them and cocked his left leg so that the boot lay against his right knee.

"Paul Bond. Sharkskin. Fourteen inches long, bulldogging heels."

"Boots hurt my feet."

"Paul can make you some that feel so good you won't want to take them off."

"Pass."

He uncocked his leg and went to sit on a leather director's chair. I set my briefcase on top of his desk.

"Get you something to drink?"

"Pass."

"Right to business, then. What have you got?"

"The people who run the smuggling ring," I said as I began pulling out papers.

"Which one?"

"The one that made a lot of money for all of you."

He grinned.

"Laura, Laura, Laura. This is so *noir*ish. The monsoon, the rain and the thunder and the lightning and the way you've made things dark. Listen, kid. You're on your way back into one of those dinky little rooms with metal toilets. I'm going back downstairs."

A monster clap of thunder rattled the glass window. I could see it shimmer, like being in a window seat on an airplane in bad weather and watching the wingtips wobble up and down. Five streaks of lightning zigzagged a few miles away.

"I love standing outside in these monsoons. It's like, I mean, did you ever stand right next to a railroad track, let the train rumble by and you want to get as close to the train as you possibly can?"

"No," I said.

"Want to stand out on the deck? Grab hold of the railing when the storm hits? This house is built to stand up to any kind of weather. I'm built that way too."

"Can I clear off your desktop?" I asked. "I need a little room."

"Don't think so. In fact, let's just stop your dog and pony show before you let the animals out of your bag. I'll get Jake, he'll deal with you."

I set the briefcase on the oak parquet floor, extended both my arms straight out, and swept everything except the lamp off the desktop. The pocket watch burst open, shards of glass flying clear across the room.

"You dumb fuck," he said, and started to get up.

"Look at these."

I laid out a dozen colored satellite recon photos.

He hesitated at the door, but couldn't resist coming to look.

"San Rafael Valley," I said. "Tank trucks. Water trucks."

I laid a sheet of paper beside the photos.

"Smuggling trucks. How many women can you get inside?"

"What are you talking about?"

"Let's say, twenty-five women. Packed in, maybe thirty-five. And why not pack them in, just like jamming women into shipping containers. So, thirty-five women. Five trucks a day. We're talking up to a thousand women in a busy week."

"So that's how they were smuggled across. Very good, Laura. But these recon photos, I can't see any names on the trucks. Where do they come from?"

I pushed the paper toward him.

"Zamora's place. The maquiladora. All but one of the trucks go out with women, only one of them comes back filled with water."

"Zamora? I don't believe it."

"Forget Zamora. Let's talk about . . . Niue."

He blanched, almost staggered. I didn't give him time to recover, didn't give him time to say anything, although his mouth was opening in protest. I took out more paper.

"Here's your money. At least, what we found in bank accounts on the island of Niue. We're looking at banks on Naura, but we don't have that information yet."

"What are you talking about?"

"This is what I do for a living, remember? I track money."

"What makes you think it's *my* money?"

"I don't."

He'd recovered enough to pull the director's chair to the desk opposite me. It was a stall, the elaborately slow movement of the chair, sitting in it, getting up to adjust its position, sitting again, tucking his jeans into the boots.

"Somebody's set up a very elaborate scam," he said finally. "Used my name on these accounts. The name means nothing."

"I agree."

"So why are you bothering to show me these things?"

"Here's what I figure. I've got account information for Zamora and Garza, but there's not much need to show that to you. I figure, they're making a whole lot of money with their smuggling scheme, and you decided that what they were paying you wasn't enough. You got me to look for this financial information so you could pressure Zamora. Get more money from him."

"This is ridiculous."

"You're not reading me at all. I don't care what they pay you. I don't care how you're involved, what you do or don't do, who you prosecute or don't prosecute."

"It's not really his money," Nasso said from the doorway.

He held a small Beretta loosely in one hand and shut the door with the other.

"You want a taste," he said to me. "But you're shaking down the wrong man."

"Call it whatever you want. I don't care. But yes. I want in. Pay me, and I'll go away. An untraceably long way away."

"Garza was greedy. You've got most of it right, except that I never dealt with Zamora. Garza set up the smuggling ring. He had connections with the El Chapo drug cartel. Garza also had connections with the Russian mafia. He knew about how they used banks in Naura to launder their money. But he was greedy. He wouldn't give me what I asked. So I set you against him. I threatened him with you."

"So how much?" Dance said quietly.

"Oh, a million dollars?" Nasso shifted his weight onto his left leg. "Two? Five?"

"You'd give her five million dollars, just to make her disappear?"

"Ten million. There's just so much money in this. Ten million is nothing."

"I've seen your Niue bank accounts," I told him. "You've got forty million in one account alone, twenty-seven million in another."

"Niue, Naura, Panama, I've got money in all those places." Dance cocked his head. "How many of my accounts do you really know about?"

"Actually, none."

"What?"

I turned over the left collar flap of my blouse, showed him the microphone.

"Jesus! What are you doing?" Dance said.

Reaching into the briefcase, I took out a digital recorder and set it on the desktop. He ran both hands through his hair, staring at the recorder, his mind incredibly transparent, thinking how quickly he could grab it. I took a small black aluminum box from the briefcase.

"Transmitter. You can take the recorder. That's what you're thinking right now, you'll grab the recorder, remove the memory card, nobody will know. But this box is a transmitter. Right up to a satellite. The entire conversation is being recorded."

"Wheatley," Dance said.

I nodded.

"Never trusted lesbians," Nasso said, raising the Beretta.

"Jake, Jake," Dance said excitedly. "Let's work something out here."

"I've already got it worked out. Outside, boss. Come on, get up, get up."

"Jake, don't be a fool."

Nasso tucked his free hand inside Dance's jacket collar and squeezed on a nerve. Dance gasped in pain and rose out of the director's chair. Nasso shifted his hold on Dance's neck and pushed him rapidly toward the door.

"Nasso, wait!" I said. *"Wait!"*

But he'd already pushed Dance through the doorway and backed him against the balcony railing. When Nasso moved back into the doorway, out of sight of anybody two floors below, he leveled the Beretta at Dance. I suddenly realized what Nasso was going to do, but I couldn't get to him in time. Just as I reached out to him, he shot Dance twice in the chest, the gunshots astonishingly loud and rebounding off the huge atrium walls.

"Here," Nasso said, thrusting the Beretta into my outstretched hand.

I took the gun before I even thought what I was doing.

"Michael!" Nasso shouted, rushing out of the doorway to Dance, who was clearly dead. Nasso propped him up, maneuvering his body over the railing as though he was trying to hold Dance from falling, but instead pushing him over the railing. Women screamed as Dance's body floated two stories down and landed with a bloodspattering thud on the marble flooring. I saw Nasso wringing his hands together, *no*, he was pulling off latex gloves and shoving them into his pocket.

He turned to me with a smile and came back to the doorway. I raised the Beretta, but he grinned wildly and waved his finger at me.

"No bullets left. Of course, nobody down there knows that. Just hold the gun up high, run down the stairway. Nobody's going to want to come near you. I'll pretend I'm trying to catch you, but I won't."

I drew back my arm, relaxing my fingers, ready to drop the gun.

"She's got a gun!"

Nasso shouted down to the people staring up at us.

"She shot him."

Two men pointed at me and started to move toward the stairway.

"Let her outside," Nasso shouted. "I've got men out there, she won't get anywhere. Stay away from her. Let her get out of the house, so nobody else gets hurt."

"On your way, Laura Winslow," he said quietly to me. "Those old arrest warrants were nothing. But now thousands of people are going to look for a murderer."

I held up the transmitter.

"Wheatley knows the truth."

"Oh, she's not a problem. Better run now. Run as long as you can. But just remember, honey. As of tonight, you are absolutely, totally fucked."

36

"Can you please come closer?" Pinau asked. "I'm not wearing my contacts, and I broke my regular glasses yesterday. All I've got are these drugstore reading things. So I can't really see you very well."

"Not a problem," I said.

"You're being hunted by every law enforcement officer within a hundred miles. Do you know that?"

"Because I murdered Michael Dance?"

"Or so they say. I'm not so sure."

"It was Jake Nasso. If you want, I can tell you what happened. But I don't really have much time."

"It's not necessary." She bent over and tapped an immaculately red fingernail on the stack of papers. "I did read all of your documents."

"And?"

She pressed her back into the chair, moved into the circle of her hotel lamp. I hardly recognized her, and for a moment wondered if it was an entirely different person. A tired, older woman, sitting in her faded chenille bathrobe, all makeup wiped from her wrinkled face, and completely unconcerned how she looked.

Seeing me look her up and down, she smiled.

"I'm sixty-seven years old," she said. "When I'm out in public, I'm a very traditional Mexican woman. Always look your finest, always be presentable to the extreme, because you are a woman in a macho society that values women mainly for their beauty. Or maybe even just for their bodies. But this is the real me."

A cigarette burned in an amber ashtray, but she seemed unaware that it was even lit. I saw a pair of worn flannel pajamas laid out on the bed. All the papers I'd faxed her were stacked on the floor beside her chair.

"What do you know about Mexico's judicial system?"

"Corrupt."

"In many ways," she said, "that's unpleasantly true. *Presidente* Fox wants to make a difference. But the corruption of the last century, the pervasive influence of the drug cartels, the underpaid *policia*, dirty money, dishonest bureaucrats—it must seem very strange to you people from *El Norte*."

"We have our own problems. Um, Mrs. Medina, I'm not here to talk politics or morality. You've read all the financial stuff? The offshore bank accounts?"

"Yes. Most of the names—I wasn't surprised."

"You provided the names, so you can't be surprised."

"Yes. That is true. But Francisco Zamora. What can I tell you about Mexico's hopes for better citizens? Better wages? Even—yes, even better water."

"Did you suspect him?"

"Garza, most definitely. Garza was always a greedy man. But Francisco? No."

She took a pack of cigarettes and an old Zippo lighter from her bathrobe pocket. About to light the cigarette, she noticed the one burning in the ashtray.

"What can you do?" I asked.

"I am the chief officer of the Public Ministry. The prosecutorial arm of the Mexican judicial system. And yet there are many things I can *not* do. Hector Garza, for example. He works for me, but he does *not* work for me. I have the power to put him in prison, but I can *not* touch him. Fox may have won the election. But hundreds of officials from the old regime didn't stand for election. Their power is fading in some circles. In other ways their ancient power is absolute. What do you *want* me to do?"

"Confirm what's in those documents."

"I do so."

"And?"

"I cannot prosecute. Embezzled monies, perhaps we can recover them from the offshore accounts you have identified. The men themselves? I am powerless."

Frustrated, she jammed the smoldering cigarette into the ashtray and quickly lit another. She inhaled deeply, like a marijuana smoker, and slowly let out the smoke.

"You know about El Chapo?" she asked.

"Guzman? The drug lord who bought his way out of prison?"

"Yes. Some people in his cartel financed Zamora's maquiladora. From the start, the entire plan was to build a model maquiladora, one that your government would hail as a champion of NAFTA. From the start, El Chapo's men planned to use the buildings as a base for smuggling. From the start, it was meant to be drugs. But in the past few years, major money has been made by smuggling people. Zamora brought his entrepreneurial spirit to smuggling women. He realized that you Americans have many appetites. Drugs is one of them, sex another. Tell me, Laura. I may call you Laura?"

"Yes."

"You must have suspected me."

"I did."

"You went to Kykotsmovi. You asked if anybody knew a young girl named Pinau. But that was a family name, almost a secret name. I dreamed of having my butterfly hairdo, I dreamed of the ceremony. People died. I was taken to Mexico. I'm not surprised that nobody remembered my secret name."

Her cell phone burred, a slight sound, almost like an insect.

"Yes? She's with me now. I'll call you back soon."

"What can you do?" I said once again.

"Do you play poker?"

"Played at it. Nickel, dime, nothing more."

"I've just raised somebody an enormous amount of face."

"Face?"

"Men. Mexican men. As I said before, men tolerate women like me. Especially men in power. They tolerate women in general, but they don't really want women to have any power outside of the home. My husband died five years ago. I've given my life to Mexico. And I play a truly vicious game of poker."

"I don't understand what you're telling me."

"In Mexico, there are both official and unofficial ways to get things done. All too often, money works in unofficial ways. But sometimes, those of us who are true to our country, we use those other methods. I have just made certain that word is passed to the drug cartels that Francisco Zamora's smuggling operation is about to be shut down. Word has been passed that he took twenty percent of the profits off the top and diverted them to offshore bank accounts. The ones you've told me about. Ten percent might be tolerated, perhaps even fifteen. Those who steal twenty percent are punished. And now, I'm tired. If you'd be so kind, an old woman would like to crawl into bed."

"I still don't understand."

"If I've read all these documents correctly, there is a scheduled delivery tomorrow of another group of women to a ranch in the San Rafael Valley. By tomorrow, Zamora will know that the cartels no longer wish him to stay in business. In the short run, it will make a difference. In six months . . . do you know much about these cartels that traffic in women?"

"I've talked with a few of the women in chat rooms."

"On the Internet? How interesting."

"Survivors. Helping each other. But only a small percentage of the women. As for the cartels, I only know what I read in that CIA report you told me about."

"By any conservative estimate," she said, "over one hundred thousand women were smuggled into the US last year. Zamora only worked a percentage of that. By tomorrow, the cartels will already have divided who gets the women supplied to Zamora. So. I'm tired. I think that's all. Oh. Please. Would you thank the woman I first contacted? The woman who hired you."

"I can't do that."

"Why not?"

"She died yesterday."

"*Madre de dios*!"

Pinau collapsed in her chair, made the sign of the cross.

"I am so sorry," she said faintly. "I think you should leave now."

"Can I have your guarantee about something?"

"In return for what you've given me? Ask. If I can do it, I will."

"*Basta Ya*. Let it flourish."

"The workers' union? For Indian women, mestizo women? I will try."

"Thank you," I said. "Thank you."

"*Señor* Johnny. Do I understand correctly, he was once your husband?"

"Yes."

"Was he a good man?"

"Once, a long time ago, I thought he'd hung the moon."

"Ah. My Cristóbal was that kind of man. I will do my best. I can't promise anything. Since the Public Ministry controls prosecution of *Basta Ya*, I can speak to some of the correct people. That's all you want? In return for what you've done?"

"Yes."

"If I were *you*," she said, "I would tell him to vanish for a while."

"He already has."

"If I were you, I would also vanish. The drug cartels will put Zamora out of business, but they will hate you for it. They have long memories."

"I am leaving tomorrow."

She stood and extend her hands, taking mine and squeezing them.

"Mexico thanks you, Laura Winslow."

Outside her hotel room, I leaned against the corridor wall, exhausted. My cell phone rang and I moved quickly away from her door.

"It's all set up," Rey said. "You say the word, I'll start the ball."

"Go," I said, and started to turn off the cell phone.

"Lock and load," I heard him say to himself. "Rock and roll."

37

We came in on horseback along a ridge two hundred yards above the ranch. While I tied the horses' reins securely to a large mesquite branch, Rey started glassing the ranch with his binoculars.

He wore total cammies. Hat, long-sleeve shirt, multi-pocketed fatigue pants tucked into cammie-patterned army boots. An M-16 slung behind his back, a Glock nine on one hip and on the opposite shoulder a Benelli M3 Super 90 combat shotgun.

During the night he'd shaved his head entirely bald.

Why? I'd asked.

It's an edge, he'd said with a shrug. A combat edge. They think they know what I look like. Now I want to show them that I'm the wrath of God.

"We early enough?" I asked.

"No truck yet. No people. Check that. Somebody just came out of the barn. Going back in."

I checked my watch, a new Timex I'd grabbed in Walgreen's when I realized that Meg had taken my old watch with the implanted tracking device.

"Seven. According to the computer records that Don Ralph found, the truck should be here by eight."

"I want you to stay up here."

"Can't do that."

"Then take the shotgun."

"Don't want to do that either."

"Damn it, Laura. You're just in the way here."

I went twenty yards away. We waited.

"Vehicle coming down the road."

"The truck?"

"A Suburban. Inside the fence, at the barn. People getting out."

"It's only seven-thirty. Who can it be?"

He lowered the binoculars suddenly, took a deep breath, raised them to his eyes.

"We've got real trouble."

Handing me the binoculars, he shook his head angrily. Zamora got out of the driver's door. I had to refocus and gasped as I saw Garza pull Alex Emerine from the car, and then Amada.

"Rey, look!" I gave him the binoculars. "What are they doing here?"

"I don't know," Rey whispered in shock. "The two of them were supposed to be driving to Scottsdale."

Rey unslung the Benelli shotgun, racked the slide, and reached into one of the pouches in his pants to take out another shell. Inserting it into the magazine, he handed the shotgun to me. I backed away.

"Two dirt bikes," he said. "I figure at least two other men in the barn. Zamora, Garza, two in the barn. I'll need you with a gun."

"I'm going to call for help."

"No time. This is a hostage situation."

"At least wait for the truck."

"Don't you get it? Laura, the truck's never going to show."

"What do you mean? It's scheduled."

"By who?"

"Zamora."

"And you trust him?"

"No, but . . ."

"The tanker's not going to show. My guess? They're here to torch the ranch. With Alex and Amada inside."

I took the shotgun by the barrel.

"Seven rounds in there. Deer slugs. Like a really big bullet, not like buckshot. You put one of those slugs into somebody, they're going down. And take this."

He reached inside his shirt and pulled out a small Beretta.

"Twenty-five caliber, nine rounds. If you have to do something up close, drop the shotgun and use this."

"Rey, you're really scaring me. Why don't we call the Border Patrol?"

"Because they might send Jake Nasso."

He started moving down the slope, keeping his body behind mesquite trees and creosote bushes. Twenty yards down, he turned to look at me. I hadn't moved. I was paralyzed. He came back up to me.

"Laura. That's my daughter down there. It's a hostage situation. I know how to handle these things, but I need you with me. And I need you *now*! Oh *Christ*!"

He raised the binoculars briefly.

"Those two guys in the barn, they just came outside with plastic gas cans. They're dropping the cans, they're picking up two more. *Now,* Laura. *Now!*"

"I don't think I can do this," I protested.

"It'll be over so fast you don't have to think about it."

"I *am* thinking about it."

"Don't think. First, last, only rule of dealing with a hostage situation. Don't take time to think. If you have to, just unload everything in that shotgun, take out the Beretta and unload everything in it. I'll be directing your fire, thinking for you."

"I can't kill somebody."

"Don't think about it. I'm going down there. Now. Be ready for me."

"Hello the barn!" Rey shouted.

A man stepped outside, recoiled when he saw Rey standing fifty feet away, and ran back into the barn.

"Hello the barn!" Rey shouted again. "Come on out here."

Garza stepped hesitantly through the door, a Tec10 in his right hand. Zamora came out behind him, accompanied by two men in biker leathers. One of them had a pistol against Amada's head, the other had his arm around Alex's throat. Rey held up his arms, showed them the M-16, and laid it slowly on the ground. Reaching inside his shirt, he carefully removed a large, thick envelope and held it up.

"I've got all of Winslow's papers. I've got the tape recorder, I've got everything right here. No copies, no computer files, nothing except what I've got right here."

Zamora made a slight motion with his hands.

"You must be Villaneuva," he said. Garza started drifting to his right.

"Let's trade."

"Why would I trade anything with you?"

"All these papers, computer disks, the recorder."

Rey dropped the hand with the envelope. Garza had now fanned out twenty feet on Zamora's left side. The two bikers remained where they were.

"You're a fool. What could I possibly have that I would trade?"

"The girls."

"I've got two men up on the slope," Rey said. "You're in their sights. Any move other than to make this trade, they take you down."

Garza looked up to where I lay behind some rocks. He held his hand over his eyes against the sun behind me.

"Thirty seconds," Rey shouted, pumping his left arm up and down. "That's their signal. If you don't send the girls over in thirty seconds, they'll take you down."

"Can we talk about this?"

"Not with me. Twenty seconds."

"Give me a minute."

"Ten seconds."

"All right!"

Garza protested, but Zamora cut him off and motioned to

the biker holding Alex. The biker lowered his pistol and shoved Alex forward. She staggered and regained her balance, not sure what to do. Zamora waved for her to walk toward Rey.

"*Both* the girls!" Rey shouted.

"There's a matter of trust here."

"Trust has got nothing to do with this. Hey, motorcycle guys. All that gasoline you've been spreading around, you realize that Zamora's going to burn you up?"

The bikers looked at each other, confused, looked at Zamora, who shook his head in disgust.

"No, really," Rey said to the bikers. "Let's talk trust here. Do you two really trust Zamora? You're nothing to him except the power you've got as witnesses."

Somebody else came out of the barn.

Jake Nasso.

He started talking to the bikers to reassure them.

"You believe Nasso?" Garza shouted. "He's Zamora's man inside the whole task force that broke up this smuggling ring. You think Nasso gives a shit about you two?"

One of the bikers started running, and the other raised his pistol. Garza shot them both with one burst from his Tec10.

"Garza!" Rey shouted. "What kind of trust have *you* got for Zamora?"

"You know what?" Zamora said. "I think you're bluffing, Villaneuva. I don't think you've got two men up on the slope. You're a loner, that's what I've always heard. I think we're going to end this. Right now."

"Hoy!"

Shouting, I stood up. Rey had given me his cammie hat, and I'd tucked my hair underneath it. Holding the shotgun shoulder high, I started down the slope.

"There's one," Rey said.

"It's that fucking woman!" Garza shouted, and began firing at me.

Rey dropped flat against the ground, grabbing the M-16

and rolling sideways, firing on full auto as his body rotated entirely around. Garza dropped to his knees and Rey emptied his clip, throwing Garza backwards. Running straight at Zamora, Rey shucked the M-16 clip and rammed home another and fired without hardly a pause. Zamora grabbed Alex, trying to get her inside the barn as Nasso reached out and grabbed Amada, snapping her head back violently as he pulled her body in front of his. Zamora dropped sideways, and Rey emptied his clip and started to insert another. Zamora raised his gun and I ran toward him, shooting, the shotgun recoil throwing the barrel too high. I pumped the slide and fired again, the deer slug screeching across the ranch yard. Zamora saw that Rey had dropped the next clip, turned to me as I pumped the slide and fired again. The slug thudded into the barn wall and Zamora stood straight up, holding his gun in both hands and sighting at me as I pumped the slide and fired, missing him *again* as his bullet whistled past my left ear so I pumped the slide one last time, stopped running, held the shotgun to my shoulder and fired.

He dropped instantly. Like a stone in a deep well. No sounds at all. Just gone.

Alex disappeared into the barn. Nasso pulled a Glock from behind his back and held it to Amada's head as Rey rammed home another clip and leveled the M-16.

"We've got a deal," Nasso said. "I take the papers, you get the woman and the girl. Is that going to happen?"

"Shoot him, Dad!" Amada shouted.

"Let her go," Rey said quietly.

"So we've got a deal?"

"Only deal on the deck is that you let her go, I let you live."

"That's the only way out of this?"

"For Christ's sake, *shoot* him!"

"Live or die," Rey said. "Your choice."

"This is your daughter, man. Don't be foolish."

Rey jumped sideways and went into a full body roll.

Nasso moved the Glock over Amada's shoulder, pointed it down between her breasts, and shot her in the right thigh. She staggered, slipped through his arms as he brought the Glock level. Rey instantly began firing, and Nasso's head exploded. Amada slipped to the ground as Rey emptied his entire clip, the bullets *whapping* into Nasso's body so that long after he was dead, his body danced and shimmered.

I threw away the shotgun and knelt beside Amada, feeling for a pulse. Alex came out of the barn, sobbing, and knelt beside me. I realized Amada was alive. Alex hugged me, Rey knelt and put his arms around both of us as we sat in that happy circle.

38

"Come on, get into the car," Taá said, clearly surprised that I wasn't alone. I'd asked her to meet me at the airport. She was driving a white Caprice. It looked and smelled like a rental car, and underneath the passenger's seat I could see one of those protective sheets of paper that rental companies put out when the car is cleaned for another customer.

Meg climbed into the front seat, while I got in back.

"So it's done," Taá said.

"Done."

"Jake Nasso. Who would have figured?"

"You're surprised?" I asked.

"I knew somebody in our task force was bad. I thought it was Dance."

"He had too much to lose," I said as she pulled away from the curb.

"With all that money, anything's possible. Nobody's beyond corruption."

"Where we going?" Meg asked.

"Well. I was going to take Laura to AZIC, show her a batch of satellite intel that just came in. But I can't get you in there, so I'll have to drop you somewhere."

As Taá turned through the airport parking lot construction area, the Caprice bumped along a dirt road. Meg's head bobbled, most of it due to her agitated state. When I'd met her earlier, I could tell that she was heavily into a manic phase, her eyes totally open, muscles rippling up and down her face and bare shoulders and arms.

"Drop me," she sang. "Bop me, drop me, pretty baby, doo wop me."

Taá stopped the car and swiveled to look at me.

"She's out of her head, Laura. Why did you bring her along?"

"Along for the song," Meg said. "Sarong, baby, sarong."

I cupped both of my hands around the back of Meg's head, wanting her to be quiet. *Sarong* obviously started out in her head as *so long* and I didn't want Taá to get that idea. Not yet. Some things didn't quite seem *right*, I tell you. Taá worked with Nasso, but how closely, and were they just partners as law officers, or partners in crime? I wasn't sure, despite the data I had to show Taá. I realized that getting into the car with Taá was a mistake.

"She'll be okay," I said. "I'll just give you the last of the data, and then you'll never see me again."

"Just like that?" Taá said.

"Rat a tat tat, just like that."

"Meg," I said. "Shut up."

"I made a mistake about you," Taá said to Meg.

"No mistake, no wake. Wakey wakey."

Taá slammed the gearshift into drive and drove away in angry silence. We got out of the airport maze onto Benton, but instead of going straight through to US10 she turned right at Kino Parkway.

"Where are we going?" I said.

Taá held up her left wrist, showing me her watch.

"I promised to pick up some meat scraps for Sophie. The butcher will close in five minutes, so if it's all right, I'll just stop by there first."

"*Puercocita,*" Meg said. "*Carnecita*. Fresh meat. Neat."

Taá turned off at 36th Street and drove into South Tucson to an old storefront building. She parked the Caprice, opened her door, and started to get out.

"Want to come in?" she said.

Meg popped out of the car and I caught Taá with a very small, satisfied grin that disappeared quickly.

Meg gave us a huge grin and nodded *yes*.

"Just take a minute," Taá said, but I grabbed Meg and pulled her to the car.

"No," I said.

Taá reached down to her right ankle, lifted the leg of her khaki pants and took out a snub-nosed .38 revolver. Holding the barrel against my right temple, she patted me down for a weapon, touching my armpits, my sides, down the outside and inside of my legs, and finally ramming her hand tight into my crotch. As an afterthought, she felt carefully underneath my leather belt, grasping the rectangular object she felt inside the belt buckle. I tensed my entire body, leaning forward just an inch, thinking I could grab the .38, but Taá took two steps backward and waved the .38 at the doorway.

"Inside," she said. "*Now.*"

The shop's door was locked. Dirty slatted blinds covered the windows and the door. Taá knocked. Somebody stuck a finger in the door blinds, drawing several slats down in a vee. Somebody unlocked the door, and Taá pushed it open. The three of us went inside, and the door closed behind us. A young Hispanic woman smiled brightly at us and locked the door.

"I was in the freezer. Sorry. Nobody else here, I had to lock the door."

Outside, it must have been at least one hundred degrees, but the butcher shop had heavy-duty air-conditioning and in my tanktop I felt chilly. The woman wore heavy jeans and a sweatshirt and what looked like long underwear.

"It's cold work," she said, "being a butcher. Got long underwear, top and bottom, shirt, sweatshirt, pants, sweat socks, boots. Cold."

"Cold, but bold," Meg said.

"Don't mind her," Taá said.

The butcher pulled on a plastic apron that went over her head and covered almost her entire body. She handed another apron to Taá.

"Got one for me?" Meg said in a singsong voice, but underneath the tones I heard the intelligence of her question and knew that however manic she was feeling, she was getting ready for what came next.

"I've got *this* for you," the butcher said, showing a SIG Sauer.

"What's going on?" I asked.

The butcher went behind one of the meat counters and stood there, looking at me, looking at Meg, and then picking up a bone saw. Taá waved her .38, motioning us to move behind the counter.

"This isn't necessary," I said.

"You had to look at the website," Taá answered.

"Money to Chihuahua."

"Yes. How did you know?"

"Until now, I didn't."

"I don't believe that," she said. "You're too smart. You're too thorough."

"Check them for weapons," the butcher said.

"This one's got something under her belt buckle."

Taá reached toward me suddenly, grasping my blouse at the neck and ripping it open, the buttons clacking on the floor as Taá kept yanking on the blouse material until she'd completely ripped it off. She pulled the miniature tape recorder out from underneath the belt buckle, yanking it violently to free the microphone cord taped up my left side. The butcher stepped behind me with a paring knife and with rapid movements sliced open my sports bra vertically from bottom to top, then severing the shoulder straps. She pealed the bra scraps from my body, uncovering the microphone which she examined as though it was a bit of cartilage or gristle in a slab of meat. Setting the microphone on a butcher's block, she smashed it flat with a meat cleaver, the way you'd mash a clove of garlic, and then she began to study Meg.

"Let's make her get naked too," she said. "See what we can find."

"I'll go for that," Meg said, and stuck her thumbs inside the top of her shorts as though to pull them off.

"Look at her," Taá said. "Shorts and tanktops and sandals. As naked as the day she got dressed. You *stupid* bitch."

She raked the front sight of the .38 along Meg's cheek, and a small river of blood ran down Meg's chin. She licked at it and grinned.

"Good meat," she said.

"Christ. She's stoned," the butcher said.

"She's on the edge of going wacky," Taá said. "I don't think she even knows where she is."

"Then let's do it."

The butcher took up the bone saw in one hand and the cleaver in the other. Several boning knives lay beside her on the chopping block, and I flicked a glance at them. Taá rapped me solidly on the back of the head, and I staggered.

"Uh uh," she said. "If only you hadn't looked at that website."

"Actually," I said, "I did more than that. I found all your offshore accounts."

She hesitated, but recovered and smiled.

"Not a chance."

"Look at the papers I left in your car."

"Not a chance."

"It was never about smuggling, was it?"

"I'm telling you," the butcher said. "Don't make a movie out of this, where you've got to confess everything before she dies. Put one in her head."

"And it was never money *out* of Mexico," I said. "It was all that money that the undocumented workers were sending back to their families. You figured a way to get a major percentage of it by hacking into the Internet money exchanges."

"For Christ's sakes," the butcher said as she strode over to where Taá stood. "Give me the piece, I'll do them right now."

"Not now," Meg said, reaching behind her and pulling the Glock from the holster underneath her tanktop. She racked the slide in an instant and slammed the Glock against Taá's forehead. "Drop the .38. Or die. Choose. Right. Now."

"You wouldn't kill me," Taá said. "We were lovers, we were friends."

"After what you did to my daughter?"

"I never touched your daughter."

"Yes, you did," I said. "Satellite tracking. Video cameras at the border crossings. That specialty software you showed me, when you lost track of all of us, you must have been watching for me, Rey, Meg's daughter, even the Emerine girl. And you never saw Rey and me, but you saw the two girls. They must have driven right through the main crossing at Nogales. You called Zamora and Nasso, and they kidnapped the girls."

"You're guessing," Taá said.

"Good Christ!" the butcher shouted, moving at us with her knives. "I told you, I fucking *told* you, don't make a movie out of this. Kill them!"

Meg staggered, blinking her eyes and shaking her head violently. I didn't know if she'd reached overload from the drugs she'd been taking, or because of the enormity of what Taá was telling her. The Glock wavered between Taá and the butcher, then slowly began to drop, as though it was too heavy to hold. Meg slumped to her knees, forcing her upper body erect, using her left hand to grip her right arm and lift the Glock.

Taá realized it was too late and tried to get her .38 against Meg's body, but Meg shot her immediately. Taá's head flew back, bits of blood and bone spattering the butcher who without hesitating picked up a boning knife and lunged at Meg. I tripped her, but she partially recovered and starting swinging the boning knife like a scythe at Meg's leg until Meg reached down and shot her in the chest.

"Jesus Christ!" Meg said, collapsing to the floor. "I didn't ever want to do that again. You stupid woman, you made me kill you."

"Come on," I said, trying to pull her to her feet. "We've got to get out of here."

"Why did she make me kill her, Laura?"

But there are some questions so basic that no answer will be enough.

And then, for a moment, she came back from the brink.

Near the front door, an Arizona Cardinals baseball jacket hung on a single wooden peg. Meg focused on the jacket with a singular purpose, like a deepsea diver watching a depth gauge and knowing there were only seconds of oxygen left to surface.

"Laura. Take this. Put it on."

She dressed me, like a mother with a sleepy child, carefully fitting my hands through the cuffs, pulling the sleeves tight, locking the bottom of the zipper, and oh so slowly and lovingly sliding the zipper to the very top.

"Now," she said. "Now we can leave this horrible place."

I got the keys to the Caprice, and we drove away from the butcher shop.

"Your daughter's alive," I told her. "I'm alive. *You're* alive."

"I need help, Laura."

Yeah. Don't we all.

epilog

When I checked into the Roosevelt Hotel on Hollywood Boulevard, I almost ran into Dolly Parton. Then I saw Liz Taylor, except it was Liz at forty. After John Wayne and three Elvises walked by, I finally asked what was happening.

"Impersonators annual banquet and performance night," the desk clerk said.

"Female impersonators?"

"No, no, nothing like that. You see a Barbra or a Liza, it's a woman. Staying just the two nights, Miss Winslow?"

"Maybe longer. Can't say."

"Mr. Villaneuva is in a connecting room. Have fun. Next?"

"You sure about this?" Rey asked.

Waiting for a taxi, we crossed Hollywood Boulevard to Mann's Chinese Theatre, and Rey knelt on Rita Hayworth's square, tracing her signature in the cement. Standing, uneasy, uncertain of what we were doing together, he fidgeted with his Hawaiian shirt, tucking it neatly into his jeans and in the next moment pulling it out.

"I wanted to knock on your door last night," he said. "I wanted . . ."

"Rey." I laid a palm on his cheek for a moment. "You're here with me. Right now, that's as much as I can deal with."

He jumped over Charles Laughton to Doris Day and knelt

again to place his palms into the impressions left by Joan Crawford.

"It's enough," he said. "To be here. With you."

It clearly *wasn't* enough for him, but I had a long way to go to sort out what kind of relationship I wanted. When I'd told him I was going to look for my daughter, he refused to let me disappear again from his life. I'm not sure what drew us closer over the past week, but Meg's breakdown was clearly a monsoon that swept our lives off course into uncharted territory.

We were on the edge of something, but I refused to step over to the other side.

One thing was clear.

I am so tired of reinventing myself. After years of many identities, I wanted to be my own person, my own self, my own soul. I arranged a set of ID papers in the name of Laura Winslow.

For two depressing days I was jailed in Tucson on a charge of murdering Michael Dance. But crime scene investigators cleared me once they'd dug through all of Taá's files. Her obsession with keeping meticulous data had led her to storing computer records of all her financial transactions, her deals with the Zamora smuggling cartel, her agreement to share profits with Jake Nasso, and, most damaging, her total contempt for Michael Dance. She'd also kept a diary of every single hour she'd spent with Meg, ending with her bitterness that Meg had no real interest in a long-time relationship. Taá drew unrealistic and obsessive details of Meg moving into the house. Meals they would plan, sheets and linen and furniture they would buy, movies to see and trips to enjoy.

Several of Meg's friends joined myself, Rey, and Amada for an intervention, finally convincing Meg to enter a drug clinic so that she could reestablish a chemical balance to offset her depression.

Many things never were resolved. Alex Emerine and Don Ralph vanished. All the LUNA chat messages vanished from AOL. New smuggling cartels were already formed, taking over Zamora's business. Jonathan Begay left Sonora, and months later I saw his face in a newspaper photograph amidst a crowd of protesters organized by the Zapatistas marching on Mexico City to demand better rights for Indians.

I didn't care.

The taxi took us along Lexington, slowing to find number 4255. It was a small two-story adobe bungalow.

"Wait for me," I said to the driver.

"You want to give me twenty now?"

Rattled, eyeing the bungalow's front door, I handed her a fifty-dollar bill. Rey followed behind me. A dog barked from the next yard when I went inside the chainlink gate. I stood so long, not wanting to ring the bell, that I didn't notice the man who came up the driveway alongside the house.

"Can I help you?"

"Ah," I said. "Ah . . . do you live here?"

"Yes. I own the house. Live upstairs."

"How long have you owned the house?"

"That's an odd question, lady, for somebody who just walked into my yard. If you're a realtor, just leave."

"I'm looking for somebody who used to live here. Maybe a tenant of yours."

"Who?"

"Ashley? Or, maybe, Kimberly?"

"I've had one of each," he said warily. "What's the last name?"

"Begay."

"Are you related to her?"

"She lives here?"

"Are you related?"

"I'm her mother."

"Ashley Begay lived here for five months until I threw her

out. By that time she'd conned me for almost four thousand dollars. Are you going to pay me for that?"

"I haven't seen her since she was two."

"Oh. Oh. I'm . . . well, I'm sorry. But she stiffed me for a lot of money."

"I'll pay you," I said, taking out a checkbook and writing him a check.

"Is this check good?"

"Yes. I can wait, if you want to call the bank."

"Hard to figure you as Ashley's mother. She's a grifter. A con artist supremo."

"Do you know where she went?"

"Pasadena."

In West Pasadena, the taxi driver took a wrong turn and we went by the Rose Bowl. It was Sunday morning, and more than a hundred people thronged on the grass and along the parking lots of the stadium. Families already had picnic baskets out, and many walkers and joggers moved on the streets, which were barricaded against traffic.

Spider had moved three times in Pasadena, and we finally found her last known address on Prospect Avenue in a very rich section of old houses. Number 449 lay hidden behind thick, high walls overflowing with purple bougainvillea. The taxi driver waited, not asking for more money.

Inside the gate, I went up a long bricked driveway and rang the doorbell. A woman with a very young baby on her left hip came to the door, leaving it locked as she studied me through the glass.

"I'm looking for Ashley Begay," I said loudly.

The woman stared at me for a long time.

"You mean Spider?"

"Yes. Is she here?"

"Try New York City. And if you ever find her, just tell her there's a warrant waiting here for her arrest. Tell her never to come back to California."

"Where now?" the taxi driver asked.

I walked into the middle of the street, looked one way, looked the other, totally undecided, lost, on the edge of wanting to find my Spider but *not* wanting to find her.

"Laura?" Rey said. "You want me to come with you?"

"I don't know where I'm going."

"Get in the taxi."

He led me to the car, a gentle but firm hand on my elbow. He settled me into the backseat, sat beside me, held my hand. Sobbing, I rested my head on his shoulder.

"Decide for me," I said. "I just don't know what to do."

He fumbled with an airline schedule, folding and refolding the pages, finally drawing a fingernail across an entry of available flights from LAX to Kennedy.

"The airport," he said to the driver.

Somewhere over Kansas, looking down through thin tendrils of horsetail clouds, I thought of Xochitl and her new life.

If I'd learned anything from all the events of the past days, it was that you *can* start again if you have the will to do so. There is no way to escape your memories, your history, your life up to now. If you ever doubt the influence of the past on the future, just look over your shoulder at the ghosts of those who survived and those who didn't. If you keep your gaze fixed on history, you are condemned forever to running from the hounds of past identities.

If you look ahead, at the edge between past and future, you can change.

I'm not sure I really believe that.

But this time, I was *going* somewhere, instead of *running* to escape my past. I turned to look at Rey, found him staring at me with concern and hope, and I took his hands in mine and smiled and grinned and leaned over to kiss him for the first time.

author's note

Sadly, the problem of illegal trafficking in women is not fictional. It has long been a global issue, but until very recently it has not been a serious issue for justice and law enforcement agencies in the United States. The President's Interagency Council on Women has basically defined trafficking as

> *the recruitment, abduction, transport, harboring, transfer, sale or receipt of persons; within national or across international borders . . . to place persons in situations of slavery or slavery-like conditions, forced labor or services, such as prostitution or sexual services, domestic servitude, bonded sweatshop labor or other debt bondage.*

Simply put, trafficking is the buying and selling of women as slaves, a horrible experience made easier by the unequal status of females in the source and transit countries. China has only recently (and reluctantly) admitted that girls are kidnapped and sold within its borders. In the year 2001, trafficking from Mexico into the United States increased exponentially to the point where smuggling people can be more profitable than smuggling drugs. Traffickers operate in small gangs, rather than more easily tracked large cartels. Traffickers use technology in highly innovative ways to establish organizational structures which hide transfers of money. (The Internet is a major vehicle for these operations.) Because trafficking in women is a relatively new criminal business and is not controlled by traditionally organized crime cartels, the United States justice and law enforcement systems are ill-equipped to deal with the problem.

For more information, use the Google Internet search engine to find articles on "illegal trafficking in women." Start with Amy O'Neill Richard's monograph (April 2000) titled "International Trafficking in Women to the United States: A Contemporary Manifestation of Slavery and Organized Crime."

Spellbinding Mysteries featuring
Cyber-sleuth Laura Winslow by

David Cole

STALKING MOON

0-380-81970-8/$6.50 US/$8.99 Can

Part-Hopi cyber-sleuth Laura Winslow is hiding from the world in the Arizona desert near the Mexican border—where life is cheap . . . and death is easy.

And Don't Miss

THE KILLING MAZE

0-06-101395-1/$6.50 US/$8.99 Can

BUTTERFLY LOST

0-06-101394-3/$5.99 US/$7.99 Can

Available wherever books are sold or please call 1-800-331-3761 to order.

DC 0102